I think you overestimate yourself, Your Grace," said Ella. "Do you think anyone in the whole world would be happy to accept you, whatever your faults?"

"But what faults could possibly override my eligibility?" the Duke of Clare asked. "I cannot think, offhand, of anyone who would not accept me."

"Well, *I* would not! And neither would Miss Prattle," she said.

"Would you not, Miss Fairmont?" he asked. "Extraordinary. Well, I think you would, and I make no doubt I could bring Prattle round my thumb, too, if I had a mind to."

"I never heard such conceit in my life!" she expostulated, half laughing.

"Do you deem it conceit in me to think myself worthy of a common gossip-monger, who makes her livelihood purveying lies about her betters? Or is it only *yourself* you consider to be above my touch?"

ESCAPADE

A NOVEL BY

Joan Smith

A FAWCETT CREST BOOK

Fawcett Publications, Inc., Greenwich, Connecticut

ESCAPADE

A Fawcett Crest Original

ISBN 0–449–23232–8

Printed in the United States of America

10   9   8   7   6   5   4   3   2   1

In Memory of
My Mother

One

Miss Puella Fairmont came to London to make her curtsy at St. James's in the spring Season of 1811. She was duly chaperoned into polite society under the auspices of her aunt, Lady Sara Mantel, a dashing matron, who was soon sure she could make a respectable match for her niece in the six weeks set aside annually to present the debutantes. The girl had some looks, some conversation, and some money—not an outstanding quantity of any of the three, but enough to make a fairly interesting combination. Her rather simply styled brown hair was no great asset, but her brown eyes sparkled brightly when she was amused. Her quiet conversation sparkled too upon occasion, and if ten thousand pounds was not a fortune, it was at least respectable.

Her season began auspiciously enough. Puella caught the eye of Sir Horace Farthington, a baronet of easy means and presentable person, but somehow it came to nothing after a few weeks. A few other gentlemen came to call; they stood up with her regularly at the balls and routs she attended, so Sir Horace was allowed to slip away. But somehow, one by one, the others stopped coming around to Grosvenor Square too. Then suddenly the season was over, and Puella had not received a single offer. No matter. She was only eighteen, and another season would see her more sure of herself, more at ease in society, more sought after.

Puella returned to her mama for the summer and again went to Lady Sara for the fall Little Season. But instead of growing more interested in the social scene, she became bored with it. She reduced her aunt to near hysterics by refusing a much sought-after voucher to Almack's in order to remain home and work on her book. During

the summer she had begun a novel, based on her first un-
successful season. *Too Long at the Fair,* she had tenta-
tively entitled it. The theme had to do with the folly of
the *haut ton.*

Lady Sara was not an intellectual woman, but she was
shrewd and soon cooked up a scheme that would get Ella,
as her niece was called at home, out to parties under the
guise of training her eye and practicing her pen on the
subject of her novel. Mr. Thorndyke of the *Morning Observer* wanted a gossip columnist to write a daily piece on
the social doings of the ten thousand, and as he was a
friend of Lady Sara's husband, Lady Sara came to hear of
it. *She* would be his correspondent officially, but in fact
the writing of the column would be largely left to Ella.
She could feel she was gaining experience at writing and
would simultaneously be forced into society. The idea appealed to Ella and was soon put into execution.

The pseudonym, "Miss Prattle," was chosen, and the
column proved a great success. That same season, Lady
Sara's mother, the Dowager Countess of Watley, came to
stay with her, and the three women managed to straddle
the narrow band that constituted society. Lady Watley
was a crony of Lady Melbourne and soon became a
bosom friend of the Prince Regent and his set as well. She
discovered all the *on dits,* the gossip, of that scandalous
tribe: who was losing a fortune at Watiers, or Oatlands,
where the Duke of York set his guests down to faro at
twenty guineas a hand, while one or the other of his wife's
twenty dogs gnawed their boots and chased their valets. If
Prinney changed his affections from one aged damsel to
another, as he regularly did, this too was observed and
reported, frequently with a venomous quote from
Richard Sheridan. Lady Sara gathered in information
from the dashing young set and older gentlemen still on
the catch for a wife, and Ella herself kept her ears cocked
for the goings-on of the debutantes and their beaux. A
more comprehensive intelligence service could hardly
have been devised for the purpose, and to add richness to

the column, Miss Prattle developed an acerbic manner of reporting that won her a wide and appreciative audience.

Almost, it seemed, Lady Sara's scheme had succeeded too well in one direction. The writing certainly increased Ella's interest in going out to parties, but it did not lead her to look for a husband. Quite the reverse, it made her a highly critical young lady, who tended to look for a fault, or at least a folly, in all the men she met. And follies she found a-plenty. Men, she soon discovered, came in three main species. They were either of the Corinthian school, who thought the world began on the riding field and finished in the green baize boxing ring; or they were dandies whose major interest was the cut of a coat and arrangement of a cravat; or they were inveterate gamblers, willing to risk a fortune on the turn of a card, or even on the progress of two flies across a pane of glass. They came, of course, in combinations of these three main patterns, with a few recognizable subspecies such as the poet, the fortune hunter, and the rake. Miss Fairmont acknowledged there were some good men in the world as well, but as they were of no use to Miss Prattle, they were hardly observed at all and never cultivated. She came, she wrote, she conquered, and became without quite realizing it a personage of some consequence herself, albeit anonymous. It was a foregone conclusion that her writing must remain a secret, or she'd have been barred from society.

Conjecture was rampant as to the author of these caustic reports who had an entree into all branches of society. It was variously reported to be Lady Caroline Lamb, doing it for a spree, or her sometime lover, Lord Byron, doing it for spite, or Beau Brummell doing it for money. Never once did it occur to anyone that it was being written by a young lady from the country, still in her teens that first year, and not even known to sight by three-quarters of the great people she lampooned with such scorn and familiarity.

Ella smiled softly to herself when her grandmama would tell her, upon returning from a soiree at Carlton

House, the Prince Regent's residence, that the Prince himself had told her in the strictest confidence that Miss Prattle was in truth a purse-pinched and illustrious peeress, or when Lady Sara laughingly reported, "Guess who they are saying we are now, love. Lady Oxford! Was there ever anything more absurd? I had it of Emily Cowper. I could hardly keep from laughing in her face, only of course I didn't, for it is she who will give Miss Prattle a voucher for Almack's."

Ella lifted an eyebrow, her brown eyes dancing. "You must certainly not offend *her*. Miss Prattle is very curious to see how her flirtation with Lord Palmerston goes on, and where shall she do it but at Almack's? Isn't it odd, Sara, that Almack's is considered such a citadel of propriety, when its very patronesses are such high flyers? I think Miss P should raise the point, don't you?"

"Miss P is becoming a crusader for respectability, is she? Your column would die on its feet if the ten thousand should turn respectable on you, Ella."

"Oh, I don't consider more than five thousand possible of conversion; the other half are lost souls," Ella returned airily, her mind following its latest bent—the shenanigans of the patronesses of Almack's. Sally Jersey too had a dozen beaux, she was thinking, as her mind flitted over the other hostesses.

"True—then, too, you always have Clare to fall back on in the unlikely case of mass conversion."

"There is no danger of *his* reforming at any rate," Ella said tartly. "One can always count on His Grace for some reportable piece of ill behavior."

"He's not so bad as some of the others," Lady Sara replied.

"You only say so because you are sweet on him," her niece charged. "You are as bad as all the other women, toadying to him, and puffing him up in his own conceit."

"Yes, Miss Prattle, but then we can always count on *you* to deflate his pretensions."

"No, I only try to. With him I never succeed. He pays me no heed."

"That doesn't stop you from trying."

"Oh, no, I will get him yet," Miss Prattle said, a determined and even martial light in her eyes. There, if only she would sparkle like that in public, Sara thought.

"Every eligible female in London wants to *get* him," Sara laughed. "That is precisely what makes it possible for him to behave so ill."

"Well, Sara, but *I* do not want to get him in the sense of attracting him—I only want to straighten him out a little."

"I know, goose, and you have about as much chance of correcting his behavior as *I* have of marrying Napoleon Bonaparte."

"Rather less, I should think," Ella said. "But still, he is good copy for the column."

"People would read it avidly if you did no more than print a whole column of his name, and nothing else. There's a sort of magic about him."

"Well, he does not seem magic to me, only insufferably rude and overbearing."

"Quite right, but he has the most winning smile in London, when he cares to put himself to the bother of using it."

"A smile is not for *using*!" Ella asserted, and the two ladies fell into a philosophical argument till dinner was announced.

Two

His Grace, the Duke of Clare, was not the premier duke of Britain, but he was certainly the *premier parti*, the most eligible bachelor. He had fallen heir to his title and estates at the age of twenty-four, when his unfortunate elder brother Joseph had killed himself by tumbling from a prime goer in a race against Lord Monkland and an Irish chairman. As a result of this sad affair, Lord Patrick had become the eighth duke and, along with his hereditary title, shortly acquired the honorary one of the season's best catch as well. Pretty girls who had not given him a thought before vied for his attention now. There had been no partying for a year after Joseph's death, of course, but the number of letters of condolence that he received, carefully worded to have somehow the aura of a billet-doux, gave some indication of his new position in society.

For two years he had been in love with Miss Artley, a delightful blond lady, and for two years she had been showing him the back of her head as she turned to admire some more eligible suitor. Now that was at an end. He was allowed as many lingering glances into her limpid blue eyes as he wished. It was not only hinted, but shamelessly said in so many word, that the offer she had formerly rejected would now be acceptable. Patrick discovered, though, that whereas he had panted after an unattainable beauty, that same beauty, when available, was less prized. But she had really divine dimples, and one afternoon about a year after his accession he was standing in her mama's saloon, for the purpose of making her an offer in form. Some malign chance led Miss Artley to embark on a discourse regarding her duty to her family. She hoped to erase any resentment that might be lingering at having refused him when a younger son, only to accept him now that he had inherited a title.

"I am sure it is my—and indeed everyone's duty—to make the best match they can. One has to think of family and connections and that sort of thing. How shocking it would have been in me—how ungrateful for all mama and papa have done for me—to have accepted an offer from a younger son, for you know I have two sisters and two brothers who must be provided for. I owe it to the family to marry well, whatever my personal preferences may have been when you asked me before."

"You hold this to be a categorical imperative?" Clare asked, some mischief dancing behind his gray eyes.

"I beg your pardon?" she asked, alarmed at such unloverlike language. She had naturally expected he would fall in with her line of thinking and swoon to hear she would have liked to accept him the first time he asked.

He delivered—right in the middle of a proposal—a short lecture on Kant's theory of hypothetical and categorical imperatives, then concluded all by himself (certainly the astonished lady had not a comment to make) that hers had been a hypothetical imperative, one arrived at to reach a specific goal. She had no bent for philosophy, but a certain low animal cunning in her detected in his sophistry that she was being led into stating she had wanted only to marry well for her own ends. She quickly denied the matter.

"Ah, then, you hold it to be a *categorical* imperative," he demanded. "One that must be followed because of its rightness and necessity? It might be taken as a general law."

This had a good sound of dissipating the blame, and she concurred readily. "Oh, yes, one must always consider one's family. That is clearly a *duty*."

He nodded his head sadly. "I feared it must be so," he said. "I am grateful for this talk, Miss Artley. My own heart dictates my offering for you, but clearly it is my duty to seek higher for a match, for the sake of my family. I am burdened with no brothers or sisters, but have a great many lesser relatives who must be taken care of. As the head of my family, it behooves me to marry an heiress, and I must not shirk my duty."

"I didn't mean *that*!" she squealed in alarm. "You need not scruple to marry where you will, with your fortune."

"But a law is a law, and a duty is a duty. If I offered for you, there would be all those brothers and sisters to provide for, whereas if I offer myself to, say, the Honorable Miss Twillingford, I should be advancing the welfare of my family."

"But she has a squint! You would not like that, my lord. Indeed you would not."

"I only mentioned Miss Twillingford as an example of the sort of lady I ought to offer for. I don't believe Kant mentions a squint at all, but certainly I must look as high as I dare for the sake of my family."

Miss Artley was reeling, but she was not down—and by no means out. She laughed weakly—too weakly to produce the dimples—which might very well have turned the trick. "You have misunderstood me," she told him. "I do not mean *you* will be expected to provide for the girls and Clarence and Edgar. Gracious, we are not so poor as that. Papa has taken care of them all, and I, as the eldest daughter, have a larger dowry than the other girls. Twenty-five thousand pounds. Anyone might live handsomely on the income of that."

"But you recall that when I offered for you before, you did not think we could live at all handsomely on your portion *and* my own. And I was not quite penniless at the time."

"What has that to do with anything?"

"A great deal, my dear. As Lord Patrick and Lady Arabella we might have rubbed along on our jointures, but a duke and duchess have such ripping expenses you don't begin to perceive the half of it. Three estates to keep up . . ."

"But you have a huge income now! Thirty thousand pounds I have heard mentioned."

"Very true, but you have made me see it is my duty to marry a fortune of similar size, for the sake of my family."

"No, indeed! I didn't mean anything of the sort. You have misunderstood me."

He smiled a deceptively bland smile. "No, ma'am, I have understood you perfectly. It is impossible for me to offer for you, but I do wish you every success in your capture of Baron Almquist. A very respectable fortune, and he will be of some assistance to your family, I believe." Clare arose from the velvet settee where they had been sitting together.

"But you asked to see me *alone!*" she pointed out. "You would not have done so only to speak to me of Kant, whoever *he* may be. Mama expects . . ."

"Mama will be disappointed, even as we are disappointed," he said, lifting her ringless fingers to his lips. The family engagement ring sat in his pocket. He was aware of an inexplicable feeling of joy at the thought.

"This is so silly, Patrick. It is not in the least necessary for us to part. I am sure papa could raise the dowry if *that* is what . . ."

"Now that, my dear, would clearly break every law you have been extolling to me. I could not allow you to act so unhandsomely."

"It is *you* who keeps chattering about laws and imperatives," she said angrily. "I never heard of Kant till you mentioned him."

"Wise young girl." He touched her cheek with one finger. "You reached his immutable laws all by yourself. *You* knew your duty a whole two years ago and acted in a manner that would be to the best advantage of your family. I am really abominably slow. *I* didn't find it out till I happened to come across Kant a few weeks ago. Barely in time to avoid making a dreadful mistake."

"But you came to make me an offer. You know you did."

"I will be eternally grateful that you reminded me of my duty." He bowed and swept majestically out the door. The impish smile on his face led the hovering butler to believe that all was well. He even dared to enquire roguishly if the duchess would like him to summon her mama when he went to the drawing room a moment later.

He was confounded when the young lady stamped her foot at him and said she never wanted to hear such impudence again. As this was followed shortly by a childish outburst of tears, he refrained from pursuing the matter.

The duke was in a pensive mood as he tooled his yellow curricle down the street to the Park. He had most certainly gone to Park Lane to make Miss Artley an offer. He was no longer a young sprig and felt vaguely that he ought to marry, as he had no brothers to inherit if he should by mischance die young, as Joseph had done. He was accustomed to thinking himself in love with Miss Artley. Clearly she was desirous of marrying him, so why had he shied off at the last minute? It was some latent resentment that rankled, he supposed, at her former refusal. The sure knowledge that since he had come into his late brother's honors, he was sought after by one and all. Hadn't more than two words to say to him when he was Lord Patrick. Each one wanted to be a duchess—that was the sum and total of it. Damned if he'd satisfy 'em. He had gone too far in goading Miss Artley, though. That had been unhandsome and uncalled for. He would see no more of her dimples after this day's work.

In less than twenty-four hours, he realized he had miscalculated the degree of his insult. Miss Artley's mama, when she discussed the visit with her daughter, decided that Arabella had set the duke's back up by alluding to former times, but felt it must be only a temporary fit of pique and sought to reawaken his interest. New gowns were fitted and great pains taken to discover where Clare might have the chance of seeing them and rekindling his passion, but the flame was well and truly extinguished.

She was replaced by a bevy of anxious beauties in the following season. There were the Misses Twitchwell, one blonde, one redhead, who refused to take offence at his never being able to tell them apart. When this joke palled on him, they were superseded by Miss Legg, famous for her killing eyes that slew a score of suitors a week. But Clare sustained no mortal wound. At a month's end he cast her off, and when she persisted in hounding him, he took to addressing her as Miss Arm, Miss Foot, or any other part of the anatomy that occurred to him.

It was reported by Miss Prattle that His Grace, the D—e of C——e, would not be Legg-shackled after all and was once more running in the London Open, as she had dubbed the marriage race. This and other interesting morsels were to be read in her gossip column entitled 'Miss Prattle Says.' It was to the third page of the *Morning Observer* that all members of the *ton* turned while having their morning chocolate, to see what scandalous and near-libelous gossip they might pick up from Miss Prattle to enliven their daily chatter. For three seasons now she had reigned supreme as the Queen of Gossip, and to add mystery to mystique, she was still unknown after all that time, in spite of strenuous efforts to learn her identity. Certainly a member of the very inner circle of society, for she knew everyone and everything. During her first year of writing, she had hit on Clare as her whipping boy. He exemplified all that she deplored—vanity, arrogance, conspicuous display of wealth, wasting of time and talents. To this were added two attributes that Thorndyke liked, too: He never threatened to sue, as some did, nor did he ever storm into the office demanding to know who Miss Prattle was; and his name was of lively interest to his readers. Miss Prattle received every encouragement to say what she pleased about him.

During the time the Twitchwells were after Clare, his intimates teased him about being color-blind, because of his inability to distinguish red hair from blonde. Miss Prattle also took him to task, but she avoided the obvious and hinted instead that it was his color blindness that had led him to appear on the strut in a waistcoat no gentleman of fashion would be caught dead in, and added that it might also account for his book at Tatt's being in the red.

"Damme, I've missed settling up day at Tatt's," Clare said when Miss Twitchwell read the article to him.

"Yes, but it is *really* a dig at you for not being able to tell me and Alice apart. Everyone says so."

"And one may always count on you to belabor the obvious, Lady . . . Alice, is it?"

"No, I'm Mary," she told him, still smiling.

"And *quite* contrary," he said, returning her smile.

Clare shrugged his elegant shoulders when Miss Prattle ticked him off for betting five hundred pounds that Miss Altmire would not be allowed a voucher to Almack's, and agreed that he ought to have made it a thousand, for it was a dead certainty no mere Cit's daughter would get her toe into the holy of holies. That she had used *his* name as a reference to Sally Jersey had goaded him into making the bet, but Miss Prattle had slipped up on that piece of business.

His failure to appear at a garden party tossed at Clare Palace for his friends resulted in the title, "The Great Absent One," but he merely quirked an eyebrow and said, "Damme, my barber was down with the quinsy; it would have been an insult to attend my own party unshaven." Miss Prattle retaliated that His Grace had had a closer shave than he realized on that day, but she knew it was untrue and unworthy of her pen. There was nothing this presumptuous lord could do that would turn society against him while he remained the richest *single* gentleman in England.

Miss Prattle once wrote an entire column, ostensibly devoted to the general debauchery and low behavior of high society, but sprinkled throughout with so many references to the D—e C——e that she deceived no one, least of all the Duke. Though he put a bland face on it, it angered Clare that it should be publicly advertised how he had failed to follow up in the House of Lords his efforts to alleviate the lot of those engaged in cottage industry, who were losing their livelihood by the introduction of mechanization. It hurt because it was true; he was well aware that he had not put forth his best efforts. Had only made the speech to support Byron—it did not affect his

18

own county—and when George had let it go, he too had forgotten it. He felt the rest—the money spent on gambling and horses—was mere nit-picking, but the slur on his sloth and disinterest spurred him, and he had resumed his activities in the House. Miss Prattle had made no mention of *that*, he observed to himself.

He was chatting one day in his study with Bippy Tredwell, an intimate friend, and the subject of Miss Prattle arose.

"The woman's turning serious on us," Bippy offered. "A regular tirade she's come up with today."

"Yes, and she's becoming a dead bore as well," Clare agreed. For three years he had been listening to people tell him what she had said about him in her latest piece. "I would dearly like to know who this curst Prattle might be."

"Might be anyone," Bippy surmised.

"Or everyone. She reports simultaneously on the dos in London, and in the country, and at Brighton. Seems to know Prinney and his set pretty well, which indicates an *older* woman."

"Knew about your bill being overdue at Tatt's, too. Shouldn't do that, Clare. Gambling debt—ought to pay up promptly."

"I cannot believe they were worried about it. There was no dun on my doorstep, and the grand total was five pounds. That one fact, though, indicates a masculine interest." (It was Sir Herbert who had added that gem, quite by accident.)

"A man, you mean? I've heard Sheridan mentioned, but surely only a woman could write such stuff as you often read, about gowns, and furbelows, and so on."

"Mmm, possibly."

"Someone you've given a heavy set-down. Think a minute."

"Lord, I could think for days. I've insulted them all."

"That's true, and the devil only knows why you do it,

when they couldn't be nicer to you if you flattered 'em all hollow."

"Yes, there's no turning them against a title and fortune. I've been trying for years. I daresay I could call a lady toad-faced and humpbacked, and she'd smile and simper till it's all I can do to keep from shaking her."

"Still, you shouldn't have said Liza Entwhistle *always* looked good in that blue gown, for her papa's in the basket, and the truth hurts."

"Is he indeed? I didn't know that, or I shouldn't have said it. Really, I was sure it was a new gown, or I shouldn't have said a word. I never *do* cast aspersions on a lady's real faults, only on her pretensions. Except, of course, when her tenacity makes it absolutely essential."

"What an odd way to go about. You don't make your insults to the point then?"

"I fear my subtleties are quite wasted on the *hoi polloi*, but I only accuse a lady of a squint when she is minutely aware that her orbs are her finest feature. Take that lamentable waddle of Sylvia Blakeney, for instance. I would *never* tell her she waddles like a pig in farrow. It would be too utterly crude. I merely imply she sings like a crow, for she's proud of her voice. Whereas Miss Stinson, who sounds for the world like an unoiled hinge when she opens her mouth—I tease about her black curls, with red roots. She has really lovely hair, naturally black. Sets 'em down a peg to think the whole town isn't admiring them."

"Beats me how they all eat up your barbs like honey, but I'm sure it's nothing to me. There's one who ain't afraid to give you back your own anyway, and that's Miss Prattle."

"Yes, Miss Prattle. Do you think I ought to do something about her—or him? Let us compromise and say 'it.' Shall I slay it?"

"How?"

"Now what was the weapon St. George used to slay the dragon? A sword, I believe. Shall I run it through, and do society a favor?"

"Got to find out who she is first."

"Not necessarily, Bip." He sipped on a glass of sherry, and held the glass to the light to examine its color and clarity. "It would be nothing without me. If I reformed, its column would sink into a dull hash of who is flirting with whom. I make Miss Prattle, as surely as Brummell made the Prince."

"By Jove! Doing it too brown. Prinney made Brummell is more like it. His father was Lord North's *secretary*. Brummell is nothing but the son of a clerk, when all's said and done."

Clare's gray eyes leaped to Bippy's face, and his tone was cool.

"Do you infer that Miss Prattle makes me?" he asked.

"Course not. Didn't mean any such a thing. The way it works, though, you wouldn't be talked about so much if Prattle didn't jot down every word you say and write it up in her column every time you buy a new bit o' blood or give a party. She *does* give you a certain éclat you wouldn't have otherwise. Calling you The Great Absent One when you didn't make it to your party that time, and Clare the Bare when you first got your hair cut *au naturel*. All that sort of nonesense. In a way, she *does* make you."

"Makes me a laughing stock!" Clare said angrily.

"Well, 'pon my word, Clare, never knew you to pay so much attention to her before. What's gotten into you?"

"Assaults on my appearance, my habits, and my manners I can tolerate, but when she takes me to task for shirking my *duty*—when she turns *serious* . . ."

"Fact of the matter is you never *did* do a hand's turn in the House, outside of that one little speech you made, till she got after you."

"I am not interested in politics. I have other concerns about which Prattle knows nothing."

"How could she, when you're as close as an oyster on the subject, and never tell a soul about . . ."

"I don't want her praise!" He glared and set down his

21

glass. Then he assumed an air of indifference again and continued, "It has got its needle into me, and I think I shall find out who it is. You were right, it is difficult to slay an invisible dragon. Now, how shall I proceed?"

"Ask Thorndyke," Bippy suggested. "Editor of the *Observer. He* must know."

"Others have queried Thorndyke. He says nothing. Has promised it anonymity, or some such thing. Damme, I think I must buy the rag."

"What, *buy* the newspaper? Devilish silly thing to do, Pa'k. Cost you a bundle, and what do you want with a newspaper?"

"It would save buying one each day, and I could fire Prattle."

"No, really! Oh, you're gulling me," Bippy said, with a sheepish smile when he realized he had been taken in. "Besides, no saying Prattle wouldn't just pick up her wages and leave when she heard *you*'d bought the paper out. Anonymity would still apply very likely, and you wouldn't even have the pleasure of firing her. Lord, Pa'k, you *would* look no how, buying a paper and finding the bird had flown."

"True."

"Everybody'd know you'd only done it to put a muzzle on Prattle."

"I should not like to give rise to vulgar tattle, but I *was* joking . . . I think."

"Wouldn't satisfy her."

"It."

"Whatever."

"If only it would stop bestowing those damned cognomens on me."

"Eh?"

"Names, titles—those ones you mentioned. Even—oh really I could strangle it at times—it even had the temerity once to label me a Dandy. Me! Now you must own that is coming it too strong. I never wear a shirt point above my ears, or more than one ring, or padding in my shoulders, or sawdust in my stockings to give me a leg. Damme, the thing is a viper."

"Yes, she ought to know you're a Corinthian."

"But we have honored it too much already with such a discussion. Who do you back in the match Alvanley has set up with his new man and the champ? The champ will take it, I think. I mean to lay a pony on it."

"Too steep for me. I'll settle for a monkey."

Clare's brief interest in Prattle was forgotten, and he made no real efforts to discover her identity.

Three

In a small but elegant mansion on Grosvenor Square, Lady Sara Mantel sat with her mama, embroidering a monogram on her husband's handkerchiefs. She was tall and dark, generally described as handsome rather than pretty, now that she was in her thirtieth year.

"I wonder if Ella has the column ready," she remarked. "It is time it was sent off to the *Observer*. Did you give her the details of the do last night at Carlton House?"

Lady Watley, who considered needlework a dead bore, fanned herself and replied, "I jotted down a few details. She is giving two paragraphs to the Bradigan do you two were at, and one to Clare, so she only wanted the high lights." She stuffed a bonbon into her pudgy red face and chewed vigorously.

"Clare again!" Lady Sara commented, snipping off a silk thread. "Lud, how she does harp on him. I declare I don't know why she has taken him in such aversion, for he is ever so amusing. We matrons all dote on him."

"He don't have to worry about you married ladies dangling after him, so he can act in a civil manner. Ella says he let fall a very nasty remark about us last night, and she means to tick him off for it."

"The corporate 'us' you mean?" Lady Sara asked.

"Yes—Miss Prattle."

"Oh, what did he say?"

"He says he is retiring to the country to be free of her, only he called us *it*, and he will conduct his amours at Clare Palace in Dorset in future to keep us at bay."

"Poor Ella. What will she do with her favorite subject beyond reach?"

"Talk will dribble back to London. We'll have to make do with hearsay. But what has upset her is that he called us FitzPrattle."

A silvery tinkle of laughter greeted this announcement. *"Touché,"* Lady Sara said.

"I'm sure I don't see the joke. Ella was most indignant, and now you fall into hysterics. What is so marvelous about adding a Fitz to our name?"

"You must know, Mama, it is the name usually given to by-blows of the great. He is calling Miss Prattle a bastard, but in his usual elegant style."

Lady Watley swallowed her bonbon before her mouth fell open. "Sara!" she gasped. "What do you mean? I know a dozen Fitzes, and none of them are—what you say. There are the FitzGeralds—John and Margaret you know, and while they are Irish they are certainly not that, for his parents are personally known to me. To say nothing of the FitzHughs, who are quite unexceptionable."

Sara applied her needle and smiled to herself. "Yes, they are respectable now, but you may be sure there is a touch of scandal somewhere in their background. Oh, *years* ago, very likely. Some great-great ancestor. FitzPrattle! Well, Ella shall let him have his own back for that, I make no doubt."

"She is doing something on his remove to Dorset, a sort of mock encomium I believe, congratulating him for realizing he is scandalizing London and taking his black soul off into oblivion."

"I doubt he'll go."

"He goes, Sara. It is a settled thing. He has already invited his two favorite flirts and their mamas. Honor Sedgley won't be left out either; the Marchioness will see to that. Bippy Tredwell will be along to play court clown, and a few other gentlemen to make up the party."

"A pity," Sara said, her needle poised in the air. "Ella could make something wonderful of it, if only she could get herself invited along."

"Oh, as to that, as well expect him to invite his tailor! He takes no note of Ella."

"Hmm, I wonder how it might be arranged. When do they go?"

"A week's time is what was being said last night."

"I see." Lady Sara said nothing else but, as she worked her monogram, a look of concentration descended on her face. After perhaps five minutes, it was replaced by a sly smile. "Do you know, Mama, I have decided to go to Almack's tonight."

Her mother grimaced with loathing. "How you can stand that dull place, with Burrell and Esterhazy staring down their noses at you. No decent gambling, and nothing to drink but a glass of lemonade or orgeat. I tell you frankly, Sara, I considered a reprieve from Almack's one of the greater advantages of your match when you married Sir Herbert. You'll drag Ella along, of course, as an excuse for going yourself. *She* doesn't care for it either, though I daresay she'll tag along and see what she can pick up for the column."

"Yes, she will go. She knows Clare is more than likely to be there, and she is always happy to throw herself in his path and see what she can glean."

At this moment, Miss Puella Fairmont entered the room, two closely written sheets in her hand. "I've finished the column," she said. "Do you want to read it?"

"I'll read it tomorrow in the *Observer*," Mrs. Watley replied.

Lady Sara put down her embroidery and took the sheets, scanning them quickly. "Why have you signed it Miss *F.* Prattle?" she asked.

25

"The F stands for Fitz," Ella replied. "I am acknowledging his hit quite openly. I haven't come up with a suitable revenge on him yet; I can scarcely question *his* legitimacy."

"Don't think of it, Ella! That would be going a good deal too far. Besides, Thorndyke wouldn't allow it."

"I know. But I take it as a promising sign that he has made a public utterance at last on my existence. He often pretends he doesn't know whom people are talking about, you know, when he is roasted about me. 'I don't believe I have the honor of the person's acquaintance,' he will say, or some such odious thing. Well, he has admitted he knows who I am now."

"Yes, and given a pretty good idea as to what he thinks of you, too." She rang a bell and sent the papers off with a footman, who knew from long habit he was to remove his livery and proceed on his secret mission to the offices of the *Observer* in a hired hack, so that no one would remark on the daily trip of Sir Herbert Mantel's carriage to that destination.

"By the by, Ella," Lady Sara said, "we are going to Almack's tonight."

Ella wrinkled her nose in distaste but made no verbal demur.

"Why don't you wear your new golden gown, and try that hairstyle we saw in the Belle Assemblée?" Sara suggested, regarding her niece critically as she spoke. She had a nice straight figure, if slightly thin. The hair was just brown, and she made no effort to be in fashion, but the face was rather pretty. If only she would look alive, and play up to any of the gentlemen who took an interest in her. She was shy, of course, but really it was too absurd of her to go on being shy for *four* seasons, while plainer girls nabbed every man out from under her nose. If she could be induced to say in public the sharp, amusing things she said at home and in her column, she would be taken up as an Original.

"Bickles is hopeless with hair," Ella replied simply.

Sara sighed. How very typical of Ella! Her abigail had been accused of being hopeless with hair for four seasons, but no effort had been made either to replace her or teach her the rudiments of dressing hair. "I'll lend you Stepson," she said.

"Thank you, Sara, and will you lend me your old white gloves as well? Mine have a finger out."

"Yes, love, but *do* buy a pair of gloves next time you are out."

"I know I am not stylish enough to please you, Sara, but I have just been reading in Hannah More a passage that expresses my feelings exactly. 'Where your heart is, there will you store up treasure.' "

Sara stared at this irrelevancy, and said curtly, "No one will fear *your* heart is on your back then, will they?"

"What Miss More *means* is that you spend your time and thought and money on what is important to you, and people who gild and polish their bodies do so only because they think in *physical* terms, like the lower animals. It is the mind and spirit that are important. I would rather decorate my mind than my body."

"Let me tell you, Ella, Hannah More is a humbug. Your heart ought to be on finding a husband at this stage of your life, and if you think a decorated mind is going to be of the slightest use, you mistake the matter."

"I know that, but I don't want to marry a man who hasn't the sense to look below the surface." This matter settled, Ella turned to speak to her grandmother.

"Will you take particular note tonight at Fenton's rout as to whether Lord Byron is present, and whom he talks to, and so on. Try to stand by him for a while and pick up a quote or two. He is highly quotable."

"Miss Prattle is finding a subject nearly as interesting as Clare, is she not?" Lady Watley asked. "You may be sure I'll be hanging on his every word, if he's there."

"I am planning a column on him. I will admire his beauty, deride his slovenly habits of dress, berate him for his affairs, and forgive him everything for his divine poetry."

"I am surprised his slovenly dress is to be derided," Lady Sara said. "I made sure you and Hannah More would approve."

"But in his case it is all affectation, you know," Ella informed her aunt. "They say he curls his hair in papers, like a lady, and I think it is true, for it is curlier sometimes than others."

"There is nothing in *that*," Sara defended. "Rain makes naturally curly hair curlier."

"Yes, but Byron's is *straighter* when the weather is damp. And his limp is a little more pronounced too though, of course, I shan't mention that."

"I should hope not!"

"It is not his fault. But what I *shall* mention is the shameless way Lady Caroline Lamb haunts him."

"That is not entirely *her* fault, for he was used to sit in her pocket a while back, and it must be a blow to be losing him."

"Yes, he must be a sore temptation, but temptation was made to be overcome. Hannah More says . . ."

"Resist the temptation to quote Hannah More at me, love," Sara said. "Nothing is more likely to put a gentleman off than to be forever preaching at him. And while you're about it, you might overcome the temptation to wear that pink gown as well. Have Bickles hem up that new golden dress, so that you won't look such a quiz at Almack's."

"Lord, Sara, you don't *still* hope to get me off your hands, do you?" Ella asked with an ironic laugh. "I am stuck on you and Sir Herbert like a barnacle." She looked worried when her aunt frowned at this instead of smiling, as she had hoped.

"Oh, do you *hate* having me? I shan't mind going back home to mama. Truly I shan't. It is only Miss Prattle I shall regret, for she is fun, but I *do* plan to write my novel you know and can get on with it when I go back home."

"Nonsense! I am thinking of you. I love having you, and so do Herbert and the children. But it is *unnatural* the way you never make the least push to form an attachment."

"I have tried, Sara, but the older gentlemen are too wise to bother with me, and the younger are too stupid for me to bother with them, so what's to do?"

"Someone in between—a gentleman no longer young—say thirty or so."

"The good ones get snapped up young, and there aren't many gentlemen at the magic age of thirty or thereabouts."

That evening Lady Sara and her charge entered Almack's and made their bows to the Patronesses before joining the throng hovering at the edge of the dance floor. Both ladies had the same prey in mind—Lord Clare—but upon discovering that he was not present, the elder did not appear disappointed. She shepherded Ella to the far corner of the room, for no reason apparent to her niece. No one was there but Bippy Tredwell, standing alone in a pose denoting an advanced state of boredom. One could not but wonder why he had come. There were more gentlemen than ladies present, so naturally Tredwell was without a partner. With a greeting, Lady Sara sallied forth and engaged him in conversation. When the music began, he asked Ella to stand up with him. Ella had feared this very contingency, and felt she might have done better for herself from all the surfeit of black jackets standing about, but Sara was smiling quite contentedly. With a shortage of girls, Ella had a partner for every dance. It was while she danced with Mr. Peters that Lady Sara once again accosted Bippy Tredwell.

"Ah, Mr. Tredwell," she began in a flattering tone. "What a pleasure it was to see you dancing with my niece. I must confess I had not observed how smoothly you executed the new waltz, till Ella said to me there was no one who did it so well as you."

Bippy's little blue eyes popped in surprise and pleasure. He was a stoutish gentleman, not conspicuously light of foot. Had she congratulated him on his fine baritone voice, he would have thought it no more than his due. Quite a fine voice. Everyone said so. But to receive a gratuitous word of praise on his dancing was a novel experience.

"Did she say so, by Jove?" he asked contentedly. It was vigorously confirmed.

"A bit of a dab at it, if I do say so myself," he admitted modestly. "Took me the devil of a time to get on to it, but I've got it down pretty pat now. Not easy to whirl around backwards, and count one, two, three at the same time. Takes a bit of getting used to."

"It's a wonder how you've mastered it so completely. I thought when Ella first said so it was her partiality speaking, for you must know she is loud in her praise of Mr. Tredwell. His very fine voice, his wit, his seat on a mount . . ."

"No, really," Bippy beamed, coloring in obvious pleasure, and beginning to suspect Miss Fairmont of more discernment than he had formerly supposed. He danced with Lady Sara, and it took no more than a hint for her to repeat her compliments and let him know Miss Fairmont thought him a wonderful fellow.

With this misinformation lodged in his brain, it was only natural that he should seek Miss Fairmont out for another dance. As it happened, she had no dances free, and as refusing a gentleman was a new experience for her, she apologized in some confusion and at length. It was enough to confirm what Lady Sara had said. The girl was sweet on him.

He did not love Ella. Indeed, before this evening he had only the haziest idea who she was, though he had spoken to her before and danced with her once. But there is some sweet seduction in feeling another admires us—a notion so flattering that some return of esteem takes place without our quite being aware. Ella liked him, and that conjured up a mental image of Ella. His satisfaction with himself spread to her, and before long the imagined esteem was mutual. Before Bippy left Almack's that night, he had decided Miss Fairmont was quite an unusual girl. Not a dasher, not an Incognita. Not a great wit or anything of the sort, but a very nice girl. He liked her.

Lady Sara observed with satisfaction that Tredwell's glance was in Ella's direction more than mere chance would warrant, but Tredwell was only the tail-end of her scheme. The major part of it had to await Clare's arrival. This happened just before the door closed at 11:00. The Prince Regent himself might arrive at one minute after, and he would not be admitted, but Clare arrived at 10:59, and the room breathed a sigh of relief. It was only an indifferent evening when the Duke of Clare did not attend.

He bowed to Lady Cowper, quizzing her on a stunning new gown, exchanged compliments with Mrs. Drummond Burrell, a joke with the Countess de Lieven, a five-minute flirtation with Lady Jersey, who exacted this honorarium from all the fashionable gentlemen and pouted at them for a week if they didn't pay up. His duty done, Clare lifted his quizzing glass to survey the room that was now surveying him. He bowed here, nodded there, and within three seconds no less than three chaperones were racing to nail him for their charges. The Marchioness of Strayward, though she had legs barely two feet long, got there first. She had a handicap of five yards on her closest running mate. Her daughter, the Lady Honor, was in her wake, not even panting, for she was taller than her mama.

"Ah, Clare, so you've got here at last," the Marchioness said happily. "We'd about given you up and were thinking of taking a look-in at Fenton's. That's where you've been till now I suppose."

"No."

"Well, you're in luck. I've had Honor save you a dance."

"You are too kind, ma'am."

Clare bowed stiffly to Honor and offered his arm, which she accepted as though it were the arm of just anyone, and not the most sought after arm in England. Lady Honor held herself very high, for she was the daughter of the fifth Marquis of Strayward. She may have been a tall, gaunt girl, with pale blue eyes and a skinny face, no conversation or liveliness and no visible intellect, but she was Lady Honor, and that she did know. She knew as well, what brains she possessed being used on matters of family, estates and titles, that the Duke of Clare was made in heaven for her. His lineage, title, fortune—all were unexceptionable. She was not aware that he was handsome, popular, a Corinthian, a charmer when he wanted to be. But she knew better than he knew himself what blood flowed in his veins, and she meant it to be transfused into her progeny when the time came. It was a settled thing in her mind. She made no effort to attract him, but still she meant to marry him, and she was supported by the full weight of her large, influential family.

Lady Sara tapped her satin-shod toe in impatience as Clare was run to ground by one mama after another. She remarked that it was not once necessary, or even possible, for him to seek a girl out. Always there was one in line, waiting to pounce. Clare dutifully paced the floor with two others after Miss Sedgley, then his civility was at an end. He strode out the door with a harassed expression on his face and headed to the parlor where the insipid beverages were served. Sara was after him like a shot and could not believe her luck to find him quite alone. He threw a wary look over his shoulder when he heard her enter.

"Relax, Clare, it's only me," she said brightly. "And I have no notion of asking you to stand up with me, or my niece."

"Sara, nice to see you," he smiled in relief. "Come and bear me company, and help stave off the mamas."

It was the very sort of remark that enraged Miss Prattle, yet after watching Clare's evening entertainment, one could hardly blame him. They hounded the man to death.

"A tedious bore, being an eligible dook, ain't it?" she teased.

"Truer words than you know, my girl, but never mind that. Where's Herbert these days? I didn't see him at Tatt's so he must be out of town."

"Yes, gone to Kent to help his papa with some estate business. He'll be gone a fortnight."

"Why didn't you go with him?"

"You forget I have a niece to chaperon."

"Oh, is that girl still with you? Taking you a devil of a long time to get her popped off. What's the matter with her?"

"She tells me the old gentlemen are so wise she bores them, and the young ones don't interest *her*. It's a problem."

"We all have our problems," he replied in a condoling spirit and led Sara to two chairs in a quiet corner, conveniently apart from other seats to allow privacy. They were old friends, coeval, and had hit London the same season. Clare had fancied Miss Watley at one time, but she had never had eyes for anyone but Sir Herbert. Still, they remained friends, met every season, and sent each other cards for their balls and larger parties. She was always happy to have a few minutes' flirtation with him when they met socially, and he was similarly inclined. Sara was now determined to capitalize on this long friendship to wangle Ella an invitation to Clare Palace. Miss Prattle would enjoy it, and while she would have no hope of attaching Clare, she would meet others there, and it would lend her a certain cachet to have been among the elect at his party. She broached the subject cautiously.

"One hears you are skipping town for a week or so. Taking a party to Clare, are you?"

"Yes, I have to go on business, like Herbert. Strayward has told me Honor is going with me, and I'll be damned if I'll be stuck with her alone, so have enlarged the party to lessen the strain of her company. Also, I might add, to lessen the likelihood of being expected to make an offer."

"They can't *make* you have her, you know."

"Can't they? I don't know, Sara. It's in the air. They expect it. I shall awake one morning and find Miss Prattle has got me engaged to Honor, and I'm for it then."

Sara squirmed in her seat at this reference to Prattle, but made no comment on it. "So you have invited a couple of your gayer flirts to enliven the party. Whom are you taking? Miss Sheridan, I gather?"

"And as Miss Sheridan is a ravishing brunette—rather in *your* style, Sara, so far as looks go—I have invited a redhead to complete the trio."

Sara felt a flush of pleasure at the comparison—it was his eyes that made one feel so special, she thought. Really, the devil was a charmer. No wonder the girls were all after him.

"Miss Prentiss," she supplied the redhead's name. Everyone knew Patrick's flirts, of course. "How interesting. Society will expect you to return caught by one or the other of them."

"My reason for inviting Sherry and Miss Prentiss was to eliminate that possibility, you recall."

"Yes, I do recall, but you don't often invite a small select party to Clare, and when you do so now, including only the three ladies from whom you are generally expected to choose your duchess, there is bound to be speculation. The time does draw near, you know. We are no longer young, Clare, you and I."

"Good God, Sara, you're frightening me to death. But I have invited some gentlemen to enlarge the party."

"I should hope so! Not even *you* would be so *outré* as

34

to invite a party composed entirely of ladies, with yourself the only attraction."

"Yes, I would," he said with a raised eyebrow and a wicked glance. "And attraction enough for 'em, too."

"What, a third of a duke each?" she jeered. "The one who got the top third, from the shoulders up, would do well enough, but truly, you know, neither your torso nor your nether limbs would be very amusing."

"My nether limbs, and *particularly* what you so genteelly describe as my *torso,* are grossly offended," he replied seriously, but with a sparkle of mischief deep in his eyes.

She slapped him with her silk fan. "That was very naughty of you, Patrick," she said severely.

"That is what one likes so much about you, Sara. You maintain all the appearances of propriety, indeed you are a very proper lady, but you don't fly into the boughs over nothing. I shall be bored to flinders with the infantry at Clare for a week with no decent company."

Sara's heart thudded at this leading remark. Surely now he would suggest her coming along.

"A pity Herbert's away, or you might have come with us," he said. "I know you would not come alone."

"Yes," she agreed, wondering how to channel his thoughts in the proper direction.

"But could your mama not come along for propriety's sake?"

"You forget my niece. Mama and I could not both leave her."

"Ah, I forgot Miss Mantel."

"No, she is not Herbert's niece, but mine."

"Miss Watley," he corrected himself automatically.

"Miss Fairmont. She is my elder sister's girl. You were not acquainted with Theresa."

"Oh, yes, I believe you told me that once before."

She had told him three times within her own memory, and very likely more, but this was no time to quibble. "I could not leave Miss Fairmont, you see. That is the only thing stopping me, for I should love to go otherwise." She waited, in expectancy of hearing an invitation extended to Miss Fairmont, too, but was disappointed. Apparently his eagerness for her own company did not stretch so far.

"A pity," he said.

At that moment, Bippy Tredwell, once again without a partner, straggled into the room and joined their party, pulling up a chair and ruining the private coze. "Asked Miss Fairmont for another dance," he informed Sara, "but her card was full. Lady Sara's niece," he told Clare.

"It chances we have just been speaking of her," Clare replied.

"That so? Didn't know you knew Miss Fairmont, Pa'k. A nice girl."

"Yes," Clare said mechanically. "A great pity you can't join us at Clare, Sara. Another time I hope." He arose, bowed, and left Sara, straining her ears to hear what they said as they left the room, but without success.

The conversation she was not able to hear was brief, but the name of Miss Fairmont arose. "I'm leaving now," Clare said. "Going to a club for a game of cards. Do you come with me?"

"Yes, surely. Might as well. Nothing to do here. A million extra men tonight. Miss Fairmont's card is full."

"Oh, yes, Miss Fairmont. Lady Sara's niece. Which one is she?" he asked, with very small interest, based solely on Bippy's having twice mentioned her name.

"That one over there in the yaller dress, dancing with Taffy Henderson," Bippy said, nodding towards her direction.

Clare raised his glass and was unimpressed by what he saw. "Very nice," he said aloud, while he thought to himself, a brown mouse. They departed together, and though only two had left the room, it was depleted of most of its interest for those remaining.

Miss Prattle composed a few lines to herself for the morrow's paper as she automatically performed the steps of the cotillion.

His Grace, the D—e of C——e, honored Almack's with an hour's visit on Thursday's assembly. Joy was confined to the bosoms of L—y H——r, Miss C——n, and Miss B——r, the three elected to stand up with him. Miss S——n and Miss P——s must take what comfort they can from the proposed party at Dorset, to which they have been invited. Don't cry, ladies! You must not expect the moon and the stars.

The next morning, Miss Fairmont was honored and deeply shocked to receive a call from Mr. Tredwell. She entertained him for a half-hour with Lady Sara playing duenna, in the latter's morning parlor. Before he left, after a very boring visit which quite tried Lady Sara's patience and powers of invention, for she was virtually the only one who spoke, Bippy offered two cards to Ella.

"Mama's having a little musical evening tomorrow, if you and your aunt would care to look in. Borelli—Italian feller—is going to sing. Daresay *I* may be called on to perform as well," he admitted sheepishly.

It was Lady Sara who accepted the invitation with delight, but as Ella also agreed to attend, the morning's visit was held by two of the three to have been a moderate success.

After he had left, Ella turned a suspicious eye on her aunt. "Sara, I believe that silly old fool is developing a *tendre* for me," she pronounced, not at all pleased.

"Do you think so, love?" her aunt replied, the picture of innocence.

"Yes, for besides having a waltz with me at Almack's last night, he asked me for another dance, which I was obliged to refuse him, and now this. Lord, what a bore it will be, listening to his caterwauling. I suppose we must go?"

"He has a very fine voice. It will be quite a select do, too. His being a crony of Clare's raises the *ton* of the crew his dear Mama can assemble."

"Yes, Clare will be there, but there's not much he can do to make an ass of himself at a sit-down musical evening."

"There's always intermission," Sara said with a cunning light in her eyes.

Unbeknownst to both ladies, a little something of interest also occurred before the musical evening. Not twenty minutes after leaving Mantel's house, Bippy encountered Clare on Bond Street, where His Grace had gone to replenish his supply of snuff.

"Ah, Tredwell," he said, coming up to him on the sidewalk. "I was wondering if I might bump into you. I thought we might have lunch at some club or other. What have you been doing with yourself this fine day?"

"Just come from Miss Fairmont's," he replied.

"Pursuing Lady Sara's niece, are you?" Clare asked, the name at last having stuck in his brain.

"No, no, nothing like that. Just securing her to attend my Mama's little soiree. Appreciates good music, you know."

"Does she indeed? I am surprised she condescended to waste her time on that Italian screech owl your Mama had the poor taste to engage then. But come, confess it is your fair self that is the attraction."

The pink glow that answered this remark was more speaking than words. *Damme, if Bippy isn't engaged in an amour, and with the most insignificant looking lady in London, too.*

"I did mention I might be rendering an air or two. Tell me, Clare, should I do an Italian aria, or a simple country song? Which would be more suitable?"

"I took it as a matter of course you would be performing a love song," Clare quizzed him.

"No, really."

"Do give us a respite from Italian tunes. Do something English, *short* and simple."

"What do you suggest?"

"How about blue-eyed Mary? Her name must surely be

Mary, to match her face." It was only fitting that such a common-looking lady have the very commonest of names.

"What, do you find her merry? Never noticed it myself. A bit of a serious girl. And her eyes ain't blue. At least I don't think they are."

"We shall go over your repertoire at lunch, and settle on something."

They strolled along Bond Street for half an hour, then repaired to White's for a meal. Bippy again broached the subject of a song, and it was becoming clear to Clare that his object was to choose something to do homage to Miss Fairmont. He had nothing to recommend regarding the song, but did say, "If this affair is serious, you shan't want to tear yourself away to come to Clare. You must not desert me, Bippy. I quite depend on you."

"No, no. Not serious at all. No thought of staying away from your party. Wouldn't miss it for the world."

"I feel the most selfish thing in nature to insist on—but my wits have gone begging! We must invite Miss Fairmont to be of our number."

"What, ask Miss Fairmont to Clare? No, really, Pa'k, you scarcely know her."

"But I am well acquainted with her charming aunt, Lady Sara. This will provide an unexceptionable excuse to lure her along. She is one of the four conversable women in London, and two of the others are not accepted in polite society."

"Who are they?"

"Tch, tch, you are much too innocent to hear such esoteric secrets. They would ruin you for Miss Fairmont. But I shall certainly drop by Grosvenor Square and leave a letter for Lady Sara. That is settled."

Bippy was not only pleased but highly flattered at this pandering to his interest. Clare did not remember either to write a letter or drop it by Grosvenor Square, but when he saw Sara at Bippy's musical evening the following day, he did make the invitation.

It was accepted with a becoming show of delight on the

part of Lady Sara, and acquiescence on the part of her niece. This calmness surprised Ella's aunt, who felt she had carried off quite a coup in arranging the visit. She was apprised of the reason on the way home.

"I sent in the most horrid article to the *Observer* this afternoon," she confessed. "All about Clare's party in Dorset."

"Naturally you must mention so interesting an event. Tell me, what did you say?"

"I'll show you my rough copy when we get home," Ella replied.

In Grosvenor Square, Ella handed a copy of her column to her aunt. "It's really beastly," she warned, biting her lip and frowning.

Lady Sara took up the sheet and read aloud: " 'History has the habit of repeating itself. The coming week will see a re-enactment of the Judgment of Paris. (He was the fairest of mortals, you Greek scholars will recall.) The three fairest damsels our Albion has to offer will be paraded before a latter-day Paris, the D—e of C——e, for him to bestow on one the Golden Apple of his favor. Bets will be taken at Brooks as to whether he will choose for his Venus L—y H——r, Miss S——n, or Miss P——s. We wait with baited breath to hear the outcome of the contest, and trust his grace will not disappoint us by once again delaying his selection, or disappoint the ladies by failing to show up at all.' "

Sara finished reading it and laughed. "Well, he shan't be surprised in any case, for he said the other evening he would wake up one morning and find you had got him engaged to someone."

"I wouldn't have sent it in if I had known he meant to ask *us*. Besides, it ruins the whole metaphor. What should we be doing at the contest?"

"Surely there were onlookers," Sara pointed out. "But you must be careful, Ella, not to make it too obvious you are there in person—that Miss Prattle is, I mean. Let a little time lapse before you send in your jottings, so it will seem plausible Miss Prattle has had time to learn of the goings-on from letters written back to town. It will be the ruination of us if he finds out Prattle is there. He will *know* it is not that utterly witless Lady Honor, nor Sherry, so that will leave only Belle Prentiss and us. You must exercise the greatest caution."

"I don't think I shall mention it at all. It is not quite *comme il faut* in any case, for me to be poking fun at him, while a guest under his roof."

"It will look mighty suspicious if you let the story go, after this build-up you have given it. Besides, it is the very reason why I . . ."

"You what?" Ella asked, her suspicions just that very moment aroused. "Sara, you sneak, you *wangled* this."

"Perhaps I pulled a few strings," she admitted, preening her hair and smiling.

"It was *you* who set Tredwell to dangling after me, wasn't it?"

"My dear, I am not a magician. I only set it up to put you in his way, and nature did the rest," she prevaricated slyly.

"What stories have you told him?" Ella asked, undeceived.

"I did nothing indiscreet, my dear, so never mind that and let us decide how the party at Clare Palace is to be covered. I think you must go on in your regular way, throwing a little jibe in here and there, but just delay sending in the stories, and perhaps you should include a few errors to make it seem it is all done secondhand."

"*Under*handed is the way it will be done. I cannot like it."

Lady Sara made little of the deceit involved, and turned the talk instead to acquisitions of toilette necessary for a week's visit to one of the finest homes in England. Ella was lamentably ignorant of the quantity of gowns and accessories necessary for it, and it was for her aunt to take her in hand during the few days allowed them before setting out in Sir Herbert's traveling coach-and-four for the holiday.

Four

Clare Palace was a huge crenelated pile of stones set deep in the heart of a vast parkland, reached by a winding road that turned off from the main post road and meandered through a meadow, a small coniferous forest, and a deer park, where live deer stood like stone statues to view the parade of carriages assembling for the week's visit. No fear or rancor marred their guileless eyes, almost as though they understood this batch of visitors had no intention of decimating their numbers. A sharp-eyed occupant of an incoming carriage might discern the glimmer of a white gazebo through the trees, done up in an oriental style, to mock the Prince's Brighton Pavilion. It was Joseph who had committed this atrocity, his last folly before falling from his horse and getting himself killed. A strange cylindrical edifice of stone, approximately four stories high with narrow slits of windows at irregular intervals, was knowingly pointed out by repeat visitors as the tower where one of the insane Clare ancestors had been incarcerated; though the fact that it gave a clear view for miles around might lead a visitor of historical inclinations to wonder whether it had not been in fact used as a lookout tower in years gone by, when England was still prey to invaders from abroad. When queried about its purpose by a shivering female guest, Clare invariably said it was Crazy Nellie's Tower, and they had best stay well away from it. He gave no hint as to whether it was Nellie herself, or her shade, who might pop out and kill them.

As they climbed the stone stairway to the north entrance, a porticoed affair with broken pediment and many columns, Ella said softly to her aunt, "Bet you a pound he won't be here."

"The Great Absent One will be here," Sara replied, with surprising conviction. She was right, but neither of his guests gave him her full attention. They were too busy gawking like tourists at his entrance hall. It appeared to soar straight up to heaven, miles and miles high, the clerestory pierced with round windows that bounced rays of light off frolicking cupids and garlands of flowers depicted on the painted ceiling. The hall was laid in black marble. Once Ella was sure she had a firm footing and wouldn't go slipping and disgrace herself instantly, she let her eyes roam around the lower walls, which were embossed with raised medallions of flowers, and took a peep through open doors into rooms as cavernous as cathedrals, and as richly appointed. The great stairway, done in oak with broad, shallow steps curved up to the right, across a landing, and down on the left, like a horse shoe.

"Welcome to Clare Palace," the host said. Ella curtsied and mumbled something, while her eyes continued darting to suits of armor, curve-legged tables with marble tops bearing great pots of flowers, and sundry oil paintings hanging on the walls in impressive gilt frames.

"The Sedgleys have already arrived," Clare said to Sara. "I hope you and your niece will join us in the drawing room after you have freshened up. Wiggins, call a house maid to show the ladies to their rooms," he said over his shoulder to the butler. With a smile he was off, and the ladies were escorted to two regal suites, each large enough to house an entire family. There Bickles and Stepson rendered them a hasty toilette, and they were ready to return below.

They met outside their doors, and Ella said in a low voice, "Do you know the way? I swear this place is as big as London. I am sure to get lost if I ever have to go about on my own."

"There are the stairs for a start anyway," Sara replied prosaically, and with this excellent starting point they made the landing, where Wiggins took them in hand and headed them in the right direction.

The Duke sat in a high-backed chair, of thronelike size and magnificence, in a room in which the chair did not seem overpowering. He looked on the verge of falling asleep, for he had been for some time in the presence of the Strayward ladies alone. He jumped up and greeted the newcomers eagerly and drew up a seat for Lady Sara beside himself. Ella took a place on the sofa next to Lady Honor.

"We were just saying, Sara," he continued the monologue she had interrupted, "we shall plan nothing for today. The others will be arriving at intervals during the day, so I must remain here. If the good weather holds up, we shall take a picnic to the Pavilion tomorrow. I hope the ladies will enjoy that. It is supposed to be one of Nash's finer efforts, though I find it a trifle gaudy. There are a dozen mounts in the stables, some of them not too wild, if any of you would care to take some exercise in the morning. I know you will want to, and perhaps your niece . . .", he turned towards Ella.

Ella said nothing, so Sara replied for her, "Oh, yes, Ella rides, if the mounts are not too restive."

"If you do not care to ride," he continued on, directing his comments to Ella, "there are several interesting walks. I shall be happy to point them out to you. Capability Brown is responsible for the east park, and Reston for the west, if you would care to compare their styles." Ella smiled weakly and nodded, still saying nothing. It seemed like a dream to her, or perhaps more like a nightmare, being pinned by the eyes of the Duke, whom she had for so long been writing about.

"Or if you would like to take a tour of the palace, my housekeeper is an excellent tour guide. The west gallery is the oldest part, built in the sixteenth century by Sir John Thynne. Many young ladies prefer the neo-Gothic addition made later." He stopped and stared at her, till she felt some reply was called for.

"Thank you," she said.

"And there are the tower and the ruined chapel. But perhaps you are not interested in architecture, Miss Fairmont?" Before their arrival, Clare had been having a similar sort of one-sided conversation with the Sedgleys, and was becoming short-tempered with people who did not care to perform their social duties.

"Oh, yes," Ella assured him, then added, "but I don't know very much about it."

"How very strange you have not learned, if it interests you," he said, and wrote Miss Fairmont off as a dead bore.

"Tell me, Sara," he turned again to the one lady in the room from whom he had some hopes of getting more than a monosyllabic reply, "What else can we do to amuse the guests?"

Wiggins then entered and poured wine, while a maid passed a tray of biscuits, which interlude gave Ella time to realize she ought to have made a better answer to his questions than she had, and to make a resolve to think of something to say.

"I imagine you have some sort of dancing party arranged," Sara said.

"Yes, a ball, but that must be at the end of the visit, for it takes a little setting up, and a few impromptu dances in the evenings. I came on such short notice everything is at loose ends. What are we to do with our *days*? I know Lady Honor does not care for riding," he bowed to Honor, who acknowledged her lack of horsemanship with a blink. "I was hoping to come up with some less strenuous entertainment," he continued, turning back to Sara.

"The ladies will enjoy being driven about the countryside in carriages if they do not like to ride," Sara informed him. "They will want to go to the village one day and go through the shops. Girls always like a shopping spree in a new place better than anything, you know. Then if they can't amuse themselves, you can always set them to decorate your ballroom for one of your dances, or get up a masquerade party that will take up an afternoon in arranging their costumes."

"I knew I might count on your good sense," he said, with a truly warm smile. Till then Ella had not realized he had such a winning smile. Sara was always talking about it, but it was not the one he usually wore to London parties, and this was the first time Ella had been exposed to it.

"Oh, don't worry about it, Clare," Sara said, perfectly at home with him. "Young people will amuse themselves. They will have their little flirtations to while away the time you must know, and no doubt you have a dozen cats and dogs around somewhere that will provide a diversion. Then, too, they will all be dashing off notes to their bosom bows back in London, telling what a gay time they are having. There is the whole palace to explore—that will take an age—and they may have some ideas of their own too. What was it we did when we were young?" Sara asked of the Marchioness, desiring for the sake of civility to include the Sedgleys in the talk.

"*I* was married my first year out and had always the job of looking after three houses, which didn't leave any time for fun," the Marchioness flattened them all by stating.

Clare flashed a quick, intimate glance at Sara, that said mutely, *you are wasting your time, my girl, trying to get an idea out of that one.*

"Well, I was always chasing after my brothers, riding anything with four legs, and fishing and shooting, which won't suit your quiet guests," Sara said. "But perhaps you young girls have some ideas. What do you think, Ella? You youngsters seem to be having such fun at Fairmont whenever I go."

The fun at Fairmont consisted of such boisterous sports as riding bareback through the meadows, poling across the lake on homemade rafts, and having frog-jumping contests, and Ella was not in a mood to proffer these suggestions to the stone face that was turned to her. She felt betrayed by her aunt, but braced herself to say *something*. "We—we know everyone there, and we visit a great deal, and have company. Perhaps we might have a sketching party one afternoon," she added desperately. She abhorred sketching, especially in parties, but it sounded a ladylike activity, which her own pursuits were not.

Sara plunged in to save her. "Yes, Crazy Nellie's Tower would make an excellent subject—from a distance, Clare," she added.

"Or that pavilion you mentioned," Ella added, determined to make at least one comment unelicited by a direct question.

"We shall contrive to be merry somehow," Sara assured him.

"Nothing is more hopeless than a scheme of merriment," Clare said rather depressingly.

"You are too pessimistic," Sara chided him.

"That, I believe, is a quotation from Dr. Johnson," Ella advised her aunt.

"*Now* I see how you amuse yourself, Miss Fairmont," Clare said, turning towards her again with a hopeful light on his face. "You are a reader. *Your* entertainment is assured, for we have a very fine library at Clare."

"Have you indeed?" she asked, with the first indication of real interest she had shown thus far.

"Yes, I will take you there later. My librarian will direct you to those subjects you are interested in." He hoped the lady might now mention her areas of interest, and contribute something to this lagging conversation, but she said only, "Thank you," in a very small voice.

Throughout the whole time, the Marchioness and her daughter sat like the well-bred statues they were and said nothing. That they were dead was obviously untrue, however, for their eyes occasionally went from one speaker to the other.

To kill time while awaiting the arrival of the others, Clare took the party to his Mama's rose garden, where the Marchioness distinguished herself by recognizing a

Queen Anne rose bush, and her daughter by telling them they had *many* finer ones at Strayward, and Ella did not distinguish herself at all. She liked roses, but like architecture, she knew little about the subject. She preferred keeping her mouth shut and appearing a fool to opening it and removing the doubt. Just before dusk, the party was considerably enlivened by the simultaneous arrival of the Prentiss and Sheridan carriages, and before long the three young gentlemen who were to complete the party—Tredwell, Mr. Peters, and Lord Harley, also came. It was time to change and reassemble for dinner, and Ella breathed a sigh of relief to escape the blighting eye of the Duke.

The meal was served on a grand scale in the formal dining room, with the Duchess of Clare acting as hostess, presiding over a table thirty feet long, laden with an array of silver, crystal, fine Wedgwood porcelain, and enough food to please the greatest glutton in the land. The visitors just arrived added sufficient variety to the assembly that conversation flourished, and the meal was a jolly one.

Mr. Peters and Lord Harley were young blades of the Corinthian set, who looked elegant in their black suits, and more at home in their riding clothes. "Doing the pretty" with the ladies was the price they were willing to pay for the privilege of getting their legs over the backs of Clare's hacks and hunters. The evenings would be dashed dull, but Clare had a well-stocked cellar, at least, to make them tolerable.

The young ladies, Miss Sheridan and Miss Prentiss, were a study in contrast. Sherry was outstanding for her ravishing appearance—crow-black hair worn in the stylish Méduse, a skin like the inside of a white rose, and eyes as black as her hair. Her conversation was insipid, but her looks so staggeringly beautiful that no one ever listened to what she had to say anyway, except her modiste. Her sole subject of conversation was gowns, and a further restriction was that it was usually her own gowns she discussed, though she occasionally offered a criticism of a rival's.

Belle Prentiss was of a different sort entirely. Not strikingly beautiful, but with a lively gamin charm. She was slight and elfin, with titian curls cut daringly short, almost a Brutus do in fact. It was the style to compare her to Lady Caroline Lamb. She was as broad in her interests as Miss Sheridan was narrow. She knew everyone, did everything, from cutting through town in her own high-perch phaeton-and-pair to reading to old Queen Charlotte in the afternoons. She sang, danced, played every known musical instrument, painted, wrote verses, drama, and novels, and still had time to take in every rout and assembly that occurred. She even read the papers and knew something about politics. It was one of her ploys to wish aloud that she were a man, so that she might be Prime Minister, and with her energy and cleverness it was not unlikely that she would have made it, had she been a man. But she was a young lady, and so would make do instead with marrying the prize of the marriage mart, the Duke of Clare.

These two young ladies were accompanied by their mothers, but as beauty and talents were unevenly distributed between the generations, neither of the elder ladies had anything to recommend her but her daughter. They were therefore of only minimal interest to the party, but of prime interest to each other, and vied endlessly for the upper hand in their dealings.

The Duke was obliged, because of precedence, to have the Marchioness on his right hand, for which he compensated by putting Lady Sara on his left. He had placed Ella beside Bippy Tredwell, as he was the only reason she was present. Since she didn't care two hoots for him, she was not at all shy to talk up to him and enjoyed a very pleasant repast. Her pleasure was somewhat mitigated to learn he would be singing after dinner, but she had some hopes of slipping off to the library and did not worry much about the concert.

"Any special song you would like to hear me sing?" he asked.

"I have no favorite," she replied.

"Like Italian songs?" he asked.

"Yes, they are very nice."

"Could do 'Tu Mi Chamas' if you like," he volunteered.

"That would be fine," she agreed, without enthusiasm.

When the ladies had retired to the drawing room, Bippy said aside to Clare that Ella wanted to hear him sing 'Tu Mi Chamas,' and did he have the music to it. Clare was still surprised at the attraction between the two, but had observed Ella's relative liveliness during dinner, and took it for an accepted thing now.

"One of the ladies will have the music by heart. Since Byron set words to it, it is all the go."

After tea, the gentlemen joined the ladies and all migrated to the music room to be entertained, first by Belle, who displayed at length her talents in singing, dancing, reciting long stretches of Shakespeare's plays that she had by heart, playing the harp, and finally—there was no end to her skills—a pantomime. The silence of this last diversion proved soporific, and the audience was in some danger of falling off to sleep after their long day, but they were soon roused by Miss Sheridan, who sang two country songs very loudly, attempting to make up in volume of sound for the paucity of her accomplishments.

Bippy's superior voice was quite a relief, but when Clare chanced to glance in Miss Fairmont's direction, he saw her yawning into her fist. Having composed her column during the other diversions, she was having a hard time to keep her eyes open. Strange, he thought, that she never once glanced at the stage to admire her suitor's prowess.

The concert finally at an end, the guests were allowed to straggle up to their rooms, amidst a volley of compliments to each other by the performers, and a dull silence from the dazed audience.

Five

Half the party slept late next morning after the rigors of the journey, but neither Miss Sheridan nor Miss Prentiss had the slightest intention of letting the other get the jump on her, and they entered the breakfast room together, pale and heavy-lidded but meticulously gilded at 9:30. By 10:30 they had both eaten and drunk a good deal more than they wanted, and could find no excuse to linger till their host should arise from his bed and join them. When Miss Sheridan decided she would risk a stroll through the grounds, Miss Prentiss insisted on joining her, fearing she had somehow discovered where *he* was to be found. Sherry congratulated Miss Prentiss on her 'interesting' gown, while inwardly wondering why she should choose to make such a sight of herself in a skimpy little mulled muslin with no bows. Miss Prentiss said it was not nearly so *fine* as Miss Sheridan's, though she was afraid that white with a ruffled bottom would get horribly soiled romping through wet grass.

While they sauntered through the park, eyes and ears alert for a trace of the owner, Clare arose and made a leisurely toilette. At 11:00 he strolled into the breakfast parlor, outfitted in buckskins and hacking jacket, for a cup of coffee. He had breakfasted in his room and came to table only to say good morning to his guests. Mrs. Sheridan and Mrs. Prentiss were there, each praising her own daughter, while mentally cursing her for being absent. They carefully noted the time so the error might not be repeated tomorrow. Lady Honor and the Marchioness were both still in bed, and never arose before noon. Shortly after 11:00, Sara and Ella came into the room, the former in her riding habit. The mothers fumed impotently when Clare invited Sara to accompany him, though he made it clear it was only a business ride, and he would be stopping at some tenant farms to attend to various matters. Again they made a mental note—tomorrow at 11:00, in riding habits.

"You don't plan to ride, Miss Fairmont," Clare said, looking at her cotton gown.

"No, I plan to take this opportunity to visit your library."

"Ella is an incorrigible bookworm," Sara explained.

"I shall take you there, and turn you over to Mr. Shane, my librarian, before we leave," he offered.

The mothers doubly regretted their daughters' absence when Clare was in such an amiable mood that he was being polite even to the Fairmont girl.

After breakfast, Sara went for her bonnet and gloves while Clare took Ella through rooms and corridors to a library composed of three adjoining rooms, whose every wall was lined with books. Ella had never seen so many assembled in one place before and thought she had landed in heaven. A tall, slight gentleman with blond hair and spectacles arose from a desk and came towards them.

"I have received a price on that Gutenberg Bible from the dealer in Belgium," he said at once, in some excitement.

"Good, order it if you think the price fair," Clare said and didn't even inquire the price quoted.

"I think we ought to talk it over," Mr. Shane suggested.

"No, no, Shane, you decide. It is *you* who is always after me to acquire one, and you too, I suspect, who will go to the bother of reading it. This is Miss Fairmont, a guest. Show her whatever she wants to see, will you please?" With a smile and a bow he was off.

As he strolled away, he heard the beginning of their discussion.

"What sorts of books do you have?" Ella asked, peering around the stacks and trying to decipher titles.

"We have English, French, Latin, Greek, German, and

a small number of Russian volumes, Miss. What are you interested in?"

"Everything," she stated comprehensively.

At the first door, Clare turned aside and pretended to study a shelf of books. He had some idea the girl was a talented linguist, and as he was interested in oddities, he wished to overhear more.

"You read all those languages?" Mr. Shane asked, impressed in spite of her plain appearance.

"Good gracious, no. I read only English, and a tiny bit of French, but I should like to *see* the others. Russian, for instance, uses quite a different set of letters from English, I believe, and I should like to see it. Shall we start with the Russian?"

Not even a dilettante, but merely a curious child, Clare remarked with a sardonic smile, and was happy he had shifted the load of accommodating her on to Shane. He proceeded at a brisk pace to the stables, from which starting point he enjoyed a pleasant ride with Lady Sara.

Around 3:00 the whole party assembled for a hearty luncheon.

"What have you planned for this afternoon, Clare?" Belle Prentiss asked her host.

"We were to have a picnic at the pavilion, but we are getting such a late start we'll make it tomorrow instead."

"And what shall we do today?" she persisted.

"Why, it is such a fine day, why don't you young ladies take a walk about the grounds and acquaint yourselves with the place?"

"We did that this morning," Miss Prentiss informed him.

"What, saw all ten thousand acres?" he asked.

Miss Prentiss threw back her copper curls and laughed. "Oh, you know we could not! Miss Sheridan and I merely went for a stroll about the gardens and to the Tower." She glanced at him with a saucy eye at this remark, for her Mama had discovered the story about Crazy Nellie's Tower being haunted, and warned her not to mention it.

"Ah," he said with an air of surprise. "I must congratulate you on your luck in being still with us then."

"Is she really locked up in there?" Sherry asked with a shiver.

"Who?" Clare asked.

"Why, your—your aunt, or cousin, or whoever she is."

"Great-great aunt," he explained. "No, she is no longer there *in person*, though really so many people report seeing her still that I sometimes wonder . . ."

"You mean it is haunted?" Belle asked, her topaz eyes sparkling with pleasurable fear.

Miss Sheridan turned pale under her black curls, and said nothing.

"I suppose it must be her ghost they see," he replied calmly.

"What is she supposed to look like?" Lady Sara enquired.

"Why, rather like Miss Prentiss. Reddish hair . . ."

"Auburn," Miss Prentiss corrected him.

"But done in an older style. Not all cut off like yours," he said to Belle, with a disparaging look at her shorn locks. Miss Sheridan smiled and ran her little white fingers through her own glossy coiffure. "She was a lady-in-waiting to Queen Anne," he continued, "but got on the wrong side of her somehow—befriended Lady Marlborough, I believe. Her husband was so displeased—ruined his court ambitions, of course—that he had her confined and she was never seen again."

"Good gracious!" Miss Sheridan gasped.

"The beast," Lady Sara added, helping herself to lobster salad. "And *you* are a beast too, Clare, to be frightening these young ladies with such a faradiddle. What does your Crazy Nellie wear? I should like to recognize her and say 'how do you do' if I should happen to bump into her while I am sketching this afternoon."

"Her hair dressed high—red, like Miss Prentiss's, as I mentioned, and a pink gown with panniers."

"I can't say I much blame her husband for having her

locked up if she wore a pink gown with red hair," Sara commented idly.

"But you must know, there is a streak of color blindness in the family," Belle teased.

Clare bit back a smile at her sally, and the others breathed a sigh of relief that he hadn't taken a pique.

"And she always carries a basket of red roses," he finished his description.

"She was clearly deranged," Sara said.

"We have a ghost at Strayward," Lady Honor announced.

Clare was sorely tempted to say there was nothing but ghosts at Strayward, for none of the inhabitants seemed to be quite alive, but he asked instead, "What sort of ghost, ma'am?"

"A monk," she replied and turned her attention to her plate.

No one was so foolhardy as to expect three consecutive remarks from her, so Clare turned again to Sara. "Do you mean to sketch today?"

"Yes, Ella and I mean to, and any of the others who care to join us are welcome. *Ca va sans dire*." She scanned the table, but with the host's plans unclear, no one else volunteered.

"Would you care to join us, Lady Honor?" she asked.

"I don't sketch," she said.

"You might enjoy the walk," Clare prodded. "You *do* walk?"

"Yes, I walk," she replied, perceiving no joke, and certainly no insult in the question.

"I shall go with you and show you the view most favored by artists," Clare volunterred. "It is advised not to get too close."

"Masonry loose, is it?" she asked, during a private conversation a little later.

"Just so. A footman was hit by a falling stone, but till I manage to get it repaired or ripped down, I find a ghost more effective than falling stones in keeping guests at a safe distance."

"You mustn't tear it down. A building in a state of decay is all the go. Sir Herbert speaks of erecting a half-chapel or so."

"We have a ruined chapel at Strayward," the Marchioness said across the table, having been straining her ears to overhear what was being said.

"And a cloister," Honor added.

Everyone looked in surprise to hear such unwonted vivacity from the Strayward ladies. There were exclamations of "indeed" and "how interesting," but they were not so easily lured into expanding.

"As you ladies have already seen my derelict tower, I expect you will want to ride this afternoon," Clare said to Sherry and Belle.

They both looked to their mothers for instructions as to what they would like to do. None were forthcoming as they hadn't the temerity to contradict a plan of Clare's. When Mr. Peters and Lord Harley began discussing what mounts they would recommend for the ladies, and which path they would take, it was too late to suggest they would prefer sketching, and so Lady Sara made off with Clare again.

Ella was not without an escort, for Bippy joined their party, to station himself at her shoulder and pester her at every line she set to paper. No artist, she performed even worse than usual and was quite ashamed of the childish, blotched sketch Tredwell snatched out of her hands to show Clare before it was even quite finished.

Clare frowned painfully and handed it back. "Very bad. Very bad indeed. In fact, I think it is actually the worst drawing of the tower I have ever seen. I can't recall having seen a worse—unless perhaps that abomination Sara is perpetrating . . ."

"I was thinking of having it shown at Somerset House," Sara joked lightly, but Ella began to think Clare was a very rude host. No matter about her own, Sara's picture was very good. She personally hated sketching and was only here because he, as her host, had not bothered his head to arrange any better sport. He ought to be glad they could amuse themselves, instead of belittling their efforts. And he was rude to the others, too, calling Miss Prentiss a redhead twice, and offending Lady Honor by asking her if she could walk. Or she *should* have been offended, if she had had any sensitivity at all. Half the town of London feared his tongue, but from long practice Miss Prattle felt she could acquit herself well enough, should it come to a verbal battle. *He* didn't care what he said or did, and Ella took the decision that henceforth *she* would not care either. She would no longer sink into herself if he asked her a question, raking her with his cold gray eyes.

She said nothing, but in her mind's eye she was envisioning the words that would soon appear in the *Observer*.

> While 99% of the *ton* twiddles its thumbs in London awaiting the D—e C——e's return from his palace, his invited guests twiddle their thumbs and try as best they might to get in the tedious days. It is reported a picnic was *planned*, but did not take place. The Misses S——n and P——s are improving their walking skills, and L——y H——r and her mama are reported to have had a good night's repose.

Her thoughts were broken into. "Did you find what you wanted in the library, Miss Fairmont?" Clare was saying. Perhaps not for the first time, as there was a certain edge to his voice. Ella knew herself to be deaf when she was preparing her column.

"Yes, thank you. You seem to have everything, and Mr. Shane was very patient in explaining it all to me. I shall know just where to find things for myself from now on."

"What sort of literature in particular are you interested in?"

"English literature," she said, not to be questioned about all those other languages she had seen. His steely eyes continued to regard her fixedly.

"Yes?" It was an invitation, almost a command, to continue, but her reading was so scattered and diffuse that, though she did read a great deal, she was no specialist and could claim no superior knowledge in any field. Her resolve to face up to him vanished under the blast of those mocking eyes.

"I see," he said, and gave up, turning once again to Sara, who proceeded to regale him successfully with a rather dull tale of Herbert and his gout.

He said not another word to Ella, and when the four returned to the house, it was to Lady Sara that he offered his arm. Miss Fairmont felt she had let herself down, and thought of a dozen witty and amusing replies she might have made to his question. Next time, she determined, she would give him a smart, even a sharp retort. She would see something but mockery in those eyes yet, even if it was anger.

As they strolled along, Clare said to Sara, "Your niece is very gauche. Why do you not take her education in hand and teach her to converse like a lady?"

"What, and set up a competitor under my own roof?" she smiled boldly, with her long-lashed eyes. Very fine eyes, he thought.

"Be serious, Sara. That little brown mouse would be no match for you, if she conversed like de Staël. Besides, you are a married lady and ought to stop hogging all the beaux."

"Oh, Ella is not open with strangers, and there is no point in trying to make a silk purse of a sow's ear."

He laughed heartily at this homely truth. "What an extraordinary experience it is, to have a chaperon admit her charge is a very plain little simpleton."

"I did not say *that!* She is well-read."

"Yes, she reads *English,* she tells me."

"When she takes to someone, she is as lively as even you could wish."

"I am no admirer of pert young ladies, but I *do* like a girl who has a few words to say for herself."

"I expect she is afraid you would give her one of your infamous set-downs, if she dared to open her mouth."

"I'm more apt to do so if she doesn't," he admitted. The conversation turned to other topics, and the group reached the palace.

"It wants a few hours to dark," Clare said. "I have some business to attend to in the village. I'll have a mount saddled up and ride in."

"And Ella and I shall take our abominable sketches in and flatten them under some books, if your Mr. Shane will permit it."

"Miss Fairmont must use her powers of persuasion," Clare said with a lift of his eyebrow in her direction. "I make no doubt they got on admirably."

This was neither meant for a compliment, nor taken for one. "Yes, I find Mr. Shane more conversable than *some* of the gentlemen here," Miss Prattle shot back, before Miss Fairmont had time to consider the wisdom of this jibe.

"Indeed!" Clare said.

There! She had jolted him out of his mockery now. But not for long. "I am happy you have found a fellow bookworm you can talk to," he said, bowed, and turned his back on them.

"I'll go round to the stables to see how my horses are doing," Bippy said, unaware that a small skirmish had just taken place.

"What came over you, Ella, to say such a thing?" Sara asked.

"He has been giving me digs all day, Sara, and I will *not* bear it any longer."

Sara's first reaction was to issue a warning, but upon consideration of Clare's recent words on the subject, she resisted. "Well, serves him right," she said. "He told me I ought to encourage you to speak up."

"You don't mean he actually *complained* about me! Oh, he is insufferable. There was no need to mention it. Everyone must know how stupidly mute I have been."

"Yes, and I have a notion everyone will soon see a transformation," Sara said with a pleased grin. "Come along, and see if you can wrest some heavy tomes from Mr. Shane."

While one party sketched, the other rode about the estate. Sherry was not long happy, cantering through fields and parks with no one to admire her blue riding habit, and by dint of repeated coaxing and sulking, she induced the others to ride with her to the local village. She hoped for no more than an ogling by the locals; a good perusal of the shops would have to await the formal visit to Kitswell. Belle did not set her jaw against the scheme, as one expected her to do, and so the gentlemen went along. When they were stuck with the ladies, riding was no fun anyway, and a road was no worse than a field. They none of them looked forward to much of interest in the trip, and were all surprised at what they discovered, though the surprise was greeted with very different emotions in them.

It was the needle-sharp Belle Prentiss who recognized the long stride of the Duke as he paced along the street. This alone made the trip worth the bother, but he was not alone. He was accompanied by a young person of ravishing beauty, a blonde girl, well-built, with her face trustingly turned towards her protector, adoration in her pretty blue eyes. For this Belle would have ridden a hundred miles. She inadvertently gave a yank on her reins when she saw them, and her mount reared up. She was not aware of the fine scene she made, controlling her frisky animal without the least difficulty. Neither were her friends aware of it; they too had spotted Clare now, and were all staring at him as though turned to stone. They were not sure he had seen them, but as he immediately bolted into the door of the closest shop—Martin's Drapers it was called—and slammed the door after him, they were inclined to think he had.

"So he did not stay with the sketching party," Sherry said. "Mama made sure he was carrying on a flirtation with Lady Sara."

There was a little smile of triumph on Belle's animated face. "Did any of you recognize her?" she asked the others.

"No," and "Never saw her before in my life," were the responses from the gentlemen. Sherry was momentarily beyond speech.

"Dashed pretty wench," Harley said, to no one in particular.

"Regular Incomparable," Peters agreed, still staring at the door through which the apparition of loveliness had vanished.

Sherry was returned to reality by the medium of jealousy. "What a very plain old gown she wore," she said.

"My dear," Belle told her in a knowing manner, "she was not a *lady*."

"Oh, what could he be doing with such a person?" Sherry wondered aloud.

"Let's go and find out," Belle suggested, smiling a challenge at them all.

"Better not," Peters cautioned, already making ready to turn his horse about to retire from the village.

"Cowards!" Belle taunted. Sherry looked about waiting for someone to decide what she was to do.

"Peters is right." Harley backed him up. "He won't be half pleased at us for seeing him. Best to get back to the palace and say nothing."

"But I don't understand what he is doing here with her," Sherry repeated herself.

"What do you think?" Harley asked angrily.

"Maybe she works for him," Peters advanced, with

some intention of concealing what was clearly to him an amorous rendezvous.

"Haha. Maybe she makes up his jackets, since they are gone into the draper's shop," Belle laughed. "He will start a new style. Weston and Stultz will no longer be the first tailors of London."

"It could very well be that she is a seamstress, doing some work for the Duchess," Peters suggested, having improved on his former excuse that she worked for Clare.

"And Clare, of course, goes with her to choose the muslin," Belle laughed ironically. "Why don't we go in and talk to him then, if it is so innocent as that?"

"Don't be such a greenhead, Belle," Peters said curtly. "Not the thing for us to be spying on him, and I for one intend to go back home and say nothing about it."

"Yes, my girl, and you'll do likewise if you're half as clever as you think you are," Harley added.

These strict warnings were enough to convince Sherry. With three horses being turned about in the middle of the road, Belle had either to join them, or go alone into the shop and accost Clare and his ladybird. Brazen as she was, she was not quite up to this, so she went along with her companions. The gentlemen killed open speculation on the way home by refusing to discuss the subject but, all the same, it was uppermost in everyone's mind.

Sherry worried to herself that Clare was showing a partiality for blondes. The young person in the village was, of course, not a threat, being of the lower orders, but Lady Honor was a blonde and the daughter of a Marquis. This point rated nearly as highly with Miss Sheridan as it did with Lady Honor. The gentlemen had no thoughts of mentioning the episode to Clare or anyone else, but Belle was as yet undecided on her strategy. True enough, Clare would dislike to be quizzed about the girl publicly, but in private she thought she might show him that she was a woman of the world by a little good-natured bantering. No more than Sherry did she see the girl as a real danger. Her interpretation of the matter was that this was the reason for his sudden bolt to Dorset in the middle of the Season, and the party he had set up was camouflage, pure and simple. It would account for his tardy rising that morning too, if he had gone out with the girl last night after the concert. She worried a little that he would take her to London and set her up in a private dwelling, thus very likely delaying any plans he might be formulating for getting married. For herself, she would not tolerate a mistress in London if she was the one he meant to have. He could keep her here in the country and welcome, but not in London, where everyone would know of her. Not the first year anyway, she compromised.

In Martin's Drapery Shop, the Duke banged his fist on the counter and exclaimed, "Dammit to hell anyway! A man can't even walk down a village street without being spied on. I'm sorry, Prissy. No, I am not angry with you. Please don't cry. You are still coming home with me, but you must stay out of sight, till these people that are visiting me leave. It won't be for long. Dry your tears now, you don't want to redden your eyes."

Six

Clare had invited a few country friends in to dinner, and with the additional young people, a small dancing party was got up in the music room to while away their second evening.

The next morning at 11:00 sharp, Miss Sheridan and Miss Prentiss entered the breakfast room, wearing striking riding habits of blue and green respectively, to set off their black and red hair. Clare had arisen early and been locked in his office for an hour with his bailiff before they came down. When the Duchess told them this bitter news, they settled for another ride with Mr. Peters and Lord Harley, but returned early to change for the picnic at the

Pavilion, where lunch was to be served under the onion dome. The food and wine were excellent, and even a picnic at Clare was not conducted without the proper number of servants attending, so no one had to serve himself. Lady Honor appeared perfectly content to sit sipping wine and staring at the countryside with vacant eyes, but to the other members of the party there seemed to be something lacking once the food had been served. Perhaps the fact that Clare sat chatting with the Marchioness and his Mama accounted for the flatness of the outing.

When everyone but Lady Honor had emptied a third glass, and sat making desultory conversation for five minutes, Belle Prentiss arose and walked over to Clare. He went with her to join the younger group.

"What would you like to do this afternoon?" he asked.

Honor yawned, and it was pretty clear that she desired nothing but to go on comparing Clare's parks to her papa's, mentally, of course. The others seemed to want to do *something,* but nothing occurred to them.

"Sara, what do you think?" Clare asked.

"Is it too late to ride into the village?"

"We have been riding all morning and have just changed out of our habits," Sherry said, with a whine creeping into her voice.

"And we went to the village yesterday," Belle added, with a knowing smile at Clare, which he ignored entirely.

"Miss Fairmont, you will not want another bout in the library so soon. *You* decide what we are to do." He was fed up with this bunch of turnipheads and not about to put himself out an inch for them.

"We might have a frog-jumping contest," she said in Miss Prattle's tart tone. If he had no reasonable plans for them, she would show him what she thought of his hospitality.

"I beg your pardon?" He stared at her with a frozen face, but she was finished with being afraid of him.

"A frog-jumping race, Your Grace. We often do it at Fairmont. We happen to have a large pond . . ."

"As it happens, I too have a large pond," he replied, with some evidence of thawing on his frozen features.

"I was sure there would be one somewhere on your ten thousand acres," she returned, quite sweetly, with just a bit of Prattle underlying the words. "We all go to the pond and catch our entry."

"It sounds horrid," Miss Sheridan said, looking at her pale pink city gown.

Miss Sedgley opened her eyes a millimeter wider and nearly frowned in distaste, but at the last moment her muscles were not up to it, so she just looked.

"No, really, Ella," Lady Sara admonished.

"But it sounds a capital idea," Clare intervened, and immediately Miss Sheridan and all the others thought it a pretty good idea too. "We go to the pond, Miss Fairmont, and catch our entrants, then what?"

"Well, catching your racer is half the fun, and it is a rule that everyone must catch his own. We set up a course about—oh, ten or fifteen yards long. We shall require some markings for a start and finish line, and of course a prize for the winner."

"What prize do you suggest?" Clare asked, listening to her explanation and never taking his eyes from her while she talked.

"Some little bibelot will do, or a guinea. At Fairmont we have an inscribed cup, since it has become an annual event."

"What a pity I have no inscribed cup, but if you assure me a guinea will do ..." His expression had not only melted, but was turning quite warm.

Ella looked, half suspecting he was roasting her, but was determined to brazen it out. "Oh, yes, a guinea will do nicely."

"Are there any other rules?"

"Yes, you are not allowed to touch your racer from beginning to end. No giving him a nudge with your toe or finger, though you may follow along behind and give all the vocal help you wish. It is the shouting and yelling that make it fun."

"By Jove, that sounds like great sport," Mr. Peters said. "Let's go to the pond straight off. I bet a monkey my frog will take yours, Harley."

"We'll see about that. Is a bullfrog allowed, Miss Fairmont?" Harley asked.

"Yes, any frog at all. Bullfrogs are excellent. But don't make the mistake of getting a toad, for they can't keep up with a frog at all."

"I know a toad from a frog," Harley replied, wounded.

"Must the girls catch their own frog, too, Miss Fairmont?" Sherry asked.

"Yes, that is part of the rules, but you may use an old pair of gloves if you don't like to touch it and take a basket to carry it in."

Clare quickly dispatched a footman for old gloves and baskets, and by the time everyone had put a question to Miss Fairmont to clarify the rules, and the gentlemen had indulged in an orgy of betting, he was back. The mothers stayed behind at the Pavilion, and in fact soon wended their way back to the house, but the young folks ran in high spirits to the pond, which was not so very far away.

Belle Prentiss entered into this game as any other with great eagerness and determination to win. She cheated a little by getting Peters to actually lift her specimen from the pond, but she put it in the basket herself and struck up a new idea by calling it Count Ugolino, from Dante's *Inferno,* because it was so grotesquely ugly.

Miss Sheridan cheated quite a lot. She smiled prettily at Bippy, and pointed out the frog she wanted, and he was kind enough to lift it from the lily pad for her and carry it in his basket. When Miss Fairmont was appealed to for a ruling on this, she allowed that as there was a shortage of baskets, it would be permitted. Lady Honor ignored all rules, as became a lady, and told Clare to get her a frog and take it to the starting line. She then went and stood under a beech tree while her will was done.

"That is definitely illegal," Ella told Clare.

"Yes, but you see I have only picked up this tiny fellow for her, and he hasn't a chance of winning. There is no point in expecting Miss Sedgley to join in any sort of a game."

The gentlemen, joining very much into the spirit, were removing topboots and stockings and wading into the pond to fish for large frogs. Ella had observed the situation and chosen for herself a fat bullfrog sitting in the middle of the pond on a log which jutted out of the water. At home she would have pulled up her skirts, taken off her shoes and stockings, and gone in after it, but she deemed that impossible here. Clare had an eye on the same creature, but was too gentlemanly to beat Ella to it. He was curious as well to see what she meant to do. The cavalier manner in which she set up the rules for the contest made him believe there was more to the brown mouse than he had supposed.

When he observed her wander off from the group, he followed her. "You have not yet got yourself a frog, Miss Fairmont," he said.

"I am looking about for a raft. I expect you must have sailed this pond when you were young, and there might be the remains of one here somewhere."

"I recall some cousins falling off one earlier this spring. I believe it may be in those rushes." He walked ahead of her and hauled out a dilapidated old raft. "I doubt she's seaworthy," he said, looking at her in a challenging manner.

She inspected it carefully before replying. "It will hold me. I don't weigh much. And even if it sinks, the water would not be over my head, would it?"

"No, but your gown . . ."

"You forget the prize," she laughed. "I shall replace the gown with that. I am sure to win with Prince Charming."

"Is that what you will call him?"

"Certainly. All frogs are princes in disguise, waiting for

the princess to kiss them and restore them to their proper form."

"And will you kiss Prince Charming if he wins for you?"

"Oh, no, it must be a *princess*. I could only turn him into a plain mister. I daresay he would rather remain king of the pond. I shall take him to London for one of the royal Princesses to transform him. Charlotte, I think, is the most likely candidate. If she is satisfied with Prince Leopold, she can take no exception to a frog."

"Prince Leopold is generally thought to be quite a handsome fellow."

"Not by *me* he isn't. Could you help me with the raft?"

"I'll get the frog for you," he offered. He wanted to see only if she *would* do it, and had no actual desire to immerse any of his guests in a stagnant pond.

"You are too heavy," she told him, "and besides, it's illegal." When the raft was at the water's edge, she picked up a stout branch, stepped on to the raft, and launched herself forth after the frog.

Lady Sara, who had been observing her all the while with Clare, now let out a horrified shriek. Miss Sheridan squealed in terror, and Miss Prentiss wished *she* had thought of such a daring way to make herself the center of attention. Lady Honor took a step forward from under the spreading boughs of the tree, but the sun struck her eyes, so she returned. Hearing such uproar all around her, Ella turned towards the shore and said, "Shh. You'll frighten Prince Charming."

"What is she talking about?" Sara asked the air.

Clare heard and replied, "It is the name she calls her frog."

"How very stupid," Miss Sheridan opined, tossing her black curls.

"Original," Clare replied. It was said in the tone of a set-down and Sherry's black eyes snapped.

"Well, I call my sweet little frog Jumper," she returned, showing that she too was capable of originality.

"Clare, *do* something," Sara begged, tugging at his sleeve. "She'll tip off that raft and drown."

"Don't fret yourself. The water is not more than two feet deep, or I should not have let her do it."

"But she'll fall in and get filthy."

Belle and Sherry were for once in accord hoping for this exact outcome. Miss Fairmont would not appear so jaunty if she fell in and ruined her gown. Though on a second glance, Sherry could not believe it would be much loss.

"She won't fall in," Clare calmed them. "She manages herself very well afloat. There, she's getting within grabbing distance now, if she doesn't frighten him off."

Ella was too experienced in the way of frogs to disturb him before he was within her grasp. She let the raft float quietly till the water was quite still. There was not a sound now but the occasional croaking of a frog. The audience was dead silent, staring at her. She approached from behind, and leaned perilously over the raft's edge, balancing herself with the pole she carried. Her other hand went out stealthily, hovered a moment over the bullfrog, then in a flash of fingers she had him secure. A little ripple of clapping from Clare, then a general whoop of congratulations went up, with Peters and Harley leading the shout.

Ella looked up in surprise. She had not been aware of the intense interest she had created, because she needed all her wits to catch Prince Charming. Such escapades were a mere commonplace at Fairmont. Indeed a plunge into the pond would not much have discommoded her at home, though she was very careful not to fall in here. She looked about her for a container for the frog, and finding none, untied her bonnet and put him in there, forming a cover with the wide ribbons.

"She'll ruin her pretty chipstraw," Miss Sheridan moaned.

"And buy a new one with her prize money," Clare said. He hurried to the pond's edge to help her alight.

"I congratulate you on a virtuoso performance, Miss Fairmont," he said.

Before she was required to word a reply, Bippy, Peters, and Harley were at her side. "By Jove, that was a famous stunt!" "Showed us all the way," and various compliments of this exalted nature were issued. Then there was a general demand to see Prince Charming.

"Tell you what, Harley," Mr. Peters said when he had seen the monstrous fellow, "I'm going to change my bet. I don't think I will win this race. Miss Fairmont will. There ain't none of our frogs can touch this fellow. Look at the hind legs on him."

"Deep-chested too," Harley agreed, as seriously as though they were rating the points of the bloods at Newmarket.

"See here, Peters," Bippy broke in. "A placed bet stands. You can't go changing your bets whenever you feel like it. We all know Prince Charming will win; what you bet is that *your* nag—frog, that is, will beat Harley's. I'm the one stuck to keep book, and I can't go changing all the odds now. Prince Charming is a dark horse—just what makes a race interesting in my view."

"There is no saying Prince Charming will win," Ella told them. "I have often seen the unlikeliest frog win out over larger and even faster ones. They don't always hop *forward,* you see. Sometimes they take it into their heads to go sideways or backward."

"What are the rules if they hop off the track?" Harley wanted to know. He disliked any irregularity in his races.

"You have to take them back to the starting line," she said firmly. "It is hard when they get three-quarters of the way to the finish line and you have to start them all over again, but you have to have rules."

"Can't have a horse race without rules," Bippy supported.

"Yes, as long as the rules apply to everyone across the board," Peters said, with a meaningful look at the young ladies, who had already flouted one bunch of rules in not securing their own entrants.

No one found anything ludicrous in this conversation. Their interest had been caught, and the race promised better sport than anything in the last few days.

Clare was now the only one without a frog, and he could not find one, so everyone began helping him, peering into rushes and looking into the murky depths of the pond. After about five minutes, a very small one leapt up on to a lily pad. In the flash of an eye Clare was in up to his ankles, but was out again so fast that the damage to his top boots was not considered to be irreparable.

"Will he do, Miss Fairmont?" he asked, holding out his hands. She had to peek into the cracks between his fingers, for he couldn't hold him up in case he should hop away.

"He's small but wiry," she decided. "You can never tell. Well, everyone has one now. Shall we go?"

As this was what they had been waiting impatiently for, they trooped off to find a likely race course. At Miss Fairmont's suggestion, they chose a shady spot in the Park, and she set the gentlemen to collect sticks and stones to indicate the starting and finishing lines. Bippy's suggestion that they just "tear up a bit of turf" was instantly vetoed. The owners all lined up with their frogs at the starting line, Clare with two as Miss Sedgley did not care to touch hers, even with gloves. Miss Fairmont was requested to call the start. "One, two, three—Go!"

"They're off!" Peters yelled. But in fact several of them were not. There was then a vociferous pandemonium of urgings, threats, and cajolings to try to get the amphibians to the finish line.

"Come on, Jumper, nasty old frog," from Miss Sheridan.

"Move, blast you, Ugolino," from Miss Prentiss.

"Get going, Prince Charming," from Miss Fairmont.

Mr. Peters' Green Boy took off in a mighty leap, and

his proud owner yelled, "That's the ticket. Show 'em all the way."

"Come on, Herbert," Sara shouted, for though a matron, she never liked to miss out on any fun.

"Sara, did you call him that?" Ella asked. They both giggled, but no one paid them any heed.

"Get a move on, Leaper," Bippy commanded. When the frog remained immobile, he stuck out his foot.

"That's illegal!" Miss Prentiss yelled. "You're disqualified. Miss Fairmont, he touched Leaper with his toe."

"You'll have to start over," Ella declared.

"Deuce take it, how can I start over? He hasn't budged yet."

"Well, don't do it again anyway."

"Move, Prattle," Clare urged, crouching over his frog.

Ella and Sara exchanged startled glances. "Move, damn you," he repeated, unaware of their interest.

Mr. Peters' Green Boy and Ella's Prince Charming were in the lead, neck-to-neck. Miss Sheridan's Jumper had gone off the edge of the track and had to start over. Miss Prentiss's Ugolino took two jumps forward, then two back, and was again at the starting line.

Harley claimed that his Prince George had pulled a tendon, and he feared he would have to withdraw him from the race. Lady Honor's entrant, called Honor's Frog for lack of the lady's having come up with a name for it, appropriately enough did not move an inch. The others were scattered about the track, only the owners knowing which was which. The frogs continued to hop about at random, this way and that, and after a while it was clear that only three had any hopes of winning. Peters' Green Boy, Ella's Prince Charming, and Bippy's Leaper were all within a quarter of the way from the finish line, with their respective owners yelling themselves hoarse.

"Go, Green Boy, Go!"

"Come on, Prince Charming!"

"You can do it, Leaper!"

What Leaper did, however, was to spot a midge, and

leap off the track to grab it. Green Boy continued hopping more or less towards the finish line, and Prince Charming suddenly sat still and didn't move at all, in spite of the most violent threats of reprisals from his owner.

"He's winded," Harley informed Ella. "Had a nag that pulled that stunt on me at Newmarket."

With a final hop, Green Boy was over the line of sticks and stones, and the clamor due to the occasion was as loud as a healthy group of youngsters could make it. There followed a spirited discussion as to why the various entrants had performed so ill. Bippy and Ella had to exchange condolences as to the nearness of their wins. "Placed and showed anyway," Bippy pointed out. Before long there was an enthusiastic request for a re-match for the three who had made any showing at all.

The frogs who were not to re-enter were jumping about and in danger of becoming stepped on or lost.

"Let's get the others back into the baskets. They should be returned to the pond," Ella said. No one paid much attention to her, and she finally began chasing around, picking them up herself. Clare went to give her a hand. "They might not survive if they're left so far from the water," she explained to him.

"Yes, by Jove. We might want to use 'em again," Bippy agreed, and he too began scuttling after frogs.

Finally they were all caught, and the three who were to run again were set at the starting line. Clare did the honor of hollering "Go," and immediately Green Boy took three long hops. Prince Charming sat still. "Told you he was winded," Harley reminded Ella. Leaper took a magnificent vault, unfortunately fifteen inches off the track.

"Curse you," Bippy shouted.

The shout got Prince Charming into action, and he was after Green Boy. From then it was a race between Green Boy and Prince Charming, for Leaper continued vaulting to the left. Bippy tried to nudge him around with his toe, but the sharp-eyed Belle Prentiss saw his nefarious plot and disqualified him on the spot.

"I don't lay my blunt on this turtle again," Bippy declared in disgust.

Prince Charming was the more powerful hopper, but he hopped only intermittently, so that the race once again went to Green Boy.

"Thought for a minute there he'd got his second wind," Harley said to Ella. "What you want to do is enter him in the short races. He ain't good for the mile—that is, this longer course. Your Prince Charming has possibilities though, for the shorter runs."

"This Leaper's worth his weight in gold," Peters declared, lifting the winner from the grass. "You're a sweet goer, feller. Made me close to a hundred pounds today. I ain't putting him back in the pond, Miss Fairmont. I'm going to keep him in a pail of water and take him back to London with me. I ought to breed him."

"He won't survive in a bucket," she counseled. "They never do. Bertie, my brother, has tried it a dozen times."

"Mean to start a new strain, and improve the breed, do you?" Clare asked sardonically. During the afternoon, Clare was never far from Miss Fairmont's side, a circumstance that she had not failed to notice.

"What you ought to do is mate him with Prince Charming," Bippy advised. "With the Prince's size and Green Boy's speed, you'd get something like."

"Don't know your biology, my friend," Peter told him. "You can't breed two stallions."

"Oh, as to that, no saying Green Boy's a boy. Prince Charming is a bullfrog, of course, but I think you'd have done better to call your champ Green Girl."

"Nosir! She ain't no commoner. I'll call her Green Lady."

There was some more discussion of this silly nature, before the guests began walking back to the Palace to change for dinner.

"We must take the frogs back to the pond," Ella reminded their departing backs, but they kept on walking away from her.

Clare had not left, nor had Bippy. "I'll help you," Bippy offered.

Clare too picked up a basket and was poking one prisoner intent on escape back into it.

"No need for you to delay yourself, Miss Fairmont," Clare said. "Bippy and I will see they are put back in the pond."

"Jolly good game you came up with," Bippy congratulated her. "We'll do this again some time, eh, Clare?"

"Next time I shall have a cup inscribed," Clare promised, smiling warmly at Miss Fairmont.

"Thank you," she replied, in a little confusion at so much condescension. "I guess you don't need me if you are both going." With a wave she ran after the others and caught up with Sara. She half expected a scold for her afternoon's wantonness, but as Clare had enjoyed the scheme, Sara held her tongue.

Trudging to the pond with the baskets of frogs, Clare said, "An interesting girl, your Miss Fairmont."

"Yes, she don't look like much, but she's nice."

"Quiet on the surface. I suppose she is shy, but when one gets to know her a little, as you do, I think she will prove an interesting addition to our circle of acquaintances."

"Glad you like her. Was a bit afraid you wouldn't, you know."

"I so seldom approve of your amours," Clare roasted gently.

"As to that, ain't an *amour* precisely. More of a friend. Platonic you might say."

"I would be unlikely to say anything so hackneyed, but I take your meaning." This explanation satisfied Clare on two points. Firstly, as to why Miss Fairmont should be so disinterested in Tredwell's attentions. If it were merely friendship, she would expect no special care from him. And secondly, it explained Bippy's interest in so plain-looking a girl. One could understand his *liking* her; loving her was something else. Bippy usually had an eye for a gaudy beauty. He had blushed in London at the mention of her name, but he was an awkward fellow, not much in the petticoat line.

Dinner was again held in the formal dining hall, and again a small party of country gentry came after dinner for a dance. This was an even more impromptu affair than the other one, and the only music provided for the dancers was Mrs. Prentiss's playing the pianoforte. She was relieved at intervals by Lady Sara and one of the ladies from the neighborhood. They played only country dances and an occasional waltz.

At the first striking of a chord, Lady Honor materialized at Lord Clare's side. It was one of the mysteries of life that she, who was never seen to move in haste, should always be there, waiting, when a partner was required. She must have hustled, he thought, to beat Miss Sheridan to the gun. He danced, perforce, with Lady Honor. One could not after all offend the daughter of one of the oldest and proudest families in all England. He was rather relieved to have it over early, in any case.

He had the next one with Miss Sheridan and complimented her on her new coiffure. "Very fetching," he said. "I like it nearly as well as the Méduse you have been wearing." Needless to say, Sherry appeared on the next and succeeding days in the Méduse.

To do honor to his country guests, Clare made sure to dance next with one of them. Belle Prentiss was not happy to be fourth on his list and considered quite seriously mentioning what she had seen in the village. She was angling to get Clare to her Papa's home for the New Year, however, so she resisted the temptation, and amused him instead with a lively account of a verse play she was writing, all about Anne Boleyn.

"I think it should be finished by the end of October, and we hope to get it mounted in time to perform it over the Christmas holidays at home in Hampshire. You recall you promised to come to us for New Year's? We shall do it then."

"I said I would *try* to come," he reminded her.

"No, no. You said you would come. We are quite counting on it. I have put in a tiny part for you, so you can learn it in a day or two and take part in the performance. I shall make you the ax-man."

"Excellent casting. I can't think I shall have to learn a line at all. And—need I inquire who will play the queen?"

"Well, she did have auburn hair," Miss Prentiss said coyly.

"Tell me, who is to play the part of your infamous husband?"

"Papa," she laughed, "for he is fat and gouty and ill-tempered, just like Henry the Eighth."

"Take care he doesn't hand me a real ax for the show. It would serve you well, hoyden."

This was just the sort of bold rallying that Belle reveled in, and she went on to explain how the beheading was to be handled in a very realistic manner, without, of course, really severing her head from her neck. By the end of her exposition, the dance was over.

Clare looked about to see whom else he must dance with and spotted Miss Fairmont at the pianoforte with her aunt, who was about to relieve Mrs. Prentiss, who had to run immediately to Belle to see what 'he' had said during the dance.

He strode towards her and asked, "May I have the pleasure of the next dance, Miss Fairmont?"

"I don't dance well," she replied. "Sara is going to play a waltz, you see, and I have not managed to get on to it yet very well, though we have had a dozen lessons."

He could hardly have been more surprised had she reached out and hit him. He had never been refused a partner since he had become the Duke of Clare.

"Surely I saw you waltz at Almack's," he said.

"I am surprised you should ask me to stand up with you if you saw that. I was all over poor Mr. Tredwell's feet."

"I'll take my chances."

"No, thank you. I have tried and tried, and have finally decided I am too old a dog to learn these new tricks." She actually turned and began to walk away. She was only an indifferent waltzer, and did not wish to appear awkward in front of Clare. Her embarrassment led to the brusqueness of her answers. Clare was more intrigued than offended, and perhaps more shocked than intrigued. He took a step after her.

"Come now, Miss Fairmont, you cannot be so old as all that."

She was surprised and dismayed to see he kept on after her.

"I am one and twenty. Well past it."

"I can give you nearly ten years, and *I* have learned the waltz."

"But you are a man."

"What has that to say to anything? A woman's limbs do not wither faster than a man's, do they?"

"It is a matter of custom. Till a young lady is seventeen, you see, she is too young to be going into society and learning the new tricks. Then when she is over twenty, she is too old."

"That leaves you four years in which to have learned them."

"True, but I have not mastered that particular trick. Nor many others either," she added. Having reached the edge of the room, she sat down, and the Duke took up a chair beside her, when she was sure he would go and find another partner.

"You have wasted your time in libraries, I gather," he prodded, fearing she was about to fall into one of her silences.

"Good gracious, don't slander me so. I counted on you to keep my dissipation a secret. You must know a lady's mind must remain unsullied of knowledge if she hopes to make any sort of respectable alliance at all. It wouldn't do for me to be knowing anything."

"You sound regretful. Was there something you wished to know?"

"Nothing in the world. Ignorance is bliss, and I wouldn't like to have my bliss disturbed." There was a rallying sparkle in her brown eyes as she made this reply, which led him to hope she was not putting an end to the conversation.

"You are a prevaricating hussy, if you will pardon my saying so, ma'am."

"I was all set to take it for a compliment till you asked my pardon. I have no notion what a prevaricator may be, but a hussy is surely only a corruption of 'housewife,' and while it is not quite accurate to call me so, it is surely no insult."

"Take care, your bliss is slipping there, with such a show of semantics." A slow smile was playing on his lips. He might have known Sara's niece would not be a dead loss.

"It has only minor pin holes in it. Nothing, I do hope, to give you a disgust of me."

"Your bliss might be in shreds without disgusting me in the least."

"But it is not. I am a completely noble savage."

"So you are blissful in the French metaphor, as well as the English."

"Surely we English are second to none in savagery. You have only to look at Bedlam or Newgate."

"Second only to the French, and particularly M. Rousseau."

"Don't taint me with so much worldly knowledge, my lord. I will be mistaken for a Blue. I already stand accused of having once read a book other than a gothic novel. I was only allowed back into society by promising I didn't understand a word of it."

"What book was it? Let me guess now. But of course, *La Nouvelle Héloïse*."

"No indeed. It was *Dr. Ward's Treatise on Drops, Pills and Panaceas*, if I have remembered the title correctly," she said with an innocent stare. "I could not but think the cure worse than the disease, when he started writing of 'vomits, purges and sweats in a great degree.' I made sure he was a quack. I do not recommend it to anyone."

"I personally put complete faith in James's Powders," he said, equally seriously, till he saw her catch her lower lip between her teeth, at which point he too broke down and laughed.

"So you refuse to come and dance with me?" he asked again.

"These withered limbs could not stand such dissipation," she told him, yet she was regretting her refusal. She would not so much mind stepping on his toes, now that she saw he had a sense of humor.

"If they could withstand balancing on that blasted raft in the middle of a pond, they can withstand a waltz. Come now, you cost me a guinea with your race, and I demand a forfeit."

"What strange ideas of hospitality prevail in the homes of the aristocracy," she lamented, but she arose with no reluctance as Sara started up the music. "And if I step all over you, it is your own fault," she added.

"You are relieved of all responsibility to my toes," he assured her as he took her in his arms. "And to think, I warned your aunt only yesterday she ought to teach you how to converse in polite society."

"So she told me, and you may imagine how pleased I was to hear it!"

"Ah, I counted on Sara to be more discreet. Blurted it right out, did she?"

"She did, but I have the irrational habit of not listening to people who tell me what to do. It is the result of an old nanny who used to make me do all manner of unpleasant things when I was in the schoolroom. Always for my own good, of course, only they never did me any good that *I* could see. What is the good of stitching a sampler so ugly your own mama refused to hang it in the house, or finishing your bread and butter, when it makes you so full you can't finish your sweet?"

"Very true."

"And what is the point in talking politely to *you,* when you are just looking for the chance to give me a set-down, as you did to others of your invited guests within my hearing yesterday."

"I am not likely to try giving *you* a setdown, however, if by any chance you should turn civil towards me. I make no doubt you would best me."

"I cannot think it would be at all difficult," she smiled.

"*Touché!* And now that you have floored me, I'll smother you in remorse by congratulating you on your inspired notion of having a frog race. What have you planned for us tomorrow?"

"One can have a deal of fun at ducks and drakes if it is properly handled."

"How is it done at Fairmont? All rules and regulations, I suppose?"

"But of course, with stiff penalties for those who fail to skip their stone at least twice."

"Poor Miss Sedgley."

"Oh, she will make you do it for her."

"Very likely. But please, elaborate as to the sort of penalty awaiting the unskilled."

"We made Bertie, my brother, hop to the barn and back on one foot, and Sara had to sing a song in French. That sort of thing."

"That should keep 'em from being bored to flinders for a few hours," he said. "Peters will bet a monkey he can skip his half a dozen times, and Harley will throw one with his left and right hands simultaneously, and Miss Prentiss will call her stone something clever."

"They enter into a game with great gusto. That makes it more fun."

The waltz was over, with no visible mutilation of Clare's toes and with Ella's confidence in good repair. He had not been so bad, once she got over her fear of him. The dancing continued pleasantly till 12:30, when light refreshments were served before they all retired.

Seven

No contest of ducks and drakes was held the next day, for England had reverted to typical weather, streaking a fine rain over the verdant countryside, and slate gray skies promising no relief in the near future. Everyone slept late, and as they wandered from the breakfast room one by one, they made no plans for the day. Miss Sheridan went to her room to have her hair done up in papers for the Méduse; Miss Prentiss dashed off a poem on the Frog-Jumping race, and Miss Prattle wrote up a column for the *Observer* before going to the library to browse.

It was there that she encountered Clare's mother, deep in conversation with Mr. Shane. She was a tall, handsome woman, who would have been called homely if she were not a duchess. Her face and nose were long, and her dark hair was turned to white in an irregular way, in a strip down the middle of her head. It was difficult not to stare at it. Although the Dowager Duchess was the titular hostess of the party, she took her duties lightly. She presided at table for the meals and was in evidence during the evening rituals, whatever form they took. In between, she could usually be found either with her long nose in a book, or in the garden, where she struggled valiantly to grow roses in the chalk soil of Dorset. The garden being inaccessible today, she was looking for a good story to pass the morning. She loved reading, but had never stood accused of even a twilight tinge of blue. She read novels, and no very edifying ones either. History, religion, philosophy and science were but words to her, and volumes on the shelves to be avoided.

It was her aim to get through life with as little bother as possible, and as much pleasure. Her joys were the simple ones mentioned. She cared nothing for crowns and coronets and went only rarely to London, preferring to have her company come to her. She loved Patrick and would be easier in her mind if she could see him married to some nice girl before she died, but she had no intention of passing away soon, and so she did not push him. She always looked with interest over the young ladies he invited to Clare and was curious to hear his comments on them. She thought the lot he had brought this time a sorry one, and wondered he had invited anyone at all when he had so much business to attend to with his charity work. Well, he would tell her all about it in his own good time. They would get together and have a good coze, as they always did. She looked at the girl before her, trying to recall the name. Lady Sara's niece; she knew that. Fairmont, that was it.

"Ah, Miss Fairmont," she exclaimed. "What a dull party my son has got up, when his guests must amuse themselves in the library."

"Not in the least, ma'am. We are having a good time, but in such weather as this our activities are confined."

"It looks as if we are in for a rainy day," she replied, glancing through the mullioned windows. "Those clouds don't intend letting up in five minutes. Are you come for a novel?"

"Why no, ma'am, though I usually devour them as though they were bonbons." The gleam of interest in Miss Fairmont's eye was met by a responding one from the Duchess.

"You'll find them all here," she was assured. "Frances Burney, Mrs. Radcliffe, Maria Edgeworth. It's a chore to find a nice story written by a woman. *They* know what we like to read."

"No doubt then you are familiar with the works of Miss Austen."

"I can't say I've heard of her. A new one, is she?"

"She has published three in the last few years—all charming."

"You must give me the titles, and I'll have Patrick pick them up when he goes back to town."

"Why, I can do better than that. I have the best one of them all with me—*Pride and Prejudice*. I'll get it for you."

Ella thought she would send the book to her ladyship's room by a maid, but the Duchess trailed right along with her and sat down for a chat while Ella jotted down the titles. This gave the older lady a chance to assess Patrick's new acquaintance. Not in his usual style—no beauty—but a taking little thing.

"You are the girl who thought up the frog race—an excellent idea. Most of the young ladies nowadays want to spend their time sitting in the shade, looking like Gainsborough paintings. It wasn't so in *my* day." She elaborated on this theme a little, meeting agreement from her companion, and left with a favorable impression of Miss Fairmont.

Ella nipped back to the library to browse amongst a selection of books on magic, ghosts, and witchcraft. She had a hearty chuckle over them later, read a few passages to Sara, and declared them absurd.

When luncheon was announced, the Dowager had to be called twice, for she was deep into her novel and the problems confronting the penniless Bennet family in finding husbands for their five daughters. As soon as the meal was over, she hastened back to her suite. Mr. Collins had just made his entrance into the story, and she was enraptured with him.

The other inhabitants of Clare Palace were less thrilled with their afternoon. The rain continued, effectively confining even the gentlemen to the house. "What shall we do?" Miss Sheridan voiced the old familiar question. She was not averse to remaining indoors, for her new yellow voile was really a summer gown, and would not do for chasing frogs, if Miss Fairmont started *that* again.

"The library here is excellent," Ella volunteered, which statement might as well have remained unsaid for all the interest it elicited.

Only Clare cocked an eyebrow and said to her aside, "Making your debauchery quite public, are you, Miss Fairmont?"

"What do you mean?" Belle asked, moving her chair closer to Clare so that she might join this private chat. "There is no debauchery in books. *I* read all the time."

"It is a private joke," Clare said in a damping voice.

"Speaking of private jokes, Clare," she said, softly now, so that Miss Fairmont might not hear, "Did I tell you what we saw in the village two days ago?"

His face stiffened, and his voice when he replied was cold. "No, ma'am, but I have observed you are having the greatest difficulty in keeping it to yourself. Let us hear it, by all means."

"Oh, I can hold my tongue," she replied, laughingly. He was looking so disapproving that she said no more on that score. "Let's play a word game," she said, to the room at large. "Do you have letters, Clare?"

"There may be some in the nursery," he replied, thus stating, either intentionally or by accident, what he thought of the idea.

"Got any jigsaw puzzles?" Bippy asked. Harley reached out and hit him, and Peters rolled up his eyes in disgust.

"We could write limericks," Ella suggested. No one was enthralled with this idea either, except Miss Prentiss who was so clever with her pen that she was sure she could out-write the others.

Belle took the idea up, and with two interested in it, it was sold to the others.

"Whom do we write about?" Bippy asked.

"Anybody you like," Belle told him.

"I know whom *I* shall write about," Miss Sheridan said, twinkling her black eyes at Clare. The angry look Miss Prentiss shot her gave rise to the suspicion that she might have the same idea.

"It's best to write about dead people," Ella advised. "Or at least people who are absent—public figures. It would be all right to do Wellington or Prinney, or Princess Caroline."

"Let's make out a list," Sara said. "Henry VIII would be a good one to start with."

"And Lady Godiva," Ella added.

"You must include Anne Boleyn! *I* shall do her, if I may, since she is the subject of my verse play, and I am familiar with her history."

"I'll do Byron then," Ella decided.

"I'll do Princess Caroline," Sara remarked.

"I'll do Prinney's other wife, Fitzherbert," Bippy mumbled.

"Who will you do, Clare?" Belle asked. "Anne Boleyn's ax-man perhaps?"

"I'll do Prattle," he replied. He told Lady Honor she would do Shakespeare, and stuck a pencil in her hand. "All right," she said.

The others made their selections, and the party was soon busy scribbling away, with Miss Prentiss interrupting at frequent intervals to remind them of such necessities as rhyme scheme and meter. No one knew what she was talking about, and Lord Harley finally told her in quite a sharp tone that it was hard to write when someone kept on interrupting you every time you thought of a good rhyme.

In about ten minutes they were finished, and their various efforts waiting to be read aloud, with blushes and grimaces attending the ordeal.

Bippy had forgotten it was a limerick they were doing and wrote nearly a complete sonnet. Lady Honor made up for his profusion by writing only one line. "William Shakespeare wrote plays," she had composed, at the end of the allotted time.

"That is true," Sherry pointed out. She was never tardy to compliment the aristocracy on an achievement.

"Dash it, it's supposed to be a *poem*," Lord Harley complained. "Never mind if it's true or not."

"Told me I wrote too much," Bippy interposed. "Now you tell Lady Honor she didn't write enough. No pleasing you."

"A poem of five lines, not a dashed epic."

"The rhyme scheme is all wrong in yours, too, Bip," Belle informed him.

"What have you got, Miss Fairmont?" Bippy asked, to avoid a reply to Belle, who would start with her old pentameters and hexameters again if he let on that he heard her.

She cleared her throat and read:

> There once was a baron named Byron
> Who found that of life he was tirin',
>   Till he journeyed to Turkey
>   And wrote a poem murkey.
> Now for Byron, all London's expirin'.

Peters, who was becoming fond of Miss Fairmont, said this was the best they'd had yet. Belle felt obliged to point out "tiring" was not a true rhyme for "Byron," and showed them how it *should* rhyme, as in her limerick on Anne Boleyn, where "head" and "dead" rhymed perfectly, and even had the same spelling so that it looked well on the page. "But that is a fine point I don't expect to find in amateur writing," she added kindly.

Lord Harley had mistakenly attributed Richard III's humpback to William of Lyons, and as Belle's interruptions had robbed him of his rhyming words—which he assured them had been quite excellent, only he forgot them—his effort won no prize.

"Let's hear from one of the ladies now," Harley requested, after he had read his effort, to resounding boos.

"I didn't do Caroline after all; I did Henry VIII," Lady Sara announced, preparatory to reading hers.

> Henry the Eighth had many wives.
> Some of them were killed with knives,
> Or axes was it, never mind,
> Their heads they never more could find.
> So you who'd marry Kings, beware:
> You'll lose your heads, also your hair.

"Aren't you clever, Lady Sara!" Sherry marveled.

"Only *two* of his wives were actually beheaded, of course," Belle had to straighten them out. "He divorced Katharine of Aragon and Anne of Cleves, and . . ."

"Yes, we know you've been reading all about it for your play, but let's get on with the poems," Harley interrupted.

"Actually, the rhyme scheme was all wrong too," Belle threw in. She was miffed at not getting to rhyme off the fates of Henry's other wives, which she had at her fingertips.

"A gentleman next, since we are going turn about," Sara said. "How about you, Clare? Prattle is it you are doing?"

"A sad comedown from kings and queens, *n'est-ce pas*?" he asked.

"Oh, but Prattle is the Queen of Gossip," Belle laughed. "I'm dying to hear what you have to say of her."

"Why don't you give him a chance to read then?" Harley inserted sharply.

After this jibe, no one else interrupted, and Clare read.

> There once was a person named Prattle,
> Who scribbled up all of the tattle
>   With a libelous mind
>   Neither cultured nor kind
> About beaux, and their women, and cattle.

"You were too easy on her," Belle asserted.

"Lady Sara or Miss Fairmont, with their clever pens could have done better," he agreed.

Miss Prentiss resented being left out of the list of clever

pens and read hers on Anne Boleyn again, while Sherry struggled with a rhyme for Beau Brummell. Finding it beyond her, she left off the Brummell and did better than anyone expected.

The others read their verses, and it was Peters who suggested a write-off, in the same manner as the frog race, with the three best writing another limerick.

After some heated discussion, and another reading of Anne Boleyn, the three chosen were Lady Sara, Ella, and Clare.

"What should we write about this time?" Ella asked.

"Oh, I know! Do Clare," Belle said.

All three of the contestants demurred, and at last Miss Prentiss had to do one herself to show them how easy it was.

"I'm not doing myself," Clare stated firmly. "I'll do Godiva. No one has done her."

Ella and Sara shrugged and began to tread the thin line between sycophancy and insult in writing a poem to their host. Sara found herself slipping into the easy trap of rhyming Clare with fair, and in disgust crumpled hers into a ball and wrote on Lady Godiva too. Ella's tended in the other direction towards insult. She wrote:

> There once was a young Duke of Clare
> Who would do anything for a dare.
>> Throw a party, not come,
>> Snub the ladies, in sum,
> What one thought of him he didn't care.

She was dissatisfied with the result, and after a few moments she too squashed up her sheet and threw it into the basket. From the corner of his eye, Clare observed the discarded papers and wondered what was on them. Ella dashed off five lines in a hurry on Farmer George, and the prize in theory, though in fact there was none, went to Lady Sara. Miss Prentiss was not an official candidate for the prize, but she insisted on reading her work anyway. It was so warm in its praise of the Duke that not only he, but anyone with a jot of sensitivity, was embarrassed at it.

After this brief poetic interlude, the party was happy to switch to cards, puzzles, and letter writing, with repeated hopes that the storm would let up soon. Clare excused himself to see to some business matters, but before leaving he tossed a log on the smouldering fire and pocketed the papers thrown aside by Sara and Ella while he bent over the wood basket.

At dinnertime the wind was still howling with rain streaking against the windows. It was impossible for any company to venture out on such a night and, after their port, the gentlemen joined the ladies in the drawing room. Upon their arrival, the Duchess forsook the elder ladies with whom she usually sat and went to Miss Fairmont.

"How are you enjoying *Pride and Prejudice*, ma'am?" Ella asked.

"Heaven. Simply heaven. I have been at it all afternoon without letup, and am only waiting a bit so that I may slip back to it without offending anyone." She glanced at the Marchioness as she spoke. "I have got to the part where Elizabeth goes to visit Collins and Miss Lucas, only they are married by now, of course, and I *think* Darcy is working up to a proposal. Does he? . . . no, no . . . don't tell me. She is the absolute end, your Miss Austen. I don't know how it comes I haven't heard of her, only I never see anyone out here in the country who can tell me what is the latest rage."

"She is not a rage precisely. Only a few have discovered her thus far."

"Her characterizations are superb. That mother!"

"And Mr. Collins. She puts him on the pan and turns up the heat bit by bit, simmering him till he is done brown."

"What a phrase! You ought to be a writer yourself, my dear."

Ella gave a start, but the Duchess took it for shyness at such praise and thought nothing of it. She chatted for a little while longer with Miss Fairmont then joined the mothers for a quarter of an hour before claiming a headache. She winked at Ella on her way out, holding a hand to her head as though it were killing her. Sara observed the pass and questioned Ella about it.

"You have gotten on mighty close terms with the mama," she said leadingly.

"I told you I lent her a book. We were discussing it."

A short while later, Clare went up to his mother to see that she was comfortable and was a little surprised to find her lounging on a chaise longue, a box of her favourite salted nuts by her side, reading avidly.

"Headache all gone, Mama?" he asked quizzingly.

"Yes, Patrick, I've left them all downstairs to bore each other to distraction. I've fed them and done my duty by praising all the young ladies to their mothers. What more do you expect of me? Why don't *you* do something to keep them entertained?"

"Shall I turn Miss Prentiss loose at the harpsichord?"

"I said entertain, not torture. That girl has no idea when to stop."

"That is invariably the way with these talented women. A definite point in Lady Honor's favour. She neither sings nor plays."

"Nor speaks, unless you draw a word out of her with a pair of pliers. Sit down if you want to," the Dowager invited, with no great sign of encouragement. Still, her son took up a seat at the end of her chaise longue.

"What are you reading, a new gothic?" he asked.

"No such thing. A very superior novel lent me by that nice little Miss Fairmont."

"*Pride and Prejudice*," he read. "Never heard of it."

"No, you never bother to dig out a new writer for me. Why could not *you* have found out about her—this Miss Austen, I mean, who wrote it. Miss Fairmont tells me she has been publishing for some years. She has given me a list of her books, and I wish you to get them and send them to me when you return to London." She fished the

91

list out from between the leaves of the book and handed it to him. He slipped it into his pocket without looking at it.

"Yes, Mama," he replied, with so much mock humility that she laughed reluctantly.

"Well, hadn't you better return to your guests?"

"Which means *you*, my unnatural mother, would rather read than talk to your only son."

"Doesn't an *unnatural* mother mean something horrid, Patrick? Or am I thinking of *natural* mother?"

"I collect you are thinking of natural son, and don't try to change the subject."

"Well, I would rather we not *both* abandon our guests belowstairs. I hope this rain doesn't continue tomorrow, or we'll have them cluttering up the house all day again. I wonder if Miss Fairmont has another novel tucked away in her trunk."

"She came prepared for the dull time they are having."

"I have been wondering why you brought them on such short notice."

"I made the mistake of begging off a party at Straywards by telling the Marchioness I was coming here, and before I got away she had kindly given me permission to bring Lady Honor along."

"But why the others?"

"You can imagine how it would be construed in town if I brought no one but Lady Honor and her mother. They are becoming damned persistent this season."

"Very wise. I knew Miss Sheridan and Miss Prentiss to be your current flirts, but Miss Fairmont is a new one, is she not?"

He smiled quite boyishly. "Miss Fairmont was a happy accident," he admitted. "A friend of Tredwell's and, of course, I have known Sara forever."

The duchess was a little sorry to hear Miss Fairmont was Bippy's friend, still she thought from his smile Patrick was not quite immune to her either. "She's nice. I like her better than those dull beauties you usually drag down here."

"Yes, Sara is nice," he returned, misreading his mother's meaning, so that she had to straighten him out.

"I was referring to Miss Fairmont. A nice sensible girl."

"Sensible? How can you say so, when I told you about her escapade on the pond?"

"Pooh, that is merely high spirits. I have been wondering, Patrick, did she actually induce Lady Honor to go chasing frogs?"

"No, Lady Honor induced me to do it for her."

"That's more like it. Well, don't let me keep you," she said, fingering her book impatiently.

"I can take a hint, Mama. I shall tell the Marchioness you are lying down with your vinaigrette."

"Tell her I took a few drops of laudanum, or she may take it into her head to drop in and see how I do. I'd hate her to catch me red-handed."

"It would serve you right," he remarked, rising.

"And don't lose my list of books," she called after him.

"I have it right here." He reached into his pocket, but felt some larger pieces of paper, and remembered the limericks.

He waited till he was outside his mother's door to read them. One had only the two lines, and he knew that it was Lady Sara who had abandoned hers after a minute. He was therefore very well aware who had written the other. He was amused—a clever way with words, due to her haunting of libraries he supposed. He was about to return them to his pocket, then read Ella's again. That last line—'What one thought of him he didn't care.' Not quite justified. Still, he supposed the general impression was that he didn't give a damn for public opinion. He shrugged his shoulders and returned to the drawing room, to find Miss Fairmont recounting a story she had read in the books of supernatural phenomena borrowed from his library.

". . . and when the heir died, all the swans left the lake, and there was a horrid eerie cry in the chimneys, and the parson passing by saw a white cloudlike thing leave by the outer chimney, only it wasn't *smoke*, but much more substantial, he said, and it circled three times around the roof, then dissipated."

"Nonsense!" Clare said firmly, a light kindling in his eye.

"Very likely," she agreed. "I am only telling what I read in a book from your library, and supposedly it happened right here at Clare Palace, in the year 1699."

"I should have warned Shane to keep those volumes away from you."

"You forget my powers of persuasion with Mr. Shane, Your Grace," Ella replied meaningfully.

"There is nothing wrong in a ghost story," Belle interjected.

"No, I imagine it is the others on the same shelf dealing with black magic and necromancy and such things that His Grace is worried about," Ella explained.

"How horrid!" Belle squealed. "You must show me where, Miss Fairmont."

"Going to write up a ghost story, Miss Prentiss?" Bippy asked.

Before she replied, Sherry had to have a portion of the duke's attention. He had not said a word about her latest gown.

"Do *you* believe in ghosts, Clare?" she asked.

"No. And don't tell me you people are gullible enough to believe, either. Now I know Lady Sara, for instance," he bowed in her direction, "is much too sensible a dame to swallow such slum."

"Except on nights like this," Sara returned. Wind came down the chimney and the flames danced in the grate. There was a whining of the storm at the windows, and somewhere in the great house a shutter banged ominously.

"That would be your great-great Uncle Ethelred come

94

back to scold you for saying he didn't rise up the chimney," Ella told him.

Miss Sheridan shivered and pulled her paisley shawl closer about her. She nudged closer to Lord Harley, who sat beside her on the settee. He looked shocked and moved away a little.

"That would be the loose shutter in the yellow guest suite," Clare contradicted.

"Spoilsport," Bippy chided. "Tell us another one, Miss Fairmont."

"We have a ghost at Strayward," Lady Honor said in a sonorous voice.

"A monk," Miss Sheridan quoted. She had a good memory for anything pertaining to the nobility.

"Yes, tell them about Crazy Nellie, Miss Fairmont," Clare added, suddenly changing his tack. An evening of ghost stories would be preferable to an evening of Miss Prentiss performing Shakespeare solo.

"I didn't read anything about her," Miss Fairmont said. "But there was an excellent story about some ancestor in the fifteen hundreds, in Elizabethan times, who was a witch. In the sketch she had one of those ruffs around her neck."

A murmur of interest ran through the collected company, and Miss Fairmont settled back to unfold the tale of Lady Matilda, as Clare informed her the ancestor was named.

"She was very beautiful," Ella began, in a hushed voice.

"It is a family characteristic," Clare added.

"Very beautiful and *ill-natured*," Ella said, with a pointed look at her interrupter. "She kept all the important and eligible gentlemen of the neighborhood dangling after her in the worst way, so that the other ladies all hated her."

"Another family characteristic," Lord Harley shot in.

"And every time one of them would start to desert her

and settle on any other lady," Ella continued, "he would meet with some horrid fate."

"Bear that in mind," Clare said to Harley.

"Stop interrupting, you two," Belle scolded. "Pray continue, Miss Fairmont."

"Well, I'm not sure I remember all the details, for there were scores of suitors, but one of them got stung on the eye by a bee and went blind. It was particularly bad, for he was an artist, and the lady he was to marry a great beauty. They had an apiary at Clare in those days, and . . ."

"Still have," Clare commented. Several hostile pairs of eyes were turned on him.

"We have an apiary at Strayward, with one hundred and fifty hives," Lady Honor said.

Sherry looked at her and smiled, and after a respectful silence to ensure that no more was coming, Miss Fairmont continued. "Another suitor went swimming, an excellent swimmer he was, but he took a cramp and drowned."

"Can't blame that on poor old Matilda," Clare pointed out.

"There was some circumstance that linked her to it— she was with the party at the time, I believe. And finally, the most mysterious bit of all, one gentleman called on Lady Matilda to tell her he was offering for a neighbor, and he was never seen to leave the house. He just vanished. Now that, you must own, looks highly suspicious."

"It's a big house. Perhaps he got lost."

"Ain't *that* big," Bippy objected.

"*You* get lost every time you come here," his host reminded him.

"Not *forever*. May wander about for half an hour or so, but I always meet a maid or someone who can show me the way. Deuce take it, this fellow's been lost since the days of Queen Elizabeth. He must have been done in by Matilda."

"That was certainly the feeling in the neighborhood at

the time," Ella resumed. "That is when it was decided she was a witch, and no one would have anything to do with her."

"Thought they dunked witches, or some such thing," Bippy mentioned.

"Not when she was a lady of so much consequence," Belle explained. What she didn't know she made up out of whole cloth, for she had a high reputation for erudition to maintain.

"That's a good story," Peters complimented Ella. "You know any more?"

"I'm not finished this one yet."

"If only everyone would stop interrupting Miss Fairmont," Belle charged them.

"Well, it seems that Matilda, not content with doing away with that suitor who came to call and vanished, lay in waiting on the road one dark night to kill his sweetheart. She had a jade sword she meant to use, but when she raised her hand to kill the poor girl, the sword was turned against her by some unseen force, and took her own head clean off."

"Rubbish," Clare scoffed.

"Yes, just missing her ruff by a fraction of an inch," Ella assured him. "And she, with great presence of mind, I must admit, picked up her own head and walked home with it underneath her arm."

"Oh, how *horrid*!" Miss Sheridan gasped, feeling her neck. "I shan't sleep a wink tonight. I know I shan't."

"And be *hagged* tomorrow," Belle teased. "What a silly you are. I wonder, Clare, if Matilda might not be your Crazy Nellie."

"No, Nellie is definitely a lady of the Queen Anne period, with a head still on, and red hair."

"Like Miss Prentiss," Miss Prentiss said mischievously.

"Just so, and a pink gown."

"The family is full of lunatics," Lady Sara said amiably.

"And ghosts," Clare added.

The shutter in the yellow suite set up its banging again, and a breeze keening through the ill-fitted French door chose that moment to extinguish two candles.

"I hope that storm lets up, or the roads will be very bad for that little party you plan tomorrow night," Lady Sara remarked to Clare. "Though if it is still raining tomorrow morning, we can spend the day decorating your ballroom. How would you like it done?"

"Why not make it a ghost party?" Ella suggested. "With so many of your dead relatives wandering around, it is a fitting atmosphere."

"Yes, let's," Belle cried, clapping her hands and envisioning an early performance of Anne Boleyn.

Honor yawned, and looked at her thumbs.

"How does one decorate for a ghost party?" Miss Sheridan inquired. "And what sort of dress ought one to wear? *I* had planned to wear my violet gown . . ."

Lady Sara had no recommendation for a gown, but for decorations thought some old sheets draped over furniture and a dimming of the lights would give the place a feeling of disuse.

"Cobwebs," Harley added.

"Where the devil do you think you'll get cobwebs?" Bippy asked.

"From spiders! Attics, barns, lots of places."

"You may be in charge of providing cobwebs," Clare told him, with a mental note to tell his mama of this delightful folly.

"Certainly, glad to help out. And the ladies can be in charge of sheets."

"Old chains, too," Ella added, "preferably hanging loosely, so that they rattle and clank."

"And *you* may be in charge of chains, Miss Fairmont," her host informed her.

"Let's all dress up in costumes," Belle exclaimed. She was finding it hard to keep up with the inventive Miss Fairmont in new ideas.

"Oh, but I was going to wear my violet gown!" Miss Sheridan said. "I didn't bring a costume with me."

"No one did, silly," Belle told her. "I daresay Clare has an attic full of old outfits. We can find something."

"Is Miss Prentiss in charge of costumes?" Ella asked Clare.

"Oh no! *I* cannot contrive an outfit for everyone. We must all get our own."

"We shall spend a delightful morning in the attics, breathing dust and rummaging through old trunks," Clare said with a mock smile.

"Jolly good sport," Peters agreed happily. "What have you got up there, Clare?"

"I have never been in the attics," he said, not quite truthfully. "Mama could tell you better, but unfortunately she is—not feeling well."

"What is the matter with her?" Sara asked.

"I believe your niece could tell you the precise name of her ailment," he returned, with a conspiratorial smile at Ella, whom he had seen biting her lip when he pronounced his mama ill.

"Just a headache, I believe she said," Ella replied in some confusion.

"Severe headache. She has taken some laudanum," Clare added, looking towards the Marchioness, who had been sitting listening with the older ladies to the plans of the youngsters.

"That is too bad," Sara commiserated. "You know, Clare, I have been thinking, if it *is* to be a costume party, you must let all the people from the neighborhood know about it."

"You're right, and there is *my* morning taken care of. I'll have to make a tour and tell them. I certainly hope the rain lets up."

"I shall go with you," Lady Honor informed him.

"You are very kind," he replied, inclining his head slightly towards her.

Her declaration raised a furor in many breasts, but

when Honor spoke a thing was settled. Miss Sheridan nibbled her finger. She would have liked very well to be of this party with two members of the nobility, one of them her beloved Clare, but a moment's consideration recalled her to the rigors of her toilette. It would be a scramble indeed for her and her mama and their women to arrange a costume for her in only one day. She could not imagine how it could be creditably contrived in time.

A general discussion followed, with everyone putting forward an idea for the decorations of the ballroom and the costumes to be worn.

"How will you go, Miss Fairmont?" Bippy asked her.

"It is a secret," she replied, and said not another word on the subject during the ten minutes he continued to prod her playfully, suggesting such unlikely disguises as a Princess, by Jove, or a flower. Lady Sara, too, was strangely silent, for she did not wish to reveal the excellent idea that had come to her, in case someone else should steal it.

The storm continued, and after a suitable period of time, yawns began to be irrepressible and someone suggested bed. Clare strolled to Ella's side and detained her on her way past. Belle Prentiss sat on the edge of a chair and untied her shoe, so she had the excuse of having to retie it to stay there and listen to them.

"Thank you again, Miss Fairmont," Clare began.

"Oh, for what?"

"For another of your brilliant ideas—the ghost party."

"I don't think you cared for it?" she said, making it a question.

"It is a host's place to provide what his guests like, and mine appear to like your idea prodigiously. Much better, in fact, than I like your limerick about me."

"But I didn't—how did you come to see it?"

"Picked it up out of the wood basket. I thought it might relieve your mind a little to know I *do* plan to attend this party. In fact, I even care what some people

100

think of me. You have been taking your impression of me from Prattle, I fear."

It may be imagined with what tumultuous feelings Ella heard this comment. When she wrote of him before, she had not really known him, except in a public way. Upon having observed him closely for a few days, she felt he was not so toplofty as she had believed, and the provocation for his cutting remarks was severe. In short, she had been unjust, and to continue writing of him while a guest was not only unjust, but iniquitous.

She could make no reply, and Clare continued in a light tone, "What, speechless with remorse at what you wrote of me, or speechless with anger that I read it?"

"I am only surprised you would have bothered."

"It was no bother. I had only to bend over a very little and pick it up."

"Still," she rallied, "one is surprised to see the Duke of Clare bend at all."

"Floored again," he said, regarding her closely in a half-smile, his eyebrows raised. "Where the deuce have you been hiding yourself all these years in London? I thought I knew all the interesting ladies, but I never knew *you* to be one of them till this visit."

"You have misunderstood the matter, milord," she replied gravely. "I did not become interesting till I was singled out by the Duke of Clare for the exceedingly great honor of an invitation to his palace. You could not expect me to go on being dull after that."

He pursed his lips and tried to frown. "No, you don't find it in the least difficult to give me a set-down, do you? And I haven't even the excuse of not being forewarned, for you told me so when I made you waltz with me."

They began walking towards the doorway, a few paces behind the last of the departing guests, only Belle remaining in the saloon now. "It was unwise of you to *make* me, *n'est-ce pas?*"

"I refuse to regret it. Till then I didn't know what a nice sharp-tongued vixen you could be. Tell me, how is it you managed to convince Bippy and my Mama that you are unexceptionable?"

"I don't know what maggot Tredwell has got into his head; he scarcely looked at me till recently, but as to your Mama, it is not me she likes, but Miss Austen."

"Oh, no, she definitely called you that *nice* little Miss Fairmont."

"A conventional epithet."

"How very poorly you accept a compliment. You've no idea how glad I am to have found out your weakness."

"I believe Lady Honor is waiting to have a word with you," Ella was happy to point out. Lady Honor had turned aside at the foot of the staircase. Flirtation was a new experience for Ella, and to be doing so with Clare as her first partner was nerve-wracking in the extreme. She preferred sparring with him.

"She'll be wanting me to tell her what she is to wear for the masquerade party. What shall we send her as? A zombie, perhaps?"

A spontaneous chuckle escaped Ella's lips before she took her leave and ran to catch up with Sara.

Belle rose slowly from the arm of the chair where she had been balancing, an unsettled expression on her face. It was an admixture of astonishment, jealousy, and anger. Three ladies chasing after Lord Clare were quite enough. She must cut this one out, before she became a positive nuisance.

Sara entered Ella's room for a chat before retiring and sat down on the end of her bed. "You are making yourself very much at home, having a coze with the Dowager, and a little private tête-à-tête with the Duke. Trying to steal my beau, are you?"

"But, of course," Ella agreed laughingly. "You didn't think I'd let a real live duke slip through my fingers without trying to nab him, did you?"

"Yes, that is precisely what I thought. And don't try to con me you are on the catch for him, for I know you've hated him any time these three years. I suppose you're collecting news for Prattle. What extravagant follies have you been eking out of the poor unsuspecting soul?"

"No folly. He's not so bad when you get to know him."

"Take care, my girl, the next step is to go tumbling into love with him! We should have Prattle's first column about the visit at Clare by tomorrow. I trust Mama padded it out appropriately with London gossip to maintain the mystery."

"Oh, yes, I sent in only a few paragraphs."

"The masquerade ball will make a good story. And tell me, have *you* decided to go as Crazy Nellie too, for I know you said your outfit was a secret, and I have decided to be Nellie myself, so you'll have to choose something else."

"You are welcome to Crazy Nellie. I daresay she's been done a dozen times. I will be Matilda."

"Not, I trust, with your head tucked underneath your arm."

"But of course, that is the whole point of it! I hope I can find something to do for a head in the attic—an old hat form or some such thing I can paint up. And how am I to hide my own head, and still see where I am going?"

"Oh, Ella, marvelous! I wish I had thought of that. How can it be done?"

"Some sort of wadding stacked up around my ears to hold a dress up to head level I expect, and I'll have to cut two holes for eyes. I refuse to terrorize a whole roomful of people and not get to see the reaction myself. Isn't it going to be wonderful?"

"But very difficult to arrange. And you'll need a ruff too."

They discussed plans happily for some while, then with a yawn, Sara was off to her own room.

But when Ella lay down in her elegant four-poster bed, fashioned with a gilded birdcage on top, it was not her outfit that worried her, but her treatment of Clare, and the degree of rancor he felt for Miss Prattle, which showed itself in little ways like his limerick and naming his frog for her. She must be on her guard, say nothing to let the truth slip out, but more even than this horrible possibility, she worried about the ethics of flaying him publicly as she had been doing for years. She would say nothing else against him personally, that was the least she could do. To suddenly cut him from her column entirely would be too odd, and too displeasing to Thorndyke, too. No, she must ease off gradually, mention the party at Clare, but not the host. For the first time in her life, she was sorry that she was Miss Prattle.

Belle was the last to leave the saloon. By the time she got to the hallway, it was deserted, and she stood for a moment, looking around her, admiring it, and thinking how she would change the pictures when she was mistress here. She heard a timid footstep behind her, and looking around, nearly fell over from shock. There, in the beautiful flesh, stood Clare's flirt, whom she had seen in the village. She was dressed in a shawl for going outdoors, or had just come in.

She took the immediate resolve to find out all she could from the girl while she had such a perfect opportunity. "Are you looking for someone?" she asked, smiling sweetly, and making her voice soft.

"No, mum," the girl said. A very common accent!

"Looking for a *door* perhaps?" Belle laughed kindly.

"Oh, no, mum. I've just come in."

"I see. Well, are you *sure* you're not looking for someone?"

"Well," the girl licked her lips, and jiggled from one foot to the other. "A housekeeper then, mum, or the dook, maybe . . ."

Belle's heart raced. He had sent to have the woman come here! "Is the duke expecting you?"

"Yes, mum. He said I was to come."

"And what is your name, my dear?" adopting a maternal attitude, though she was not more than a year older than the young girl.

"Prissie. Prissie Muckleton. My pa works here, in the stables," she volunteered.

"We must certainly let the duke know you are come," Belle said, gloating inside with her triumph.

She had a vision of herself conducting the person to His Grace's chamber, but this ultimate glory was denied her. The butler came into the hall to extinguish lights for the night, and upon spying Prissie in conversation with a guest, took the wench by the arm and said, "Here, you. What are *you* doing in here?" in a very rough manner.

"I was asked to come," Prissie said, fearfully.

"Not in the front door you weren't," the butler replied.

"I didn't come in by the front door, but the little side door by the garden."

"The back door for the likes of you," the stern butler decreed and carted her off.

Belle's feet barely touched the stairs as she flitted to her room. She lay long awake, deciding how to use this piece of information she had chanced across. She settled on nothing, but the possibilities were endless to one of her inventive talents.

Eight

The morning brought a respite from the rain, but no sunny skies, and Ella nurtured a secret hope that by nightfall they would be enjoying another storm. With a heavy day's work arranging her costume before her, she arose just before 9:00, thinking she would be the first one up. Several others were of the same opinion, and a full crew, even including Lady Honor, had assembled round the table before 9:30. Ella heard her name—her Miss Prattle name—mentioned by Miss Prentiss as she entered the breakfast room. She held the *Morning Observer* in her hands and was regaling them with the first column to have reached Dorset, though others were already printed in London.

"FitzPrattle has no good idea of your hospitality, Clare," she said. "Only hear what she writes of our little party. 'Those patrons who thought they were poorly entertained at the Concert of Ancient Music last night may thank their lucky stars they were not at C——e Palace, where the tired guests who had traveled all day were required to sing for their supper before they were allowed to go to bed. Miss P——s must have been exhausted, for rumor has it she was made to sing, dance and act two excerpts from Shakespeare. The D——e of C——e, we are happy to inform you all, was home to greet his guests. Let us hope he has something better planned for them than amateur talent nights. The momentous announcement we are all waiting for with bated breath has not been made, but Miss P——s must have got a neck ahead of the others, if entertaining is one of the requirements for the post of Duchess.' Well, that is very bad of her," Belle said, smiling from ear to ear.

Miss Sheridan grabbed the paper to make sure no mention was made of Miss S——n's performance. "She hasn't said a word about *me*," she pouted.

"Take heart," Clare told her. "This is only the beginning. It will get to you soon enough."

"He means Prattle," Bippy advised Miss Sheridan. "Calls her it."

"This paper is days old," Belle said. "I wonder what she will say about our frog contest."

"She'd better say I won with Green Boy, or I'll write her a letter," Peters said.

"Accuracy is not one of its concerns," Clare warned him.

"She doesn't mention any of us but you, Miss Prentiss," Sherry said, when she had investigated the paper thoroughly. "Not even Lady Honor. Everyone will be wondering if I even got here, though at least they know *I* was invited. It never said you and Miss Fairmont were coming, Lady Sara. Strange that Miss Prattle did not say you were here, too."

"Clare only invited us at the last moment," Sara said. She was secure enough in her social position that she could admit it without shame.

"Yes, and, of course, she would not have named Miss Fairmont as one of the three in the Judgment of Paris contest."

"You take FitzPrattle too seriously, my dear," Clare told her. She did not catch that he was saying he had no intention of choosing a bride from among the three, but Miss Prentiss, who alone knew of Prissie Muckleton, put this interpretation on his words. Of the three original girls, she had always felt that she had the inner track. And of the three, she was also the only one who had noticed his new partiality for Miss Fairmont. Being a worldly girl, Belle had assumed Miss Fairmont was along to lend an air of respectability to Lady Sara's presence. She was one of his long-standing flirts. But the presence of Prissie Muckleton shot that theory into a cocked hat. No, Miss Fairmont was not her aunt's chaperon, but a threat in her own right. After that flirtation—really it went beyond conversation to reach the elevated status of flirtation—she had overheard between them last night, she was on her guard. She might have to take steps to eliminate Miss Fairmont.

Clare turned to Miss Fairmont. "No doubt your name will appear in tomorrow's column, Miss Fairmont."

"I can't think she will consider me newsworthy." Ella well knew her name would never appear in Prattle's column.

"You underrate yourself," Clare replied. "If Fitz does not see fit to name the inventor of the contest, we must certainly write it a blast of a letter."

"By Jove, yes. All your idea," Bippy backed him up.

"Ella is not disappointed to be omitted," Sara told them, enjoying this little game to the fullest.

"No, indeed."

"It's a damned impertinence the way she rakes us all over the coals. But why are we discussing such a tedious subject?"

"It's time to go," Honor told Clare. "Get your hat."

"Yes, ma'am, and *you* get your bonnet." So *that's* why she's up before noon, he thought. By God, she must be serious, to have hauled her carcass out of bed at this hour.

The others went to the ballroom, except for Lady Sara, who went to inquire of Clare for keys to the attic.

"Sara, I'm glad to see you alone. You *must* come with us," he said, in a very urgent voice.

"What in the world for?"

"I have had a chat with mama, and she pointed out what I should have seen for myself. It is as good as announcing an engagement if I go making a call to every home in the neighborhood with Lady Honor. Just the two of us—it will be bound to be misunderstood, and I daresay that is precisely what Honor had in mind."

"You overestimate her."

"Well, I suppose such cunning is beyond her, but she *thinks* she is going to marry me—her whole family thinks it—and no doubt it seemed entirely appropriate to her that she come with me."

"You refine too much on it, but I'll come if you like."

"I *insist*—dash up and get your bonnet, or she'll have me into the carriage and off before we know what has happened. How does she do it, Sara? I pay no attention to her outside of what common decency demands, yet here she is at my home. I am standing up with her first at every dance; she is coming with me on these calls, and if I don't watch my step, she'll marry me when I'm not looking."

"She is strangely indomitable for a girl who doesn't do anything."

"Hurry!"

Sara hustled off for a bonnet and pelisse, but in spite of her haste, Honor was down before her, pulling on her blue kid gloves in silence. "Are *you* coming?" she asked Lady Sara.

"Clare has asked me along. Do you mind?"

"No," Lady Honor replied. Her gloves smoothed to her satisfaction, she said, "Come along, Clare," as though she were already his bride—or his mother.

Insulated from gossip by the presence of Lady Sara, Clare's morning passed with no great discomfort. He even had someone to talk to. Back at the palace, there was considerable bustle and merriment and hurrying around of footmen and maids to obtain old sheets, chains, and a few skulls that Bippy knew to be hiding in a little-used study.

"There, I think we have made it pretty horrid," Miss Prentiss said. "What do you think, Miss Fairmont?" Belle was by degrees insinuating herself onto a closer footing with Miss Fairmont to see what she could discover of the girl.

"If only a storm will be so obliging as to come up, it will be an excellent, scary party."

Belle took the notion that armor, axes, and halberds would add to the gloom, and these were lugged in from the armaments room. Harley tried in vain to detach spider webs from the barn and rehang them, but his efforts were in vain, so he brought in any spiders he could find instead, and ordered them to get busy. Miss Sheridan squashed as many of them as she could without his seeing her, but still there remained more than she cared to contemplate. When Clare, Sara, and Honor returned from the calls around 1:00, the room was ready for inspection.

"How do you like it?" Belle asked Clare. "I have had these weapons brought in from the armaments room, you see. Wasn't that a clever idea?"

He glanced around, but the effect was not marvelous by daylight, and it took a good deal of praising her own efforts to encourage him to believe it looked anything but messy and dirty.

"It is fine," Lady Honor said, looking at the chandeliers, then the floor.

"It will be great, you'll see," Belle told them all. "Have we time to go to the attic for costumes before lunch?"

"It will be dusty up there. I'll have lunch served early so that we may get on with it."

Lunch was served almost immediately, and the sole subject of conversation was the ball. After lunch, everyone tramped up to the attics. Lady Sara looked in vain for a pink dress with panniers in the Queen Anne style, but found nothing remotely like it. Watching her discard gown after gown, Clare said, "If your great secret is to set up as Crazy Nellie, you'll find Mama has the entire ensemble downstairs. Somebody always wears it to our costume balls."

Sara glared at him. "You certainly know how to take the wind out of a person's sails."

"But I know how to put it back again too. You will look quite ravishing, Sara." He smiled that disturbing smile, and she forgave him all. "She also has the red wig—pity to cover your own hair—and Mulch will give you some red roses."

"I see this original idea of mine is down to a fine routine."

"Just so. How is your niece going?"

Sara laughed. "I shan't spoil her surprise, just because you've spoiled mine. And I bet no one has ever had *her* idea before."

He looked across the room at Ella in a speculative manner. "Now what idea has she got in that strange little noggin of hers?" There was a tender undertone in his words.

"You'll see. What about Lady Honor? Someone ought to get her a costume, I expect. I see she didn't come abovestairs."

"She walks, but she don't *climb*. We'll toss a sheet over her and pretend she is a sofa done up for safekeeping. No one will know the difference."

"They will if they try to sit on her."

"Sara, my dear, I don't hold that sort of party at Clare."

"Where *do* you hold that sort?" she asked pertly.

"Where proper society matrons are unlikely to attend. Hush! Here comes your niece."

Sara's eyes widened at this spontaneous warning. She could not remember Clare ever having cared a hoot who heard what he said before, except for his Mama. But here was he, turning his most charming smile on Ella. "Mystery lady," he was saying. "You are going to take the shine out of us all, I hear."

"Sara, you didn't tell him!"

"Of course I didn't, but he knew who I plan to be."

"I expect Crazy Nellie has attended many parties here over the years."

"She never misses a ball, according to Clare."

"I have already atoned for my foray into veracity by saying *you* will be the most exquisite Nellie ever," he reminded Sara, then turned to Ella. "Now won't you tell me how you mean to go, Miss Fairmont? I'll see if I can't find a costume to match. I'm devilish tired of being my ancestor, the third duke, with that uncomfortable ruff cutting into my neck and chin. After the portrait in the long gallery," he explained. "It, like Crazy Nellie, is one of our standard guests at the balls, since we have the outfit and it's so dramatic."

"No, I won't tell you," Ella replied nonchalantly.

Sara thought to see some show of resentment or ire, but no, Clare accepted it in quite good nature. In fact, the unfathomable creature was smiling. It had just occurred to him that what he liked so much about Miss Fairmont was that she didn't care two straws for him. Had he so much as hinted to Sherry how he meant to go, or Miss Prentiss, they would immediately have set about matching his costume, uninvited.

Miss Prentiss, observing that Clare was once again with Ella, came running over. "What do you think of this green shot silk as as a gown for Anne Boleyn, Clare?"

"Very nice," he said, hardly looking at it.

Sara, noticing that the style was not more than ten years old, said that it would require alterations, though there seemed to be plenty of material.

"Come and see what I have found for you, Clare," Miss Prentiss continued. "There is a velvet top and white silk stockings—it looks quite like the rigout Henry VIII wears in the pictures one always sees. A little three-cornered hat and some chin whiskers and you might pass very well."

"I wouldn't be caught dead in that outfit," he said firmly. "In the first place, it is as hot as a quilt with the buckram and wadding under the velvet top, and in the second, I don't like the long silk hose."

"What are you wearing then?" she persisted, wondering if she might yet regulate her costume to his.

"I don't know. I'll find something."

"You won't if you don't start looking," Ella warned him. "There is Bippy in the Henry VIII tunic, and Harley getting into the cavalier's suit. That would have suited you."

"I am flattered," he said.

"*Fit* you is what I meant," she corrected.

"Thank you again," he said humbly.

"She's right," Sara told him. "You'd better pick up something fast, for the rest of us are about ready to leave."

"Let's go then," Clare said.

"Going to go as a match to Lady Honor, are you?" Sara teased.

Belle's ears perked up, but no explanation was offered to this private joke. "Miss Fairmont has no costume," she said.

"Mine isn't up here," Ella replied mysteriously. She had secreted a likely dress behind a trunk and meant to come back for it later.

They all trooped downstairs and separated to attend to the pressing and renovations of their costumes. Ella was busy all afternoon. She had to find a papier-mâché hat stand, paint its face, get a wig for it, and put red paint on the neck to stimulate blood; then she had to arrange the wadding that was to hold her gown up over her own head, and also to get Bickles to put eye holes in it without utterly ruining the gown. Sara and Stepson helped too, as Crazy Nellie's costume was ready to put on. Stepson even found a crimping iron in the basement and made her up a ruff.

The hoped-for storm did not come up that evening, but a pleasantly eerie wind was blowing outside, and echoes of its soughing came in at chimney flues and loose windows. With less than half the usual quantity of candles lit, and the ghostlike sheets and Bippy's skulls decorating the room, it was felt to be a fair representation of a haunted house. Harley complained that he had never seen such a stubborn set of spiders, who refused to spin a single web after all his trouble in bringing them into a nice warm house. It was the Dowager's addition to atmosphere to blow out the tapers in the entrance hall, and send the butler to the door with one single candle held high. More civilized accommodations prevailed in the ladies' dressing room and the dining room, but the house was a fine mess, just the way it was when her husband had first brought her there, the Duchess declared.

The guests began arriving, and Clare and his Mama were well pleased with the ghosts, goblins, and sprites who had come to their party. Many of those invited had the same inspiration, or lack of it, that had got Honor into her sheet. With so many ghosts present, Clare accidentally stood up for the first dance with a neighbor's daughter who chanced to be standing beside him when the music struck up, but no one knew it but themselves and Lady Honor. He remedied this, or rather she did, by appearing at his elbow for the next dance. He felt she had never been so appropriately dressed before. When the ghost said not a word, he had a pretty fair inkling who it was, and when it reached out and clamped his arm, he knew for sure. Lady Honor had no difficulty recognizing Clare, since he had

113

come as Admiral Nelson in an old admiral's uniform of his uncle's, and his disguise consisted of a patch over one eye. He also had one arm supported in a sling, but he removed this impediment for the dancing.

Nelson was busily scanning the room for a mystery lady by the end of the second dance. He could not find her, but Crazy Nellie was spotted flirting with two country gentlemen, and he went to inquire of her regarding Ella. He met his Mama on the way, and she walked along with him.

"She ran into unexpected difficulties with her head, but should be here presently," Sara told them, laughing gaily and refusing to explain.

At the moment they heard a shriek from Miss Sheridan, who, finding nothing half so beguiling in Clare's attic as her own mauve ball gown, had worn it with an egret half-mask.

"Good God!" Clare exclaimed, looking at the ghastly spectacle which had just entered. Around the room a series of squeals and shouts went up, as one after another of his guests looked towards the door.

"It's Matilda to the life!" the Dowager shrieked.

"To the death," Clare corrected.

"Who the devil can it be?" his Mama asked. "It must be a gentleman—look at the height of it."

"You forget there's a head under those shoulders," he pointed out, "as well as under the arm. A head—why it's Miss Fairmont!" He hurried towards her, fighting his way through a crowd that had gathered to admire her ghoulish ingenuity.

He separated her from the group. "Come, Lady Matilda. We are a fine pair of derelicts, for I have lost an eye and an arm, and you have lost your head."

"I very nearly did," she said. "I thought Miss Prentiss would pull it right out of my hands. Isn't it *real* looking?"

He reached out and took the dummy head from her. "Charming, but I think I prefer the one you usually wear. Where shall we stick your spare while we dance?"

"Do you know," a serious little voice emanated from the bodice of the gown, "I don't see how I *can* dance. I can hardly even breathe in here. It is excessively hot. And the costume would look very odd if I put down the head."

"My dear, it looks excessively odd in any case."

"Yes, isn't it horrid? Do you like it?"

"Original, as I have come to expect of Miss Fairmont."

"Oh, you knew it was I! How could you tell?"

"By your voice. Besides, I couldn't find you anywhere when I was looking for you."

A thrill ran through Ella's whole body. "Were you looking for me?" she asked. Clare had been introduced to her three times in London, without once remembering her name. It was very strange and exhilarating indeed to learn he had been looking for her in a room full of girls.

"Yes, I wanted to make you waltz with me again."

"I'm through with warning you. You know I've two left feet. And in this outfit . . ."

"Serves you right. You might have come as Lady Hamilton if you'd bothered to ask me what I was wearing, and then you'd have been perfectly comfortable."

"But I wouldn't have looked anything like her."

"Dash it, Miss Fairmont, I wish you'd take off that dress—I mean lower it over your face or something. You've no idea how foolish I feel, talking to your collar."

A muffled snort came from the bodice. "I'll ruin my costume, and not everyone has seen it yet."

"We'll tour the room, bowing and nodding to everyone like royalty, and *then* you will make some arrangement to get your head up out of there. Come along. Shall I carry the head?"

He lodged it in the crook of his left arm, gave Ella his right arm and together they toured the room, with Clare holding out the head and introducing it to everyone, in mock solemn tones.

"By Jove, you are up to all sorts of rigs, Miss Fairmont," Peters congratulated warmly.

"Be sure to save me a dance, Miss Fairmont," from Harley.

"I thought of going as Matilda, but didn't want to put anyone to the bother of making up the outfit," Belle said.

The rounds completed, Clare placed the head on a pedestal in front of a bust of Homer and said to it, "Be good, Matilda, and if you don't cast any spells while we're gone, we'll give you back your body tomorrow. Now for *you*," he turned to Ella.

"Not here. I'm stuffed with cotton wool. Is there somewhere I can go and get it out?"

"Come along." He took her hand and led her to a small parlor, and they both began pulling bits of wool from the neck of her dress.

"You must be baked alive in there," he said.

"I am *melted*," she said, as her head popped free at last.

"Lord, what a mess you look, Ella—Miss Fairmont."

"My name is Ella. If we are on an insult basis, I suppose you may use it. I have a comb here in my reticule somewhere. I should really go upstairs . . ."

"Since we are to be on an insult-and-first-name basis of cordiality, I shan't hesitate to tell you I am mighty tired of waiting for you. There is a mirror." He pointed to the far wall. "See if you can't make yourself presentable, and let's go and dance."

She went to the mirror and rearranged her locks hastily, in a careless fashion adopted from Bickles. She was ill at ease, with Clare watching her perform this feminine ritual. Looking at his reflection in the glass, she said, "At least it's good and dark in the ballroom, so no one will see if I look a mess."

"*I* will see," he told her.

"But it's your fault, so I shan't mind what *you* think."

He expected no better of Miss Fairmont. *I shan't care what* you *think!* "You have a knack for making a fellow feel insignificant," he said, smiling while she pulled the gown down around her and rearranged the belt.

"A new experience for *you*, Your Grace."

"An entirely new experience. Only Prattle has treated me so shabbily till now, and I never favored her with my gallantry."

That again! She recovered and retaliated, "Do you call it gallantry to tell a girl she looks a mess, and you are tired of waiting for her?"

"Come, Lady Hamilton. I don't want to miss that waltz." He held out his hand impatiently.

She took a last look in the mirror. "I don't look much like *her*."

"No, for she was fat and long in the tooth when *I* met her. Much inclined to pose and prose too, I might add."

"But she looks so lovely in that series of Romney's portraits!"

"She must have been something in her youth. To do her justice, she had gone well to seed before I ever made her acquaintance."

"A lady of *any* age would not feel she had been done justice if you should *say* so, however."

"I know you would like to stand here all night arguing, shrew, but *I* should like to dance." He took her arm and marched her swiftly to the ballroom.

The first sight they met was Miss Sheridan, looking exquisite in her mauve gown, her black curls framing her face. "It was foolish of me to wear this costume and end up looking so awful," Ella complained.

Clare followed her glance and stood observing Sherry a moment. "Beauty is only skin deep, Ella. The world is full of beautiful pictures and statues and faces. All very pleasing to *look* at, but it is intelligence and imagination and, of course, charm that hold the interest in the long haul."

"I should concentrate on trying to be charming," Ella thought aloud.

"Just what I was thinking myself for, of course, you have no intelligence or imagination!"

She looked hurt for a minute, till she saw he was quizzing her. "Well, that was horrid of you."

"Wasn't it? Ah, the music at last."

They twirled around the floor in rhythm. The near darkness and the intimacy of the waltz added a heady excitement, almost a sensation of unreality to these moments.

"Three more days, Ella," Clare said. "How shall we amuse our guests?"

The words sounded awesomely strange to her ears. She could not imagine what madness had come over him. But, inexperienced as she was, she had a sharp idea what madness was coming over her. At least she retained enough sanity to know it was madness. She racked her brain and recalled another pastime from Fairmont.

"Why don't you gentlemen put on a curricle race for us? You can wear our colors—a ribbon round your arm or hat, like knights of old."

"It will be done, milady, providing I may wear *your* color."

"To save Paris the bother of making his choice?" she asked.

"Any rumors of an impending engagement have been greatly exaggerated—in fact they are sheer invention." Still, he knew that if he didn't secure Ella's favor for the curricle race, Honor would slap a blue ribbon round his curled beaver and put yet another knot in the noose tightening round his neck. "What is your color?" he asked.

"Our servants wear gray livery."

"How cheerful. I shall go in half-mourning."

"Do you think you might have a jousting contest too?" she asked, relieved, though not entirely happy, to get the conversation down to earth.

"Where we have at each other with those great long poles? I'm afraid not, Ella, even for you."

"Bows and arrows?"

"Pistols it will have to be. We're not set up for bows and arrows. Besides, I shall most assuredly win for you if it's pistols."

"You're very cocksure, Your Grace."

"Tell me, why is it I am still 'Your Grace,' while *you* have been Ella this quarter hour?"

"You didn't tell me your name."

"Ah, and in my vanity, I assumed you to know it was Patrick, when you must have heard my Mama call me so fifty times."

"But you did not ask me to call you so. Bippy calls you Pa'k, I notice, like they call me Ella."

"Is that not your name then?"

"Only half of it. The whole is Puella. Papa is a Latin scholar of sorts, you see. I'm glad he didn't take into his head to call me Hera or Athene or some such horrid thing."

"Girl. *Puella* means girl. I wonder if he oughtn't to have made it *Mulier*."

"Good gracious, it sounds like a disease. What is it?"

"Why, it is the most beautiful word in the Latin language—woman. But I like Puella. It has a nice generic sound to it. I shall call you Puella."

"Not if you wish me to answer, you won't."

"Pue?"

"Worse! I beat my two brothers to a pulp to cure them of the horrid habit."

"You say *horrid* too often. All you young ladies do."

"You're very fussy."

"Surely that is established beyond question. But the most charming face is ruined by a common bonnet, and the most interesting speech by a dull repetition."

This coming on top of Clare's former gallantry was a disagreeable surprise. She began to think him in need of another set-down. "Upon my word, I never heard such gall."

"You can't be abreast of your Prattle. You must know when I condescend to attend one of my own parties, I demand perfection from everyone. Miss Sheridan is perfectly lovely; Miss Prentiss is a perfect imitation of Caroline Lamb . . ."

"And Lady Honor?"

"She is a perfect *lady*—did you expect some indiscretion to escape me? Sorry to disappoint you. And *you* must be perfectly conversable."

"You have left yourself out of this list of perfection."

"An amazing oversight! I must blame it on the waltz. But it is perfectly obvious I am *here*. And now perfectly plain that this perfect waltz is ended—you see how a word palls after a while?"

"Perfectly. I ask nothing more than that this *horrid* waltz be finished."

"I despair of ever getting the last word with you, Puella," he said, giving her his most charming smile. Intimate, disarming—and on that odd note it was over.

No denying all other partners were dull after him, though they came with a flattering regularity. Bippy, Peters, Harley, and the gentlemen of the neighborhood, so that sitting out a dance was unnecessary, and in fact impossible. But always from the corner of her eye she was aware of the Admiral's uniform. Knew at exactly what moment he reached up and pulled the patch from his eye with an impatient gesture. Could almost hear him say 'damned nuisance.' She had to take herself sharply in hand to prevent trailing him around the room with her eyes, as all the other ladies were doing. She had her Prattle duties to help her, mixed blessing that they had become.

She would have been gratified to know she was as much in Clare's thoughts as he was in hers, while he danced and made himself polite to everyone. His next partner, one of the daughters of a neighbor, found a ball a suitable time to tell him her papa was interested in buying a little ten-acre field adjacent to their farm that he apparently never used, and even asked him what price he would take for it. He told her he made it a practice not to sell off any land, but he might rent it, if her papa cared to call on his bailiff tomorrow. He was invariably polite to his neighbors, however strong the inclination to be otherwise. Miss Sheridan next regaled him with the thrilling saga of her efforts to find a masquerade costume, and why it was she was wearing a ball gown. He had failed to notice this tremendously important fact and stung her to the quick by saying no one else would notice, either. Lady Sara had her turn about the floor with him, for she adamantly refused to sit against the wall all evening like a dowager, when she was not quite thirty and adored dancing.

Three times she tried some bantering conversation with him, and three times he returned to the subject of her niece. Had she always been such an outrageous little baggage, and how did it come Sara had not put her in his way before. In vain she told him he had met her years ago. He insisted he had never *really* known her. By the dance's end, such an untenable idea had entered her head that she felt weak. But no, he had only decided to make her his latest flirt, for a lark. She must warn Ella not to go falling in love with him. Looking out for Ella around the room at various times during the evening, she noticed she was paying no heed to him. Never came within a right angle of looking at him. Well, the Great Absent One would find *that* interesting.

When everyone had retired to his chamber after an enjoyable evening, Lady Sara undertook to hint her niece away from Clare.

"I see Clare is setting up a flirtation with you," she said, in an offhand manner. "What an odd creature he is. I suppose he does it to let the three beauties know he doesn't plan to make his selection from this year's crop."

"Very likely," Ella agreed.

"Not falling for him, I trust?"

"Oh, no, after following his amorous exploits all these years, I am on to his tricks."

Sara looked at her niece levelly. "He can be mighty charming. I'm half in love with him myself, when he smiles at me. But only half. He doesn't mean a thing by it."

"I know," Ella said and turned to the mirror.

"That's good. I felt it my duty to mention the fact, for it is becoming rather clear he's singled you out for special attention, and it would be a wonder if it didn't go to your head."

"A good thing I wasn't wearing any this evening," Ella replied in a droll voice.

Sara nodded, satisfied that her niece's heart was not at stake. "Well, so long as you realize the situation, I see no harm in playing up to him. It will set you quite apart and will make the other gentlemen sit up and take notice when we go back to town."

"Yes, that's what I thought," Ella said, keeping her back to her aunt, while she fiddled with her hair in the mirror.

Her duty done, Sara retired to her room, and Ella considered this good advice—the same she had been giving herself all evening. She had a shrewd notion her main attraction for Clare was his belief she didn't care overly much for him. If she took to languishing after him, he'd be finished with her in two minutes. All right, then, go on just as she had been doing, and *try* to keep her heart in line. The best means of accomplishing this would be to stay away from him as much as possible.

Nine

Keeping away from Clare proved exceptionally difficult for Miss Fairmont in the following days, for it was soon clear to everyone that he had chosen her as the special object of his attention.

"Ella has had another of her inspired notions," he announced at breakfast next morning, using her first name in the most casual manner in the world. Sherry's mouth fell open, and Belle's topaz eyes narrowed. If Lady Honor had been there, she would likely have blinked. "We are to

122

have a knights' contest—curricle races, pistol match—and no, Ella, no jousting."

"By Jove, a very good idea," Bippy remarked, buttering a hot scone of a sort he could find nowhere but at Clare Palace. "Knight errantry ain't dead by a long shot. Will you do me the honor to let me wear your color, Miss Fairmont?"

Before she could reply, Clare informed him, "Ella has done *me* the honor of being her knight."

"Oh, I say, that ain't fair, Pa'k," Peters jumped in. "I wanted to be Miss Fairmont's knight, or swain, or whatever you call it. Soon as you mentioned it, it came to me I'd wear green, in honor of Green Boy and Miss Fairmont."

"It seems Miss Fairmont is not so *green* as we had thought," Belle said in a spiteful tone.

Ella could hardly believe her ears. It was a Prattlelike comment, and she realized how her own sharp words over the years must have stung.

"Ella's color is gray," Pat said to Peters, ignoring Belle's ill humor entirely.

"Gray?" Belle asked. "Why, that is a mourning color."

"*You* ought certainly to wear green though, Peters, for Miss Prentiss' eyes."

"My eyes are hazel," Belle retorted angrily.

"They have a definite tint of green at the moment," he told her, smiling lazily.

He means jealousy, Ella thought, and glanced at him. He was still observing Belle, but she fancied there was a slight twitching of the lips.

"No way of getting a *hazel* ribbon," Bippy said, in a rare streak of practicality.

"No, nor a gray one either," Belle continued, "unless you happen to have some mourning ribbons around the place."

"It will be arranged," Patrick assured her, in unimpaired humor.

"I'd like to have a go at the jousting, Pa'k," Harley declared. "Be famous fun. Get some long barge poles or some such thing, and pad up the end of them so we don't break each others' ribs. Love to give it a try."

"And I know some Elizabethan madrigals I shall sing for you later on in the evening, to continue the theme," Miss Prentiss added.

This was greeted with an unenthusiastic silence till Miss Sheridan said, "We could all dress up in Elizabethan outfits!" with her mind as usual running to gowns.

"What a good idea, Sherry," her Mama congratulated her.

The Straywards, worried at Miss Fairmont's sudden entrance into the chase after Clare, had left word to be roused early and made a dragging entry at this point. Honor had orders to be lively, and she spoke up immediately.

"We have a gown at Strayward belonging to Queen Elizabeth," she informed them.

"It has eight hundred seed pearls on the bodice alone," the Marchioness added.

"How ambitious of you to have counted them, ma'am," Clare praised her. "But we haven't enough Elizabethan costumes here to go halfway around."

"Good," his mother murmured in a low voice.

"About the jousting," Harley returned to his favorite topic. "Do you have any long poles in the barn, Pa'k?"

"No."

"We'll have to chop down some saplings then and strip off the branches. And don't tell me you have no saplings in the home woods, for you've hundreds of them."

"The boys at home use turnip rooting sticks," Ella volunteered.

"We don't grow turnips at Clare," the host said, "and if you chop down so much as one sapling I shall sue you for malicious destruction of property."

"We grow turnips at Strayward," the Marchioness said, for Honor had been passed a plate of scones and was too busy to speak.

"Get 'em from the side of the road then," Harley said, ignoring this bulletin.

"It sounds terribly dangerous," Sherry offered.

"Yes, it'll be great sport," Peters said. "We'll hack down to the home woods after breakfast and choose our poles. You coming, Tredwell?"

"Oh yes, might as well, you know."

"I shall have three warrants drawn up then," Clare said casually. No one, of course, paid him any heed.

"You must each choose your lady first," Sherry reminded them, dimpling prettily at Harley. He was a far cry from a duke, being only a baron, but held the only other title of all the gentlemen.

"Yes, shall we draw straws?" the callous fellow suggested.

"I'll give you a blue ribbon," Lady Honor told him. No more than Miss Sheridan did she intend to bestow her color on a man without a title, and Belle had already told her in a gleeful aside that Clare had chosen.

"Thank you," he muttered. There was something unchallengeable in the graven face of Lady Honor.

"Guess that leaves you to bestow a ribbon on *me*," Bippy said to Miss Sheridan, who happened to be sitting beside him. "What's your color?"

"I look best in pink," she said, a trifle sulkily.

Peters looked to Belle Prentiss. "Green," she said in disgust.

Breakfast over, the gentlemen went to select and prepare their jousting poles, with the exception of the Duke, who rode to the village to attend a meeting with his local banker and some other gentlemen. The young ladies, at the instigation of Belle Prentiss, decorated the curricles with flowers and ribbons. Lady Sara did Honor's work for her, and the lady was kind enough to say, "That is all right," when she was finished.

"You're welcome," Sara replied pointedly.

During the morning's work, the young ladies called each other by their first names so often that Sara's ears were ringing with Belles, Sherrys, and Ellas. No one, however, was brave enough to drop the "Lady" before the name of Honor, but in any case, few remarks were addressed to her, as she had taken up a comfortable seat on a bench some distance apart from them.

A clearing in the park was chosen for the tournament, and chairs lugged out to allow comfort for the ladies and their Mamas. Several kitchen maids and footmen were allowed off work to attend, and the parson's six children were invited, when they accidentally dropped in at an auspicious hour, so that there was a fair-sized audience for the contest.

Belle had been closely observing Miss Fairmont's success with the Duke and decided the time had come to put a spoke in her wheel. She was not so unwise as to charge Clare directly with what she knew of Prissie Muckleton, for he had pokered up angrily at even the mention of having been seen in the village. She thought the better course to reveal his behavior to Miss Fairmont who was a bit of a prude.

"What a tease Clare is, singling you out for special attention," she began when they were off away from the others.

"He is no more than polite to me," Ella said brusquely, arranging a loop of ribbon higher, so it did not catch in the wheel of the curricle.

"Pshaw, Ella, you are not such a flat as that! It is always 'Miss Fairmont will do this', or lately, '*Ella* will tell us that,' and 'What do *you* think, Ella?' It would be enough to turn a girl's head if she didn't know the truth."

Ella disliked this conversation very much, but was too human to ignore that tantalizing phrase, 'the truth.' "What do you mean?" she asked, her heart thudding fast, she hardly knew why.

"Oh, Ella, you *don't* mean you don't know about the lightskirt he has picked up in the village?" she laughed. "We are all on to him. We saw them together a few days ago in Kitswell. He nipped into a doorway with her, try-

126

ing to hide from us, but we all saw her—Sherry, Peters, Harley, and myself. She was very beautiful—he is so fastidious about his *real* flirts' looks. *His* women must be the fairest of them all. *I* think the only reason he has brought us all down here is to cover his traces, the rogue. And *you*, of course, are the one he has chosen to pretend he is interested in, to turn us off the scent."

Ella stared at Belle and had for one instant an overpowering desire to claw her hazel eyes out of her head. But sense overcame passion in the same instant, and she naturally did nothing of the sort. To her credit, she even managed a smile, a sardonic parting of the lips. "That's rather pointless, isn't it? Throwing you off the scent when you all know about it and have even seen his girl friend."

"But that is the best part of the joke! He doesn't know we saw him. Peters and Harley won't let us say anything to him. Well, they have convinced us we ought not to, and only the four of us know. We didn't tell our mothers, Sherry and I, and your aunt doesn't know, I suppose, unless *he* told her. But I made sure *you* would know," she finished up, with some thought of remaining on a friendly footing with Miss Fairmont, just in case.

"I don't know how you thought I should know, when you four who spied him appear to have made a pact of silence," Ella said, her anger channeling itself to the bearer of bad news, as it so often does when the doer is beyond range.

"We were not *spying* on him!" Belle took her up immediately.

"I said when you spied him—happened to see him was all I meant. My, you're touchy, Belle." Ella had been shocked and angered to hear Belle's story, but Miss Prattle was advancing to the fore, curious for reportable details, and it was Miss Prattle who spoke out, in Ella's voice. "This girl, what did she look like?"

"As pretty as could be," Belle informed her, with a thrill of pleasure. "A petite blonde. She was clinging to his arm. We caught only a glimpse then, but she is young and attractive, as I learned later, though *very* common—a servant I think. Prissie is her name."

"Did you see them again?"

"Haha, I most certainly did, and you might see her yourself if you open your door one night, when we are all supposed to be asleep. He brings her right here to the palace! I was downstairs late one evening, and she came in wearing a shawl, asking for the 'dook'—a very common accent. I was surprised he had her come here, with his Mama in residence, but it is supposed to be a secret from her, I make no doubt. The butler gave her what for, for not slipping up the back way."

Ella's senses were reeling, but she had enough pride to hide her hurt from this prying witch. "I am shocked that he brings her under his mother's roof," she said.

"Yes, so am I, for he is usually very discreet. But then it saves him the trip into the village, I suppose, and so far as that goes, he would be well known there and more likely to cause gossip by haunting her house, than by having her here. So *that* is why he has latched on to you—to fool us all."

"But I see you are not so easily fooled!" Ella said calmly.

"Yes, and I am glad I told you since you didn't know, for it is too bad of him to fool *you*."

"He isn't fooling *me*," Ella said in a steely voice and began to work on the carriage with great concentration, till Belle hopped away.

Ella did not rate her attractions high. She had been as much amazed as the others at her meteoric rise to favor in His Grace's eyes and was entirely ready to accept Belle's reason for it. Even without Sara's warning she would have believed it. She had held a grudge against Clare for many a long year—and was aware of his arrogance, vanity, conceit. She had not known him to be a rake, but Belle had mentioned his discretion. That would account for it. She had been a fool to think he cared for her—indeed she had never thought him serious. But she had not thought he was using her in this sly way, to conceal his own lechery. She had been a fool, and as if that weren't bad enough, everyone at the party who mattered, all the people her own age, *knew* she was a fool and were laughing at her. Well, she was in a position of pre-eminence to turn the tables on Clare, and she soon set about doing it.

She slipped up to her room before lunch, dipped her pen in vitriol, and wrote her revenge. Without taking a cool second look at what she was doing, she dashed off in colorful phrases the atrocities of Lord Clare, to be read and discussed in London. She addressed it to her grandmother and took it below for posting. This activity acted as a catharsis for her emotions, and when she met His Grace, she could treat him calmly, knowing that retribution was in store for him.

Ten

The first event in the tournament was to be the curricle race. The vehicles were tooled up to the starting point by the drivers, each with a band of ribbon streaming from his hat. They made a gay sight in their decorated carriages, and a pleasant cheer arose from the gathered crowd. A footman had been given a hurried lesson on the long horn by Miss Prentiss, and blasted four hoots to initiate the race. The ladies, always excepting Lady Honor, stood cheering their knights on, and from then till the drivers had disappeared down the road, executed an alarmingly sharp turn, and come back into view, there was little for the girls to do but talk and call each other by their first names some more. Miss Prentiss, now Belle to all, sought to ingratiate herself with Ella, when she observed that her tale-bearing had not turned her against Clare, as she had hoped. It had seemed to have almost the reverse effect, for Miss Fairmont was a little livelier than usual.

She formed the excellent notion of inviting her to her home for New Year's, to take part in the play about Anne Boleyn.

"Come for the New Year, Ella. Clare is coming." As things stood, it seemed a good deal more likely he *would* come if Ella were known to be of the party, and one could always forget to remind her later if the friendship with the Duke petered out. "We'll get together in London, and you can choose a part. Jane Seymour is not taken. I have given her some very good lines." She had to cut the conversation short as Sherry was lending an ear, and *she* was definitely *not* to be invited, however strongly she hinted. Belle needn't have worried. Sherry hadn't the slightest notion of inviting herself until Clare's plans were stated.

In a short time the sound of wheels and hooves bespoke the return of the charioteers, and the ladies had once more to urge their knight on. Harley and Clare were bolting along, neck to neck, with Bippy two lengths behind, and Peters out of it. He had made a poor turn, and lost a minute righting himself after the disaster. Every one of the young ladies was cheering Clare on to break the tie. Even Lady Honor said in a calm, deliberate voice, "Clare must win." It was impossible he should not when Honor had decreed it, and he edged Harley out by a half a length, to be welcomed from his curricle by a shouting mob. Belle had been defoliating roses under the disapproving eye of the Duchess while she stood chatting, and had two handfuls of red petals to shower over him.

"That's one for us, Ella," Clare said when he had shaken himself free of petals. "Have you no favor to confer on me? A token of your gratitude?"

She reached down and grabbed a sprig of red clover from the lawn and handed it to him. "In the lapel, if you please," he said. She felt extremely awkward and forward, inserting it in his lapel, as though she were a brazen hussy like Belle Prentiss. But it was all a part of the show he was putting on, of course, pretending he liked her.

This was too much for Belle to tolerate. She elbowed Ella aside, and stuck a nice red rose on top of the clover, while the Duchess glowered at this repeated desecration of her garden.

"There, that's more like it," she said saucily.

But before he returned to his curricle, Clare pointedly reached down and pulled the clover to the front, with a smile at Ella.

"Time for the jousting contest," Harley called. "This time I'll take you, Clare."

"No, you won't. I'm not jousting."

"What, afraid?" Belle taunted.

"It's dangerous, and I don't think you others ought to either," he stated, yet there was a certain look of longing on his face as they began hoisting the prepared saplings.

His mother arose from her chair and walked over to him. "I wish you would not, Pat."

"Don't worry, Mama. I'm not about to risk my neck till I've produced an heir." They stood chatting a minute, and Belle turned to Ella.

"It's because of his brother, I suppose. *He* broke his neck falling from a horse. I ought not to have said anything. The title would go to his cousin, George Foley, if anything happened to Clare."

During an enthusiastic morning of preparations and discussion, Harley had decided the contenders ought to carry shields for protection. These had been duly removed from the armaments room and brought to the site, but were soon found unwieldy and were cast aside. Next they had to discover the proper grip for their swaddled saplings. Harley maintained that the only possible position was tucked firmly under the right arm, while Peters found it rested more comfortably against the abdomen. Clare advised them that both hands ought to be used, while using the legs to keep a seat on the horse.

"That's easy for *you* to say; you ain't competing," Harley responded.

"Ask Miss Fairmont how they do it at Fairmont," Bippy advised.

"Yes, she'll know," Harley agreed. He was nearly as strong a supporter of Miss Fairmont as Peters was.

"It is a matter of style merely," she reported. "Bertie, my older brother, always uses two hands, but Tom uses a shorter pole and holds it in one—up quite high so that he strikes the opponent in the shoulder. But a blow to the head is illegal."

"Have we got the sticks the right length?" Peters asked her.

She examined them, and pronounced them just right. "You don't want them too long or you can't strike a true blow."

"They actually *do* joust at Fairmont?" Clare asked her.

"Certainly, and no one has ever been hurt. Badly, I mean. Bertie got a black eye, and Ronnie MacIntyre has had several nose bleeds, but that happens if you look at him too hard, so that's nothing."

"If they do it at Fairmont, *I* do it," Clare declared and took up a pole.

"Perhaps you shouldn't," Ella said, glancing at his mother.

"What, worried about me, Ella? But how flattering!"

"No, I'm worried about your mother."

"You do a very good job of cutting me down to size," he said, glancing at her sideways. She smiled to think how much better that remark suited the situation than he knew.

He picked up a pole and looked inquiringly at his mother. She shrugged her shoulders, to indicate she was washing her hands of him, and he turned back to Ella. "I shan't kill myself. The way these Johnnie Raws go at it, I see it isn't the lethal sport I imagined. And if we do it at Fairmont, then I must get in some practice." He gave her one of his warmest smiles, designed, she supposed, to lure

132

her into falling in love with him. But she was on to him now.

"But it is not likely *you* will ever be at Fairmont, is it, Your Grace?"

"Not by invitation, it seems," he replied with a frown.

The remark annoyed him, but with the gladiators all eager to be slaying each other, he was diverted from considering it. They had only three poles, so that only two men could tilt at a time, and Peters insisted he deserved a turn before Clare be allowed to replace him. The horn was blown, dreadfully off key, and with his pole firmly lodged against his abdomen, Peters galloped towards Harley, who stuck to his decision of tucking his under his right arm. Harley's tactic gave him more maneuverability, and besides he was the better rider, so that with these two advantages, he unseated Peters on the second tilt. Peters suffered a hard fall, but no broken bones, and Bippy replaced him. They were unanimous in giving Clare last place, as he was the last to agree to enter.

Tredwell tried to do it with both hands on the pole, and his horse shied. With no hands to aid him, he sailed over the horse's head and hit the ground with a thump. The ladies rushed forward to succor him. "Believe I've broken my leg," he said apologetically. But when he was dragged from the ground, it was discovered he could put some weight on it, so he was provided with a pair of crutches from the lengths cut off the jousting poles and encouraged loudly to refrain from succumbing to a broken leg. Within two minutes he had forgotten all about it and discarded the crutches. Within three, he was jumping up and down as hard as Belle and Sherry.

"Don't try it with both hands on the stick," he warned Clare as his turn came up.

Clare ignored his advice, and when he went thundering towards Harley, he was tossed from his horse as easily as the others.

"By Jove, this is great sport," Harley beamed, the victor. "Who wants to do it again? Just beginning to get the hang of it. Tuck 'er under your right elbow; that's the ticket."

"I'll try it again, your way," Clare said, picking himself up from the turf, with Belle tugging at one hand and Sara at the other. "And I'll unseat you if we have to joust all afternoon."

It soon began to seem as if they would. Two more times Harley sent Clare flying from his saddle.

"Are you glued to that damned horse?" Clare demanded. He was streaked with grass and dirt from head to toe but picked himself up to go again.

"I've thrown you three times. That's enough," Harley decided. "There's no competition here." He hopped down from his mount and went to Miss Fairmont. "Where exactly do you and your brothers live, Miss Fairmont?" he asked.

Clare listened in consternation as she told him, and in pique when she suggested he must come down and have a go at it with her brothers. I believe she's trying to make me jealous, he thought. He did not yet acknowledge that she was succeeding.

"I'll toss Peters once more for practice, then we'll go on to the pistol match," Harley said, and the arrogant fellow made good his boast. The others were all tired of hitting the ground, so Harley was the winner of the jousting tournament. He seemed to have forgotten he was representing Lady Honor, for he never once looked towards her for commendation. He was too busy congratulating himself, but she had wandered off to examine the weeds in Clare's grass and didn't notice.

"We've missed this round, but the pistol match is a shoe-in for us," Clare assured his lady. "Can't expect to win 'em all," he added when she showed no enthusiasm.

"Your face is dirty," she replied.

"Rub it off, will you?" he said and handed her his handkerchief.

She dabbed at his cheek in exquisite embarrassment, while Belle looked on in envy. The targets were set up, the pistols loaded, and an ear-shattering interlude of pistols going off at no great distance from them was enjoyed by the onlookers. Sherry stuck her fingers in her ears and closed her eyes, and passed the interval in this interesting manner. Clare, who made a fetish of his shooting, was the winner by a wide margin, and the tournament was over. Of all the contenders, it was only he who came to report to his lady at the termination of each event.

"I am expecting something better than a weed for my reward this time," he told Ella.

"We didn't bother to make up any prizes," she replied.

Belle, who was never far from their side, told them that the lady's hand was the prize in days of yore.

"It wasn't *that* kind of contest," Sherry shouted, thunderstruck at the stupidity of Belle, who thought she was so knowing.

"A pity," Clare murmured, throwing a teasing look at Sherry.

She said 'oh', and ran to her Mama to report this latest turn of events.

"But the imaginative Miss Fairmont will think of something," Clare continued.

The imaginative Miss Prentiss certainly thought of something and wished the lot of bestowing a reward on the winner was hers. Ella turned aside and addressed a remark to Harley.

Refreshments were served under an awning, to preserve the ladies' complexion from the odd burning rays that might filter through the hazy sky, their bonnets, and parasols. Ella headed for the lemonade, but Clare detained her.

"We victors deserve champagne, don't you think?" He handed her a glass. "To the victor's lady," he said and drank.

She was aware of everyone watching them, aware too that they all knew he was making sport of her. She swallowed a lump in her throat and sipped a little champagne.

Clare was surprised to see that the more gallant he became, the more she withdrew into herself. He had not much experience with shy ladies. There were so many of the other sort putting themselves in his way, that he had come to believe the breed extinct. In spite of his experience with ladies, he had really very little occasion to court them. They were too busy courting him. It seemed he was actually going to have to *pursue* the little brown mouse to win her favor. His pride, which he called determination, did not allow him to think of giving it up. He turned to Ella with one of his winsome smiles. "Well, Ella, I hope you enjoyed your contest."

"It has been fine up till now," she snapped back, her patience becoming exhausted.

This was beginning to sound more like pique than shyness, and he asked bluntly, "Have I inadvertently said—or done—something to offend you? If I have, I beg your pardon."

"No, I don't believe you are doing it *inadvertently*," she answered and walked away from him.

He was left standing looking after her, in confusion and some resentment. Belle and Sherry were eager to take her place, and he did not bother Miss Fairmont again that afternoon, but when the refreshments had been partaken of, he walked over and gave Lady Sara his arm for the walk back to the palace.

"Sara, you witch," he said, with an easy confidence, "have you frightened your niece off from me?"

"Not exactly," she replied, unoffended.

"But you spoke to her?" She nodded. "May I ask what, exactly, you said?"

"Why, I only told her you are a flirt and a tease, and she must not take your attentions seriously. I felt honor-bound to do that much. In spite of her years, she is the veriest greenhead, Clare, and would not understand the way you carry on."

"But I have not been *carrying on* with her in the least. I thought I had found a friend, and I take it as unkind in you to frighten her away. Friendship is possible between the sexes, don't you think?"

"Very likely, I wouldn't know from experience, and neither would you. But a girl of her age is not looking for *friendship* in an eligible man. Oh, don't turn white and tremble on me. She isn't setting her cap at you.".

"I know. That is why I wonder you found it necessary to speak to her."

"Well, she isn't *yet*, but if you continue in your quite singular attentions, I can't guarantee she won't get ideas."

"And that's *all* you said? It doesn't quite account for ... You didn't perhaps in an excess of auntly concern intimate I was a rake, or anything of that sort?"

"Certainly not. I wouldn't say anything to make you more attractive than you are, and besides, it's not true. Only I think you might distribute your charms a little more widely. That's all it will take."

"Ah, but it is dangerous to distribute my charms on the others. They *have* an eye on the coronet, you see. I don't dare go for a stroll with one of them after dinner, or they'll have the banns announced. Besides, they're bores, and Ella is fun, like you."

Sara's mind was busily at work throughout this conversation. If there was a chance in a million he might become serious about Ella, she wouldn't throw a rub in his way for the world. It seemed an unlikely match, yet he had spurned the beauties for seasons past counting and must surely mean to settle on someone soon. She must not turn him off completely. "I told you she is lively when she is at ease with someone. Don't you remember?"

"I *think*, if I remember correctly, you said she was lively when she *liked* someone."

"Well, what's the difference?"

"The difference is that till today she has been at ease with me, ergo *liked* me, but today I am being held at arm's length, and I'm damned if I know what I've done to make her dislike me."

"It wouldn't take much," Sara laughed, remembering

the large store of malice behind this new friendship, at least on Prattle's side.

"Fraught with revealing obscurities, just like a woman. What do you mean, or have you any idea yourself?"

"Ah, well, you do have that odious reputation to lug around with you, Clare."

"I have Prattle to thank for that."

"*Au contraire*, you have yourself, but that's what I meant in any case."

"She's too sensible to be put off by a vicious gossip columnist, and it don't account for her latest snub."

"Did she snub you? I warrant you deserved it."

"I don't think I did. But I may be spoiled by all my other ladies, who wouldn't say boo to a goose."

"To a *dook* you mean!"

"We needn't look far to see where she gets her sharp tongue, my dear. Runs in the family."

"So it does. You should hear Theresa—her mother."

"I can't think I am likely to. I have been told it is unlikely I will ever be at Fairmont, when I hinted for an invitation."

This was beginning to sound more and more serious, and Sara was rapid to undo any harm she might have done formerly. "Surely your charms and graces are up to conciliating one very green girl," she said, making it a challenge.

"Have I your permission to continue in this *friendship* then?"

"Much difference it would make whether I gave it or not."

"But, my dear, I should haunt her to death if you forbade it."

"Oh, well, in *that* case, you have my permission to pay your addresses quite openly."

They were at the house and went their separate ways. Sara was dying of curiosity, but the affair was progressing so satisfactorily that she feared to ruin it by intervention and so said nothing.

No extra company had been invited in for the evening, so after the gentlemen had rejoined the ladies in the drawing room, the whole party went into the music room for Belle's madrigals. The attic had not yielded Elizabethan garb for all, but the enterprising Miss Prentiss had found one gown for herself and had her woman press it up while she attended the tournament. She regretted having only two inches of hair, for long coils would have been more authentic, but she found a veil that gave a good effect and mounted the platform. She appeared to know a good many madrigals, or she may have repeated some of them several times, for they had a way of all sounding very much alike. When Peters and Bippy, who had taken the precaution of seating themselves near the exit, slipped out, Mrs. Prentiss gave her daughter a sign that meant 'enough,' and no one else performed that evening.

"I will take a glass of wine before retiring," Lady Honor told Clare, so wine was served to all. Before long, eyes began drooping, and it was time to retire.

The Dowager had been very good all day, attending the tournament and sitting through the concert, so felt she had earned the reward of a late night's reading and a good sleep-in in the morning. She said to Ella on her way out, "I read it again, *Pride and Prejudice*. I wish I could get hold of Miss Austen's other books. Such a nice sharp dig as she can slide into the middle of a polite conversation. I adore her. Have you found anything to read in the library?" It sounded on the surface a strange question, considering the thousands of books residing there, but they knew themselves to be discussing novels.

"I haven't had time," Ella confessed. "We have been very busy."

"Yes, thank goodness you thought up that tournament. Harley was a wonder with the pole, wasn't he? I could see Patrick was ready to slay him. He'll make poor Billy, the groom, practice with him till he can pry Harley off his horse. Well, it's early yet. I plan to read for a couple of hours before bed. I'll see if I can't find something you'd like, if you'd like to come along with me. Shane will be gone, and we'll have the place to ourselves. I always feel I ought to be reading philosophy or something when he's there. A very bookish fellow. Was at Oxford with Patrick, planning a diplomatic career, but he has the nerves and couldn't handle it."

They went together across the hall towards the library. Miss Prentiss and Miss Sheridan exchanged disheartened glances, and Lady Honor, her wine drunk, went to bed without saying goodnight to anyone.

In the library, the ladies wasted no time on serious books, but headed immediately for the two shelves that interested them. They read titles to each other and exchanged views on authors in nearly perfect harmony for several minutes.

"You've read this *Vicar of Wakefield* thing?" the Duchess asked in a disparaging tone.

"Yes, but Primrose was too prim for me to swallow."

"Wasn't he too good to be true? And much too good to be likable. Yes, the sad fact is, a story character needs a wide streak of nastiness in him before you can really take to him. Now, here's one you might like—quite horrid."

"You too, Mama?" a voice said behind them.

"Oh, Patrick, you scared the life out of me, sneaking up behind us like a thief in the night. Are you after something to lull you to sleep too?"

"No, I find Belle's madrigals wonderfully soporific. I am only curious to see what you two are up to. Perverting Ella's taste with your trash, are you?"

"I am delighted to see it is perverted already, and we see very much eye to eye in the matter of novels."

"*Horrid* novels," Pat augmented, with a glance at Ella, who had quite successfully avoided his glances all the evening. "Might I suggest . . ."

"Never mind any of your silly suggestions," his mother cut in rudely. "We don't want to read Kant or Goethe or any other old foreigners. What we want is a nice story, don't we, Ella?" Ella was surprised and flattered to be addressed by her given name.

"I don't know why it is mothers are always wanting to have *sons*," the Duchess grumbled on. "I wish *I* had a daughter. Any foolish notion this gudgeon takes into his head he tries to palm off on me. Was making me read all about Kant a while back—all to do with imperatives and categories and I don't remember what foolishness. But that's how sons are. They sneeze and we must catch cold."

"I am not familiar with Kant," Ella said.

"I do not recommend him to you," the Dowager advised. "You'll find yourself wondering whether the whole world should do as you are doing, and who is to say whether the whole world likes nuts or lobsters or whatever it is you want."

"That was not the point, Mama."

"Oh pooh! There was no point to it. I studied it a week and didn't learn a thing but that Germans are fools, and I had a pretty good suspicion of that already."

Lifting a book from the shelf, the Duchess turned to Ella again. "Monk Lewis, here's what I was about to suggest when this son of mine came crawling up on us. It's horrid; you'll love it, Ella."

"Thank you. I haven't read this one. Good night," she curtsied to them both and hurried from the room, her book under her arm.

"What a nice young girl she is," the Dowager said, looking at her son in an innocent manner.

"And you always wanted a daughter," he added.

"It's a pity she isn't a little better looking, for she would do very well for my daughter, but is not quite handsome enough to make you a wife, I fancy."

"I must concede appearance is not her long suit," he said, but not in a condemning tone at all.

"What do looks matter when all's said and done? I was no more than passing pretty myself, but your Papa never complained."

"Hush, Beauty!" he held up a finger and waggled it under her nose. "I won't have my Mother's charms denigrated so. There is no one a hatchet face and a hooked nose become so well as you, Mama."

"And while you're into the butter boat, don't forget my hair. So original the way it has decided to go white in a streak down the center, instead of at the temples, like everyone else."

"Sets off the beak to a nicety, ma'am. Isn't there some eagle with a white streak like that?"

"You're thinking of a skunk, Pat. Well, it's too bad we are both so unhandsome, Ella and I, but it's always the way. If a woman has so much as one striking feature, she thinks of nothing else and is a dead bore. And if she happens to have a good head of hair *and* fine eyes, she is insupportable. Not mentioning any names, but if a certain beauty has any more mirrors lugged off to her room, the rest of us won't know what we look like. She has had the pier glass lifted from the green corner room—couldn't see her shoes or some such thing in the one she has, and now I discover she's taken the ormolu hand mirror from the room we used for the ladies the other night. Says she needs it to see the *back* of her head. If she decides to have a look at her backside, she'll be stripping the big gilt mirror from my saloon."

Pat bit back a smile and peered over his shoulder to insure their privacy.

"Oh, she's not listening. She's up looking at the back of her head."

"I sincerely hope so."

"And if your Miss Prentiss has any more accomplishments, I hope she didn't bring them with her."

"Not *my* Miss Prentiss. A genius of that magnitude belongs to the world."

"Her mother, the odious woman, tells me we are going to them for the New Year. You may have got yourself trapped into it, Pat, but pray don't go promising to deliver *me* to listen to Miss Prentiss present a three-act play. I'd sooner spend my New Year in a damp basement. Told her my brother was coming here, so don't go and let out of the bag he's been bed-ridden these three years."

"Said Ernie was coming, eh? I wonder if that might be sufficient excuse for me to beg off as well."

"You can't very well. She's written you into her play. Lucky you!"

"But I am only the hatchet man. I can't think my lines will be many."

"Go! It's the chance of a lifetime. And mind you have that hatchet well-honed."

"You are an incorrigible old witch."

"Yes, but I don't sing, or write plays, or play any musical instrument."

"True, you make up for your ugly temper by a total lack of accomplishments."

"Go to bed," she scolded and hooked her arm through his. In perfect harmony they strode through the rooms, blowing out candles as they went. At the door she sighed. "If only she had a *little* more looks."

"And a little less temper," he said, cryptically.

Eleven

The threatening clouds had returned the next morning, so that the much-discussed trip to the village was postponed till afternoon, in hopes that the clouds, in the interval, would either open up and disgorge their rain or blow away. With nothing more interesting to do, everyone lingered over breakfast, talking and planning future excursions. Clare's mother enquired of Ella how she was enjoying Monk Lewis.

"If I tell you I stayed up till two, reading, you will have some idea. Ambrosio is a marvelous villain. Is his streak of nastiness wide enough to please you?"

"With him it is not so much a streak as a total coloration. I thought of half a dozen others you would like after you had left the library. I'll bring them to you after breakfast."

"I still wish you would take a look through Kant's *Critique of Pure Reason*, Ella," Clare mentioned, obviously to all, not for the first time.

"Critique of Pure Drivel I call it," his mother challenged. "I don't see why you must go improving Ella's perfectly well-formed mind."

"But I will give you the book," he smiled at Ella, "and ask you what you think of it."

The Dowager shook her head and exchanged a conspiratorial smile with Ella. It was impossible to give Clare a set-down with his mother at the table, so Ella said no more. Clare hoped she was getting over whatever freakish start she had been in and was feeling happier.

It was Belle Prentiss, with her sharp wits, who first recovered from the shock of this conversation. It had been noted by all the degree of condescension with which Ella was treated by her noble hosts. "If you are interested in literature, Ella, I wish you will take a look at my play on Anne Boleyn—the one I was telling you about. You are to play Jane Seymour, you recall. I hope you have not forgotten."

"What, are *you* going to Belle's New Year's party?" Clare asked, with interest.

"I am not at all sure I can go. We never make our plans so far in advance. I don't know what Mama may have planned."

"You must come," Belle insisted. "Clare is to be my ax-man, and lob off my head in a horrid scene at the end, then you and Papa, who is playing Henry VIII, have a lovely scene to close the drama. And you can show me how you made Matilda's head too."

"But really, it is too soon for me to say," Ella repeated. "However, I should love to read your play."

"I'll send for it."

Several of the gentlemen scowled at this idea, and Ella said, "I didn't mean right now."

"But there's nothing else to do," Belle countered and sent off for her manuscript.

While the table was being cleared of everything except coffee, a few judicious guests slipped away as well. Harley and Peters vanished. The Marchioness returned to her bed, leaving Honor to guard Clare, which she did by closing her eyes and dozing quietly. Mrs. Sheridan tripped upstairs to look over Sherry's gowns, and Mrs. Prentiss followed her to see what she was up to. The others poured another cup of coffee to keep themselves awake. Sherry took up the *Morning Observer*, and the reading was begun. As there was as yet only one copy of the play's manuscript, Belle undertook to read all parts herself, varying her voice ingeniously to indicate kings, queens, sundry ladies-in-waiting, and attendant lords. At the end of a very long first act, she stopped and asked, in a purely rhetorical spirit, "Do you like it so far?"

"Very interesting," Lady Sara volunteered.

"Devilish long speeches," Bippy added. "Mean to say you expect people to memorize all that stuff?"

"The fact that it is in blank verse makes it easier to learn. There is a rhythmical flow to it, you see."

"Didn't notice," Bippy commented.

"I am taking the hardest part myself. I have the longest speeches."

"Yes, I noticed that. Don't know how you could have written it, much less get it all off by heart. Must be a devilish clever girl."

Belle colored prettily at this judgment, though it was hardly a new one. She looked around for some repetition of this praise. Ella sat in appalled silence. She had never heard such nonsense in her life. To suppose that Anne Boleyn could have stolen a king from his lawful wife and changed the course of history, if she were the prim little soul Belle had made her, was unthinkable.

"What do you think, Ella?" Belle asked directly.

"It is very good, only—it is not quite my idea of what Anne Boleyn was like."

"I have read several books about her. It is historically quite accurate. I checked all the dates and everything."

"Oh, indeed, I didn't mean to criticize in that way."

"She's too mealy-mouthed," the Duchess said bluntly. "Put a little rumgumption into her. Our Miss Austen would know how to go about it, eh, Ella?"

"I do feel your main character lacks liveliness," Ella said, putting her thoughts more modestly.

"Yes, but what do you mean exactly? She is very lively. I have her playing on a lyre for Henry, and doing that little dance, you know, when he is having dinner at her Papa's house . . ."

"Oh, yes, she don't lack for talents," the Duchess said, in a strange voice.

"I meant in the speeches," Ella explained. "You know, where Henry is trying to lure her to marry him."

"No, he is merely trying to seduce me, at first."

"I wasn't quite sure, but it seems to me Anne ought to do more than keep repeating that she has too much regard for the marriage vows, for in the end she *hasn't*, you recall. I thought of her as being more active—actually trying to get Henry to get rid of Katherine of Aragon in some manner."

"It is clear she must have been a conniving little hussy," the Duchess continued. "You don't show that side of her, and that is her most interesting side. What do you think, Pat?"

"She didn't get to my part. I have been waiting in expectation of a few early scenes with me honing up my ax."

"The ax-man has only the one scene, but if you will promise to learn the lines, I will make you someone else. Archbishop Cranmer has not been cast yet."

"No, I wouldn't like to give up my ax."

"Pat has great plans for his scene," the Dowager said playfully, but refrained from exchanging a look with her son, though she gave him a sharp nudge with her elbow. Across the table from them, Ella looked up, and the Dowager winked at her. A strange feeling of its all having happened before came over her, then she remembered it was on the occasion of the sick headache.

"Have you thought up a good piece of business with the ax?" Belle asked. "I am very happy to get ideas from everyone."

"I thought it might be effective if I—ah—hesitated a little, as though I could not bear to sever such a lovely head from its shoulders. Then too it will prolong that really minuscule part you have given me. No more than a walk-on."

"That is an excellent idea, and you might say—well, what you just said, about severing such a lovely head."

"Not historically accurate, I fear."

"There is no way of knowing at this late date what was actually *said*. When I spoke of historical accuracy, I was referring to the general lines of the story—the names of the characters involved, and the dates, and so on. We must add the little realistic touches to make it . . ."

"Realistic," Bippy supplied.

"Yes, that's what I meant."

"Jolly good idea."

"And I shall put in *your* idea too, Ella, and make myself more conniving."

"That was the Duchess's idea," Bippy pointed out.

Belle smiled and thanked them all for their help, while wondering at their temerity in telling *her* how to write a play.

At the termination of the discussion, Sherry came forward from the end of the table holding the *Observer* in her hands. "Only see what that horrid Prattle has said about us today," she chirped, pink with pleasure to see her exploits mentioned in print again.

Belle was so eager she dropped her manuscript all over the floor in an effort to wrest the paper from Sherry. Ella's mind leapt back to what column this would be and tried to make herself inconspicuous. Belle, whose voice was up to anything, took it upon herself to read once more.

"She has left all those blank letters, but I'll supply names," she explained before beginning. "This is what she says—it's about the picnic. 'London may now breathe a sigh of relief. At last we have word of the wondrous doings in Dorset, at the palace of the Duke of Clare. The promised picnic was held in the Chinese Pavilion, where English food was served to English guests on English dishes by English servants.' How strange! What does she mean by that?"

"It's taking a knock at my Chinese pavilion," Clare explained. "Did it expect us to eat rice with chopsticks?"

"I should say not," Sherry replied. "I would be bound to drop it all over and ruin my gown."

"But then you would have the pleasure of changing your gown," Clare said.

Belle continued: " 'The hedonists, not satisfied with a picnic, were later regaled with a frog-jumping contest.' " Turning aside she said, "She doesn't mention that it was *your* idea, Ella. 'The contestants were not even thoroughbreds, but having been reared in the Duke of Clare's pond, some blue blood may have seeped into their veins. Mr. Peters' Green Boy was the winner by a length, and it is being said around town that Lady Honor's nag did not leave the gate. One wonders whether there was not some Strayward blood in that frog.' "

"Oh, how horrid!" Sherry gasped, with a fearful look at Lady Honor, who dozed on oblivious. "We must not let her see this column. She will be so angry."

"Not she," Clare contradicted.

"There's more," Sherry announced, and continued reading. " 'We have it on the best authority that a trip to the local village is planned, and an evening dancing party with guests from the neighborhood. So far, the host has been in attendance, in body if not in mind.' "

"That is too bad of her," Sherry said to Clare. "What does she mean?"

"I don't believe it approves of our entertainment. It expected a round of formal balls and *fêtes champêtres* no doubt," Clare replied, concealing a twinge of anger at the justified criticism. "Is there more, or does it save the rest of its space for London doings?"

"A little more," Sherry replied. " 'The undoubtedly bored guests may take consolation from the fact that the play at Covent Gardens . . .' Oh, she only goes on to pan the play, and say who was there. Well, shall we go on with Act II of my play? I have started it."

"Why don't you save your voice to sing to us this evening?" the Duchess replied very promptly. "Your first act was very enjoyable. Just give your Anne a little sharper tongue, and you will have a good play there. Do you want to come along to the library with me now, Ella, and I'll give you those books I was speaking about?"

Happy for any excuse to avoid further readings from Anne Boleyn, Ella hopped up and set off with the Duchess.

"Don't forget to give her Kant, too," Clare called after his mother.

"Pest of a boy," she grumbled, and gave not another thought to Immanuel Kant or his writings. She did spare a passing thought for her son though. Odd he should be pushing his dull old books on to Ella. He only did that with people he cared for. Yes, he was coming to like the girl better than he knew.

When Mr. Shane handed a heavy tome bound in Russian leather to Miss Fairmont, explaining it was the book His Grace said she wished to read, the Dowager laughed and said merrily, "He means to improve your mind, Ella, whether you like it or no." Why, the rascal had made a special trip to the library, and if *that* didn't mean he was interested, she was no judge of her own son. She bent her mind to helping the affair along and decided Miss Fairmont must know something of Pat's better nature.

During the morning the threatening clouds blew away, and it was decided to leave for the village early and stop for lunch at the Green Man. A little sight-seeing at the church, the river, and a visit to the roundhouse by the gentlemen were to make up the afternoon. When the disposition of carriages was being discussed, Lady Honor materialized at Clare's side.

"I will go with you," she told him.

"Very well," he said curtly, with the briefest of glimpses towards Ella, just enough to make her think he had been about to ask her to go with him. "I'm taking the curricle," he added, hoping to make her change her mind.

"Yes," she replied, unblinking.

With Clare's partner taken care of in a manner to neither please nor yet quite displease them, Belle and Sherry could chat quite amicably and decide that they would go with Bippy and Peters, for neither one was willing to risk her neck with Lord Harley, who was known to drive like a man demented.

"You come with me and Belle," Bippy said to Ella. "You won't want to ride with that hellcat of a Harley. He'll be racing any rig or farmer's gig he overtakes on the road. Ain't safe."

"All right," she agreed.

"Deuce take it," Harley stormed. "You've got *one* girl, Tredwell. No need to go turning Miss Fairmont against me. That's the way you all feel about it, I won't go at all. Rather do a bit of shooting anyway, if it's all right with you, Pa'k."

"You could do with the practice," Clare replied. "But don't go shooting the glass out of the windows as you did at Tredwell's hunting lodge."

"You know perfectly I was ape—that is to say, ain't such a gudgeon as that."

"Well, now, it seems you've gone and made your plans without considering us," the Dowager said, coming up to the group with Lady Sara.

"Will you mind taking your own carriage, Mama? We're all taking our curricles, and you won't like that."

"It's coming around. Lady Sara is coming with me, and we hoped Ella would accompany us old fogies to keep us amused. You won't like being wedged three in a curricle, my dear. Come along in a civilized carriage with us."

"Perhaps Lady Honor would like the closed carriage," Clare suggested hopefully.

"No, I will go with you," she stated firmly and took his arm.

"Come along, Ella," the Duchess said, as her chaise was drawn up the drive. Everyone piled into their chosen vehicles, with the Duchess's the last to leave.

"I have a little business to transact in the village," the Duchess confessed to her companions. "Won't take very long. You can drop me off at the orphanage, and I'll have Wooster pick me up in half an hour. Or perhaps you'd like to see my son's children?" she added as an afterthought, though it had been her intention all along to show his philanthropy off to Ella.

Lady Sara's eyes nearly started from her head, then she laughed. "Lord, what a start you gave me, Ma'am. He supports the orphanage, I collect?"

"Yes, he is the founder and sole supporter of the Dorset Home for Boys. He is having a new wing built, which is why he came to Clare at this time. I told him I'd stop off to pick up some papers that Ulmhorn, the manager, wants him to see. He doesn't want the others to know about it . . ."

"Well, it is surely nothing to be ashamed of!" Lady Sara said.

"It's not modesty, Lady Sara. Once it got talked up that he is bankrolling the place, there would be a hundred organizations after him. That is why he keeps it quiet. The fact is, he was fleeced of quite a large sum by setting up a place in Wiltshire, and he wants to keep his charities centered around home, where he can keep an eye on them. *I* tell him he is ashamed to let the world know how he mistreats the poor little rascals. Only funning, you know."

When all three were deposited at the door of a large red brick building and ushered in by an obsequious Ulmhorn, there was no fault to be found in the home provided to the parentless boys. Three rooms of them were bent over their books with masters attendant, and another lot were being released for a turn in the yard. The Dowager declined a tour of the building, which her guests would rather liked to have seen, and excused herself to go into an office with Ulmhorn, while a matron brought tea to the other ladies. But they were little interested in tea. They preferred to stroll around and examine everything.

"Here's a plaque. Some sort of dedication," Sara said. Ella trailed over to read it. " 'This home founded in memory of Joseph Beresford, Duke of Clare, who died in 1808,' " she read. "It's very short, isn't it?"

"What more is there to say?"

"It must be very expensive to keep up," Ella said in a low voice.

"Well, love, he isn't exactly a pauper, you know."

"All the boys look well fed and nicely clothed. Not like some of the orphanages one sees. Remember the one near Fairmont?"

"It doesn't have a noble patron."

"No." Ella looked around. "Sara, I feel terrible."

"What, are you ill?"

"No, I mean about all the awful things I have written about Patrick—Clare."

Sara noticed the Patrick, but chose to ignore it. "Well, he *does* squander a shocking amount of money on himself as well."

"Yes, but I had no idea he did anything like this. He is very generous, and I have made such fun of him. Besides, I see now that I have observed him at close range that those nasty things he says—well, whomever he says them *to* always deserves them. It must be very trying to be always chased after by women."

"I can think of worse fates. *Not* to be chased, for instance."

"Be serious, Sara. What am I to do?"

No advice was given, for at that moment the Duchess came out of a door and joined them for a cup of tea. "Mr. Ulmhorn is tallying up some accounts, so I'll join you for a moment," she said. "What do you think of the place?"

"Your son is not the fashionable fribble he would have us believe," Lady Sara returned.

The Duchess smiled softly to herself. "He saves his idiocies for London. At home he behaves just as he ought. His next project is to set up a place similar to this for girls. Why should they be left to fend for themselves, poor tykes? The females are the ones who need help, and so I tell him. We can't harbor them all at Clare. I have six more girls than I need right now, and if he don't get busy and set up a house for them, I'll do it myself, though my purse isn't so deep as his. The last girl who came to us is a sad case. Muckleton is the name."

Ella stared, her pulse racing, but the lady continued on, unnoticing. "Her Papa works for us, in the stables—a widower. His daughter, Prissie, was left home to mind the two boys, and a *wretched* old neighbor took to pestering her. Would have assaulted her, I think, but the two little boys—they're only eight and nine—beat him off with pots and pans. They had the presence of mind to notify their father, who told Clare all about it. We've taken Prissie in for the time being, and the boys are here. She is very pretty, and the best thing would be to find a husband for her, that she might give them a home. It won't be hard. What a havoc as she is creating among the footmen! But I think it is the ferrier who has the inner track. Ah, here is Ulmhorn already, with the bills." She arose and went back into his office.

Ella felt as though the bottom had fallen out of her stomach. She had believed *that* of Clare! Had been rude and offensive to him, and—oh God! The column she had sent in. Announced to the world that he was a philanderer, and on Belle Prentiss's say-so.

"Oh, Sara," she wailed. "What have I done?" But Sara, alas, was not aware of that particular column. She had been so eager to villify him that she had sealed it up and posted it off without showing it to her mentor.

"You have been mistaken in him. It's not your fault."

"Oh," she moaned, and couldn't find the strength to confess.

"Perk up, my girl. She'll be back soon, and how are we to account for your vapors?"

"I can't face her."

"Don't be such a wet goose, Ella. She has taken a great fancy to you, and don't think *that* will do you any harm in Clare's eyes, for he is very close to his Mama. You might get him yet." It was the first time Sara had mentioned such a high hope to her niece, and she looked for some reaction. The wilting face on her niece was not the reaction she expected, and she rallied her. "You make too much of the column, Ella. He took it in quite good part this morning, didn't you think? *I* think he rather appreciated that bit about Honor's Frog not moving, though he was too well-bred to show it."

"Oh, I wish I had never *heard* of Prattle."

"You're not all of Prattle. Mama and I do a bit too."

"*I* am the Prattle who has pilloried Clare."

"He's none the worse for it."

"He will be! He hates her, you know. He goes on saying little things . . ."

"Nothing can be done about the past, Ella, though I begin to think it is time to retire Prattle."

"We have a contract till the end of the Season."

"Drink your tea. She'll be back in a moment."

In fact, it was several moments before the Duchess returned, allowing aunt and niece time for more discussion of the same fruitless sort. Sara had her own ideas why they had been brought to the orphanage, and her hopes were riding so high that she did not quite realize the depths of Ella's feelings. She was ridden with guilt and remorse but could see no way to undo the harm she had done. No further accounts of Clare would be included in Prattle, but that was so small a drop of balm as to do no good whatsoever.

"We'd better hustle," the Duchess said when she came back to them.

"You—you must be very proud of your son," Ella said in a small voice, as they went back to the carriage.

"So I am, but mind you don't *tell* him so. We wouldn't want his head getting too big."

They proceeded on their way to the village.

"Ah, there is Tredwell's rig. Let us get down and join the others. We shan't say where we've been. I'd just as lief you not mention it to my son either," the Duchess said.

The group was reunited for a stroll through very inferior shops, where not even Miss Sheridan could find any allurement for her frocks except a few yards of pink ribbon, and Belle was limited to the purchase of a set of colored patent pens to decorate the cover for her play on Anne Boleyn. Lady Honor, looking neither to right nor left, pulled Clare up and down aisles with her. "We will go now," she decided, when she had completed her unseeing tour. "I am ready for lunch."

"I hope your shopping spree has given you a good appetite," Clare said.

"I didn't buy anything," she remarked.

"No doubt the shops are better around Strayward," he smiled.

"Yes."

The party occupied the largest private parlor at the inn, and made merry for an hour over a cold luncheon, before flocking to see the church, where the martyrs' tombs were considered to be the showpiece. Belle regretted she had not come prepared for taking rubbings of the brasses. Outside, Ella suggested that it would be a fit subject for sketching, with its interesting Norman architecture and little row of miniature statues.

"Not for *you*, Ella," Clare said, "too demanding. Remember Nellie's tower." He had taken up a post beside her in the church, and as she was not snubbing him today, he continued on there.

Ella was in despair. Her peace was ruined, but life must go on. She pushed her troubles to the back of her mind and determined to be as charming a partner as possible during these few occasions when she would be with Clare. "I think it was the tilt of Crazy Nellie's Tower that defeated me. I daresay I could do this building very well."

"Let us stroll on and see the view from the bridge over the river," he said, offering her his arm. She was quiet, for the echo of her abuse of him would keep rising in her mind. They had to walk right past the orphanage to reach the river, but they neither of them glanced to the left. In fact, Clare made a point of showing her a milliner's shop on the right as they passed by. "I'm glad Sherry isn't with us, or we'd be hauled in to watch her try on bonnets," he said.

"I can't think she needs any more. She brought *seven* with her."

"You can't expect her to repeat herself. In *bonnets* I mean."

"You are being *horrid*, and don't expect me to stoop to talking about her behind her back. If I were half so pretty, I would wear a new bonnet every day, too."

"Then I thank God you are not."

"So do *not* I!"

"What, still bemoaning your insignificant little face?" He peered at it while he delivered this amiable insult. It appeared less insignificant than formerly. Almost its planes were taking on a pleasing air for him.

"No, and please don't tell me beauty is only skin deep. I know it already. And much good it does, when our eyes only *see* skin deep. What is the point in having a pretty skeleton, or set of veins, I should like to know."

156

"I believe you are misunderstanding the point of that particular homily. It refers to character, or some such thing."

Another wave of remorse washed over her. "Very likely," she agreed humbly.

"I think you are unconscionably hard to please, Ella. Here am I wearing myself to the bone trying to please you—and having very poor luck, I might add. Harley was sore as a boil that you wouldn't ride in his curricle; Tredwell asked you to go in his carriage. Pretty well for a girl who likes to complain about being plain."

"Yes, you are all very kind," she said.

"Lord, next you'll be accusing us of charity." This topic was too prickly to be pursued at all, so they watched a squirrel instead, till they were caught up by the others.

It was Lady Sara and the Dowager who overtook them first. "Great luck, Ella," the Duchess said. "You'll never guess what I found at the book store. Another by Miss Austen. *Sense and Sensibility* it's called. Are you familiar with it?"

"Yes, and it's good too, only not quite so good as the other. Still, I think you'll enjoy Mrs. Dashwood. She is a marvelous harpy."

"I like the title. That promises a good conflict of personalities. Oh, there is Miss Sheridan with a huge parcel. She must have found a mirror she couldn't resist."

"Mama!" Clare warned.

"I have bought the loveliest bonnet," Sherry gushed, running forward to impart her news. "Would you like to see it?" She was already untying the string.

"Why don't you wait till we get home, dear?" the Duchess said in the sweetest voice in the world. "You will want to get it set on your head properly with the help of a *mirror* or two, before you model it for us."

"Yes," Sherry agreed, "for it sits at an angle, so sweet, only I haven't decided whether to wear it perched over the left or right eye."

"You will have to give that a good deal of consideration," she was advised by the irrepressible Duchess. "Have your woman take you up an extra brace of candles to give you a good view."

"Thank you, ma'am. I do find it a little hard to see if I am tidy, for my mirror is in quite a dark corner."

"What a shame!"

"But Mama's room has very good lighting, so I usually go in there for the finishing touches when I am dressing in the evening."

"So that is how you achieve such an admirable effect," Clare congratulated her. She beamed happily. "Sherry has found a new bonnet, Ella. Didn't I prophesy she would be interested in the millinery shop?"

Sherry felt a surge of triumph when Ella frowned at him. How ludicrous of Belle to think they had anything to fear from this plain-faced little creature. "Did you really, Clare?" she asked. "But you know I am not so lofty as to think only London or Paris could produce a bonnet worthy of me."

"I bet you could find a suitable bonnet anywhere," Clare said and turned again to admire the view of the river.

Lady Honor, Belle, Peters, and Tredwell strolled along next, and everyone had to wait a while till Belle had jotted down a few notes for a sonnet she meant to compose on the view, then tell her whether the trees she was admiring were willows or elms or beech, and where was east and west, and what were those lovely little yellow flowers called.

"For I like to get everything accurate, you know."

The gentlemen could not forego a stop at the roundhouse, and after this they all returned to the palace. They passed a quiet evening of charades and word games, which diverted Ella's mind from her troubles, and she became quite lively, not once insulting Clare. When he found an opportunity to speak to her privately, he said, "All over your sulks, Ella?"

"I can't think what you mean," she said, in guilty confusion.

"Hmm. No doubt I imagined that cold shoulder you were showing me yesterday." She shook her head and smiled in terrible embarrassment.

"No, seriously, I wish you will tell me."

"It—it was nothing."

"A misunderstanding perhaps?" he asked helpfully.

"Yes," she grasped at this thin straw.

"I see." He supposed Sara *had* said something more to her than she admitted, but at least she must have unsaid it, whatever it was. "Are we all straightened then? Still friends?"

"Yes, certainly," she said, feeling like the worst traitor ever.

"Good," he smiled one of his intimate, devastating smiles, the memory of which kept her awake for hours.

Twelve

The next day was the last one prior to departure from the palace. No lady had received an offer, or anything remotely resembling one. Belle and Sherry were becoming desperate, and even Honor felt an uneasiness which she did not recognize as impatience. Ella too was uneasy, for reasons different from the others. The large ball was to be held that evening, and with their toilettes to prepare, the ladies required no other pastime but to help out a little with the decoration of the ballroom and continue wooing the host.

It was Belle who organized the young group after breakfast to gather flowers. In vain did the Duchess tell her they usually just brought in pots from the greenhouse. She had already sent for baskets and shears, determined to destroy the rose garden. She garnered Clare to her side for the purpose of selection and a-cutting she would go. Lady Honor took no part in this outing. She went with a book to the drawing room and sat with it open all morning, though she did not turn any pages. Miss Sheridan was fidgety and ill-natured. She was by no means sure a mere afternoon in papers would set her curls bouncing as she liked, but on the other hand, it would be madness to let Belle have Clare to herself all morning. She went along, but she was in the sulks and took to silent pouting when Belle chastised her for cutting the roses with stems only three inches long. Clare did not stand up for her in the least, and she soon flounced off to her room in high dudgeon to have a quick bout with the papers before luncheon.

"Old silly," Belle said when she was gone, with a sly glance at Clare. "I shudder to think of the poor man who ends up with *her* for a wife. She has no idea of anything but bonnets and gowns."

"But you must own," he replied, "she is an expert on that."

"Yes," Belle replied prettily, "by beginning *now* she will have the grandest outfit of us all."

Ella had her back to the pair, trying to deter Harley from adding poison ivy to his bouquet, but she overheard the conversation and could only wonder at Belle's folly. Nothing was more likely to put a gentleman off than to hear one lady rip apart another in the latter's absence. She had always assumed Belle to have the inner track with Clare. It had appeared so in London, but since coming to Dorset, she was seeing all these people in a new light.

Sherry was as beautiful at close range as from afar, but when one came to realize the expenditure of time and energy that went into her magnificent appearance, one could not take her seriously. She was a beautiful shell, ravishing at all times, with every hair in place, but it was a full-time job to keep her in looks, and so she hadn't a moment for conversation or diversion—the epitome of what Hannah

More wrote about. Belle was as clever and talented as one had always supposed, yet her cleverness was too widely spread, and too thinly spread too. She did everything poorly—wrote, sketched, sang, played, danced, rhymed. And Lady Honor, on the other hand, did nothing. It was clear to her why Clare hesitated in conferring his golden apple. He might opt for looks, cleverness or breeding, but whichever he chose, he would get nothing else.

Harley had moved on from poison ivy to weeds, and she had to stop him again. "That is not a flower," she said, pulling a dandelion from his careless armful of blooms.

"No, really. Dashed pretty thing. No one will notice it ain't a flower."

"Yes, but it smells after it has been inside a while."

"All flowers smell."

"Dandelions smell *badly*. They stink," she said, when he did not appear to understand her first utterance.

"Really? Well I never knew that before. You are full of all kinds of useful information, Miss Fairmont. Maybe you could tell us what to feed Green Boy. Peters' frog is looking pulled today, I can tell you."

Peters turned to them at the sound of his name and joined the conversation. "He isn't eating a thing. Been off his feed for two days. I hope he don't go and pop off on me before I get him home to breed him."

"No, I can't help you. I told you they always die if you put them in a pail. They eat all sorts of insects, of course, but they never do in captivity. The best thing would be to return him to the pond, and let nature cure him. He's lonesome."

"I'll never find him again," Peters said, doubtfully.

Harley, away from Ella's scrutiny, grabbed up a bunch of dandelions and added them to his bouquet.

"You may not, but at least he won't be *dead*, and he surely will be if you try to keep him in a pail. I lost three that way before I gave up on it."

"Ten to one I wouldn't recognize him again if I *did*

happen to spot him. I might tag him, I suppose. Tie some sort of a string around his leg, or a ribbon."

Ella confessed that this idea had never been tried at Fairmont. Peters left the flower-gathering to the others and went to tag his Green Boy. But within minutes he was back with his wooden bucket, requesting Ella's help to hold the fellow's leg, as he wouldn't hold still a second. The others interrupted their flower cutting to watch this performance, and when it was done, Peters and Ella went together to launch Green Boy back into the pond. They each had a hand on the handle of the bucket and were laughing as they went.

"Just like Jack and Jill," Belle said. Noticing that Clare was frowning after them, she added, "They make a nice couple, don't they? He is becoming quite particular, I have noticed."

"I haven't noticed," Clare answered.

"Ah, but *you* have other fish to fry, Clare. How is your other fish, by the way?"

"I beg your pardon?"

"I haven't told a soul! About Prissie I mean."

"So you *did* see us in the village."

"Oh yes, and *here* too." She hadn't meant to say anything to him, but he seemed quite docile today, and she was always eager to show off.

"If you saw her here, I must suppose you have been down to the kitchens. She is working as cook's helper," he replied dampingly.

Belle realized that Clare would not so abuse one of his flirts, and realized as well that she had misread that whole affair. It had come to nothing in the end, for it had not even turned Miss Fairmont against him, as she had hoped. "I was only funning," she laughed merrily and nipped into the house to escape any further discussion of the matter.

Bippy Tredwell at once came over to Clare. "Know what I think?" he said. "I think Peters is more taken with Miss Fairmont that he lets on."

Clare was relieved that the question was about Ella rather than Prissie and replied, "Quite cutting you out, in fact."

"Oh, as to that, you've been cutting me out any time this week. Thought you was developing a *tendre* for her, but if you ain't . . ." He stopped, for he just realized from the discomposed scowl on Clare's face that he was right in his assumption. "Always saying he'll have to ask Miss Fairmont this or that or the other. Stood up with her twice at all your dances, and Miss Sheridan was telling me before she left that *she* hasn't stood up with him once since we've been here. I do think he's making up to her."

"Are you jealous?"

"No, told you it was Platonic with her and me. *I* ain't jealous."

"Certainly *I* am not," Clare assured him with a waving gesture of his hands, and he turned purposefully away from the direction of the pond.

Belle came back and demanded Clare's assistance with a rose whose thorns were particularly severe, so Bippy wandered off to add some ferns to his flowers.

It was more than half an hour later, with all the blooms taken in for Belle and Lady Sara to arrange, that Bippy again went out to the garden. He saw Clare still there, ostensibly admiring his lawn, but looking in the direction of the pond. "Been gone a devil of a long time," he said.

Clare didn't bother pretending to misunderstand this cryptic statement. "The pond is only three hundred yards away," he replied.

"Pity we can't see it for that bunch of bushes you have there. Wonder what they're up to."

"It wouldn't take ten minutes to toss Green Boy into the water and get back here."

"No, he's up to something. I'd give a monkey to know what. Wonder if they've taken that raft out for a sail."

"They might have fallen in."

"That's as good an excuse as any to go after them,"

163

Bippy replied, and they strode together at a rapid gait towards the pond.

No such awful fate had befallen the miscreant couple. They had not gone near the raft at all, but were skipping flat stones over the pond, laughing and shouting, and amusing themselves very agreeably.

"So, this is where you've got to," Bippy charged in an injured tone.

"We came to put Green Boy back in the pond," Peters said.

"Did that more than half an hour ago," Bippy said.

"Are we late for lunch?" Ella asked. "Oh, I hope we have not kept everyone waiting. I had no idea it was so late."

"It ain't. We just wondered what was keeping you two."

"We were afraid you might have fallen into the pond," Clare explained, feeling unaccountably foolish in the face of Bippy's accusing tone.

"This puddle's only two feet deep," Peters replied. "Said so yourself. We are playing ducks and drakes. Miss Fairmont can skip a stone *six* times, Pa'k. Did you ever see such a girl? I can't get mine to go more than four."

"You only did that once," Ella told him. "And I *still* think that last skip was only a frog surfacing, for it didn't arc at all from the last one."

"No, by Jove, it was four, I swear."

"Don't contradict a lady," Bippy adjured severely.

"I ain't, only I'm sure it skipped four times."

"You can't do it again anyway," Ella challenged him.

"I can so, only I'll have to take off this curst jacket. Stutz makes 'em so tight you can't get a proper throw at all." He proceeded to remove the jacket, and was roundly roasted when his next stone sank ignominiously immediately it hit the pond, without even one skip.

"It was clearly the *coat's* fault," Ella commented.

"Ho, *I* can do better than that," Bippy proclaimed.

"You could hardly do worse," Clare said, reaching

down for a stone with which to test his own prowess. It skipped only the once, and Bippy had no better luck when he tried it.

In view of their shocking ignorance of the noble art, Miss Fairmont took pity on them and explained that the secret was in getting the throwing arm laid out at a right angle to the body, so that the stone would skim parallel to the pond's surface. Without the least difficulty, her next stone skipped the pond's surface five times before sinking from sight.

"This girl's double-jointed," Peters complained. "I can't get my arm out at such an angle to my body. Do it again, will you?"

Ella complied, and again the stone skipped five times.

"The stones are too round, that's the trouble," Bippy said, when his next effort produced only two hops.

"If they ain't too round for Miss Fairmont, they ain't too round for us," Peters replied, and on his next throw he repeated his former success of four hops. "Let's see you match that, Clare."

Clare reached down and selected a handful of the flattest stones he could find. His skill was equal to Peters', and a good deal better than Bippy's, but though they all skipped stones and insulted each other mutually for close to half an hour, no one could match Miss Fairmont, who regularly and effortlessly hopped her stones five or six times. She once outdid herself and achieved seven hops. Only Peters saw this feat, and he was reduced to great shame.

"Deuce take it, what a bunch of flats we are, that not *one* of us three *men* can equal a *girl's* record. You must be double-jointed, Miss Fairmont. I swear you've got your arm skewed out at an angle different from the rest of us."

"I have been practicing on and off since I was a child," she explained in a placating and slightly smug manner.

"So have I," Peters admitted. "That's no excuse."

"It's us that need an excuse," Bippy said. "Miss Fairmont don't need an *excuse* for beating us all hollow."

"No, by Jove, she is always up to anything," Peters agreed, recovering his spirits. "And she was right about Green Boy, too. He was back in form, snapping up flies and what not within minutes of being put back in the pond. We knew it was him by the string we tied on his leg."

They all began scanning the pond for Green Boy, and while they were engaged in this fruitless task, a footboy came down the hill and summoned them for lunch. Some rather extensive cleaning up was required after their game, and it happened that they all four reached the front hall together about ten minutes later, ready for luncheon. Ella was completely unaware of the consternation she caused when she walked into the small dining hall, accompanied by three of the four gentlemen who made up the party.

Sherry was still pouting and patting her curly locks, but Belle immediately sought to turn attention to its proper quarter. "Have you been in the ballroom admiring our flower arrangements, Clare?" she asked.

"No, but I shall certainly do so after lunch. Sorry we have kept you waiting."

"We've been down at the pond skipping stones," Peters blurted out, a fact which the more circumspect of the group would have as lief not mentioned. "Miss Fairmont can skip a stone from one side of the pond to the other."

"How talented!" Belle said angrily. "Ella appears to be skilled in the *unlikeliest* areas. Tell me, Ella, do you sing at all, or paint, or play the pianoforte, or do any of the things *ladies* usually do?"

"Only a very little," Ella replied frankly, wondering anew at Belle's spite and lack of finesse in showing it so obviously.

"You must have ruined your gown," Sherry said. "We can't get the brown spots out of the muslin *I* wore the day you made us all chase frogs."

"Try lemon juice, dear," Lady Sara counseled.

"Yes, you brought a whole bag of them with you,

didn't you, Sherry, to bleach your freckles?" Belle asked innocently. With time's winged chariot pushing them so mercilessly, they were all on edge and trying any device to detract from the competition.

Even Lady Honor entered the fray, in her own irrelevant manner. "I planted six lemon seeds, and three of them sprouted, at Strayward," she said.

Sherry was so miffed at the falsity of Belle's charge that she didn't even acknowledge this utterance from the daughter of a marquis. "*I* am not subject to freckles, Miss Prentiss," she retorted. "They usually go with *red hair*. Mama does have some lemons though, if you would like to try some to bleach out *your* freckles for Clare's ball."

"One of them is three inches high," Lady Honor added.

This dictum too was ignored. "No, no, *I* don't spend all day worrying about my looks, the way *some people* do," Belle shot back, while still smiling politely.

"A pity," Mrs. Sheridan said, with a quick perusal of her daughter's tormentor.

Mrs. Prentiss could not allow this slur on her daughter's appearance to go unchallenged, and she went into a spiel on the far-flung accomplishments of her daughter.

"Oh, yes, we know *Belle* is up to anything," Mrs. Sheridan snapped. "There is no end to her accomplishments, and her interminable demonstrations of them." She sat huffing in agitation, and sprinkled sugar on her cold cuts by mistake.

This was too lively a discussion for Lady Honor. She retired from the fray and busied herself with the plate of smoked salmon. Ella felt acutely uncomfortable and kept her eyes on her plate, but Sara and Clare exchanged a silent smile. Such scenes of jealousy were no novelty to him, and this one pleased Lady Sara very well. Any chance either of them had ever had was effectually laid to rest now.

The Dowager feared the meal would turn into a cat fight, as she later told her son, so to forestall the possibility, she made public a piece of news she had received by the morning's post. She had meant to give Clare a private warning first, but it proved impossible.

"I have had a note from Lord Strayward this morning," she said, addressing herself to the Marchioness, who did not appear much interested to hear it. Clare, on the other hand, was deeply alarmed. His fork clattered to his plate from the involuntary and quite violent jerk of his wrist.

"Yes," the Duchess continued, "he will arrive today and accompany you and Honor back to London."

"Why did he think it necessary to come so far out of his way?" Clare asked. "Strayward is miles east of here. The ladies might have stopped on their way to London and gone on with him from there." The question was neither necessary, nor was it really answered. There was no doubt why he was coming. He was making himself available to accept an offer for his daughter's hand. Plain as a pikestaff. Not satisfied with shoving that pale lump of a girl on to him to entertain for a week, he now meant to make her a life tenant. Action must be taken, and it was bound to be unpleasant. He would *not* be coerced into offering for Honor, if he had to shove the whole family out the door by main force.

"I don't know," his Mama said, giving the reply a questioning tone, in hopes that the Marchioness would enlighten her.

"He didn't write to *me*; not a line," she was told.

"Very likely it has something to do with the election at Bournemouth," the Dowager suggested. "He'd be backing Sempleton."

"Yes, he will be for the Tory," his wife asserted. Strayward was active in politics.

"Then he will be backing the loser," Clare said. What little partiality he felt in politics was for the Whigs.

"*England* will be the loser in that case," Lady Honor said, with an uncharacteristic emphasis. She nearly frowned at Clare.

"When does he come?" Clare asked.

"He expects to arrive late this afternoon," his mother replied.

Not so bad then, Clare thought. The party were all leaving early next morning, and there was the ball this evening. He would play least in sight and try to avoid a confrontation. It was damnably unpleasant to offend these well-connected peers that one must go on meeting everywhere.

Clare hid in his study after lunch and around 4:00 rode to Kitswell to round up his business at the orphanage. He intended to return home only in time to change for dinner. How his guests spent their afternoon he neither knew nor cared. The ladies, he supposed, would be busy preparing for the ball, and Bippy and the gentlemen could amuse themselves out of doors. The weather was good. Clare left Kitswell just before 6:00—no country hours for dinner on the day of the ball. He cantered home alone, his mind ranging over a wide field of thought.

The ghost of Lady Honor obtruded itself, of course, and a morose picture followed of himself married to that lifeless body. He could vividly picture her setting her arm on his sleeve and saying "I will marry you," as she said "I will go with you," whenever there was a trip in the offing. Impossible! Still it was time, and past time, to marry someone. Sherry? A beautiful little widgeon. How Mama would rail if he offered for her! And how dull life would be, once one was accustomed to her beauty. Truth to tell, her physical charms were beginning to pall already. No, she was fine to look at, and her absurd utterances were mildly amusing, but one did not marry a mannequin. Belle? She was lively enough. Always had some rig running. And yet, there were those interminable demonstrations of her talents, as Mrs. Sheridan had so sweetly pointed out.

The other nubile lady under his roof he considered the longest of all. Miss Fairmont had definitely caught his fancy. Not beautiful—yet not quite plain either. A surprising prettiness—something in her eyes—when she

169

smiled at you unexpectedly. Mama liked her, which was nice, but not necessary. Yes, of the four, she was the only one he could envisage living with without running mad. A soft smile curved his lips to think of her surprise when he told her. What would she say? Something outrageous. Yet she was no stranger to masculine attentions. Harley and Peters were infatuated with her and, of course, Bippy was really the one who had discovered her. In fact, twice that very day it had been pointed out to him that Peters was dangling after her. A little tension stirred in his breast when he recalled her setting off for the pond with Peters and staying so long alone with him. She might be with him now. He urged his horse on to a faster pace, without realizing he was doing so, or why.

He rode into the stable and was relieved to see Strayward had not arrived yet. He walked around to the front of the house to see if his carriage was coming. It wasn't. Deciding to go in at the east entrance to have a look at the ballroom, to satisfy Belle who would certainly demand praise, he walked back in that direction towards his Mama's rose garden. It was sadly depleted after the morning's foray, and he looked around, frowning slightly. He heard a rustling behind him, from the stone bench on the other side of a planting of yellow rose bushes. He turned and saw Ella just arising, with a book in her hand.

"Ah, Ella," he said, smiling. "Looking into that book of Kant's I recommended, are you?"

"No, sir, I am enjoying the cynicism of La Rochefoucauld. What a nasty person he was to be sure. Suspected everyone of being as vile as he was himself."

"I like him excessively," Clare replied, solely for the sake of a little argument.

"Now isn't that a coincidence?" she replied. "I thought of you while I was reading his maxims and made sure you *would* agree."

"With the cynical, venomous old rascal," Clare added agreeably.

"Just so."

"Tell me, which of his maxims brought me to mind. I can think of nothing more interesting than a discussion of myself."

"It was rather the *tone* of them than one particular maxim."

"Cynical. No, really. Is that what you think of me?"

"Well, not precisely, but I think that is what you would *like* people to think of you," she said.

He walked around the rose bushes to join her. "Perhaps I give that impression. I hope you are coming to know me better." He took her hand, indicating that she was to be seated again on the stone bench.

She remained standing. "Oh, yes, now that I have seen you ruthlessly ordering your guests about and making fun of them—us, behind our backs, I have a much truer picture of your character. And I prefer *not* to sit on that dreadful, hard, and very cold bench," she added.

"Let us take a stroll then, and see if we can find a rose-bush that is not totally destroyed. Strange you did not find the bench uncomfortable *before* my arrival, by the way," he said, to add a little fuel to the discussion.

"I found it so uncomfortable that I was about to leave when you came. But then a man who will put *stone* benches in his rose garden obviously has not the comfort of his guests in mind. At Fairmont we have lovely little wicker settees."

"Which must be brought in every time rain threatens, or they squawk like a beaten dog when you sit on them," he riposted.

"Yes, they do squawk a little," she admitted, "but they do not cause a chill to the marrow of your bones at least."

"If you have taken a chill, Miss Fairmont, I shall personally bring you a posset, or embrocation, or whatever treatment you require," he bowed formally. "What was recommended in that one book you read by—Doctor Ward was it?"

"He most particularly advised staying away from stone benches."

He smiled, and they walked on, but he soon remembered Strayward's imminent arrival, and the smile faded from his face.

"Is it the prospect of my taking ill that has put you in the hips so suddenly?" she rallied, "or the even more awful one of your having to quack me?"

"Neither. I know you were bamming me, of course. It's something else entirely."

"You are thrown into the dismals at the thought of your party breaking up perhaps?"

"No, it is rather the addition to my party that frightens me."

"Strayward? Is he so bad as that? He seems a harmless enough sort, from what I have seen of him about town."

"Well, he isn't coming for the fun of the drive, you know."

Ella had a pretty good idea why he was coming, but hardly felt in a position to say anything, though she *did* feel Clare wished to discuss it with her, which was singularly flattering.

"It is this damn . . . diabolical Prattle that has put about the idea I instituted this party to choose a bride." Ella winced, but as Clare was looking in the direction of the road, he did not observe it. "Well, I can tell you *she* is not the bride I have in mind."

"Have you one in mind then?" Ella asked, alarmed.

"Oh yes," he smiled, and looked at her so oddly that she felt weak.

She hardly knew what she was saying. "Well, I think you overestimate yourself, milord. I doubt that Honor would even accept an offer now that the truth is out. That you are a *Whig*, I mean."

"Not a chance. I might be an anarchist for all she'd care."

"Upon my word, you have a good opinion of yourself,

sir! Do you think anyone in the whole world would be happy to accept you, whatever your faults?"

"But what faults could possibly override my eligibility?" he asked, only half-joking, she feared. "I cannot think, offhand, of anyone who would not accept me."

"Well *I* would not! And neither would Miss Prattle," she said, unsure whether he was joking or not, for while he was not smiling, he did not appear totally serious, either. There seemed to be some hint of playfulness about his lips.

"Would you not, Miss Fairmont?" he asked, quite struck at the possibility. "Extraordinary." Seeing her state of uncertainty, and wishing to goad her a little further, he said, "Well, I think you would, and I make no doubt I could bring Prattle round my thumb too, if I had a mind to."

"I never heard such conceit in my life!" she expostulated, half laughing.

"Do you deem it conceit in me to think myself worthy of a common gossipmonger, who makes her livelihood purveying lies about her betters? Or is it only *yourself* you consider to be above my touch?"

"I didn't mean that!" she gasped, stung more by his castigation of Prattle than the latter part regarding herself.

"Then what *did* you mean, for that is certainly what you said."

"I—I only mean it is conceited in you to *say* such things openly, even if you do *think* them."

"I am lacking in hypocrisy, in fact. Certainly a grave deficiency in a gentleman."

"I didn't mean that either. Oh, it is horrid of you to say so. You are only trying to make me angry."

"And do you know, I think I am succeeding better than I expected. You should allow your temper to run away with you more often. The flush becomes you." Naturally she flushed more deeply at this sudden compliment.

Into the pause that followed, a clatter of hooves was heard approaching.

"Oh, God, it's Strayward," Clare said, in a resigned voice. "What *damnable* timing!" Then he suddenly smiled and said, "We shall continue this discussion on whether or not you will marry me another time. I'd better go and welcome him." In a sardonic voice he added, "And you accused me of a lack of hypocrisy."

The color deserted Ella's cheeks, and she was left with her mouth hanging open. He could not be serious! It was all a joke, of course. Clare strode round to the front of the building, and it was Ella who went in at the east door, in a trance, her mind boggled at the conversation she had just held.

A short, pudgy gentleman of middle years descended from the elegant black traveling carriage with the Strayward crest on the panel. Strayward was even shorter than his stubby wife, but they were so seldom in each other's company that it was no inconvenience. He wore a well-cut blue jacket and faun trousers, but there was no hope of fashion with such an unfortunate physique. His face was round and his cheeks rosy.

"Clare, my boy," he said in a hearty voice, offering his hand. "Nice to see you. Are you taking good care of my girls, heh?"

"I trust they have been tolerably amused, sir," he replied, shaking the hand that was stretched out to him.

"Ho, amused! I should say so. Yes, indeed. That little vixen of mine, Lady Cynthia—no, or is it Honor you have here?"

"Lady Honor."

"Yes, yes, so it is, the saucy minx. She is always amused. Anything amuses her."

"It certainly takes very little to keep her entertained," Clare agreed.

"And my lady? How does Eleanor go on?"

"Fine, sir. Will you not step in and see them?"

"I'll see you first, Clare, what? We have some arrangements to make—business arrangements."

Clare felt the noose slip a little tighter about his neck

and unconsciously tugged at his cravat. "Let us not discuss politics on an empty stomach," he replied with studied obtuseness.

"Politics? No, I didn't mean that. Never discuss politics with a Whig. They don't know anything about politics. But you ain't political, Clare. No one ever said that of you."

This was meant for a compliment, Clare assumed, and he nodded.

"No," Strayward rattled on, linking his arm in Clare's, "I didn't mean political business." They proceeded towards the house. Looking around the grounds, he continued, "Fine place you have here. Very fine place. Next to Strayward I cannot think of a place I like better. Blenheim is a barn of a place. I hate yellow buildings, but your place is very fine. She will like it."

There could be no misreading this hint. Clare actually felt the flesh creep on his back. He said nothing but suddenly regretted he had not rushed on and made a direct offer to Miss Fairmont.

They entered through the double portals to the hall, and Strayward said, "Shall we talk now or later?"

"What is it you wish to discuss, sir?" Clare asked, with a blank look on his face.

"Why—why business, to be sure."

"Yes, so you mentioned, but I am at a loss to know what business you refer to."

"The settlement, of course."

"Settlement of what?" Clare asked, trying earnestly to sound sincere and uninformed.

"By Jove, I must speak to Eleanor," Strayward said, a little embarrassed and not in the least happy. "I understood you and Cynthia—thought it was all settled."

"Cynthia?" Clare asked, in no real doubt, despite Strayward's inability to distinguish between his daughters.

"T'other one then, whoever is here with Eleanor."

"Ah, Lady Honor."

"Yes, yes, that's it. Honor."

The butler had rung for a footman at the gentlemen's entrance, and he now appeared. "Would you like to go directly to your room, sir, or would you care for a glass of wine first?" Clare asked.

"I'll go up to my room. Might have a bottle sent up, if you'd be so kind."

"A pleasure. Claret, or . . ."

"Brandy," Strayward said firmly. If he had come here on a fool's errand, a hundred miles out of his way, he would need more than claret to keep his temper.

"See to it," Clare said to the footman, then to Strayward he added, "We dine at seven thirty, sir. We are holding a ball this evening to entertain the ladies. You will not want the bother of dressing twice."

"Knee breeches," Strayward muttered unhappily. "I daresay my man packed them." As he hobbled up the grand staircase, he was grumbling to himself about getting decked out in a monkey suit and silk stockings, and all for nothing. Clare breathed a sigh of relief. But he knew his relief was only temporary. They wouldn't give up on him so easily.

He remembered that he had intended to look at the ballroom and went there before going upstairs to change. He looked around at the large baskets of flowers and ferns and didn't see a thing.

Thirteen

The guests at Clare Palace were to sit down to dinner in the great dining hall at 7:30. This evening, the dinner and ball formed the highlight of the visit, and comprised the one event to which more than a casual attention had been paid. The ladies had all kept their most elaborate gowns for this night, and it was on this occasion they felt, or at least hoped, that Clare would announce which of the ladies had won his favor. There was no real reason to believe he would do so, but by constantly talking of it among themselves, they had kept the hope alive. To be sure, he had an opportunity to see each of them alone, should he desire it; both Sherry and Belle were downstairs, rigged to the nines, by seven o'clock. When Belle could not find him, she conceived the plan of going to his office, where he spent much of his time, to ask him if he had seen the ballroom. She felt it to be an inferior sort of excuse, but such speed and cunning were necessary to evade Sherry that she had only a second and half a mind to think about it.

Clare was not in his office. He feared it was the first place Strayward would go hunting for him. He stayed abovestairs with his door bolted till twenty minutes past seven. Sherry actually exposed her body and her best peau de soie gown to the elements in an effort to find him. She ventured into the rose garden—such a romantic spot to receive an offer in—but he was not there. She took two steps beyond the crushed shell walks to the lawn beyond, but there was a spot of moisture on the grass, so she came back. Water was fatal to white satin slippers and their paste buckles. Ella and Lady Sara, the former in her good yellow gown she had worn to Almack's, the latter in deep blue crepe and diamonds, went to the saloon at 7:00 and sat conversing with the Dowager Duchess, and looking at Lady Honor, who did not say anything. Mrs. Prentiss and Mrs. Sheridan were also there, sparring with each other, and sitting aside so that they had a view of the hall, and the hunt. The Marchioness was still upstairs with her husband, trying to convince him that Clare had indeed been dangling after Honor in a most marked manner all season.

"Hunting mares' nests," he said, in a voice becoming plaintive from brandy and disappointment.

"No such a thing," she maintained inaccurately. "Speak to him after dinner."

"Hadn't a notion what I was talking about."

"Pshaw, you have bungled it, Strayward. Put it to him straight. No doubt he misunderstood you."

"Thought I was talking politics. Never talk politics to a Whig. Whigs don't understand politics. They only want to spoil the farmers and workers by showering them with gold, and to give the Papists in Ireland a lot of power. Nonsense."

The Straywards did not go downstairs till 7:30. Ten minutes before that, Clare descended and met Sherry just coming in from the east door through the ballroom.

"Oh, Clare, so that's where you are," she said, with great relief, and a sharp eye about her for Belle, who had given up her search and gone to the saloon.

"Yes, have you been looking for me?"

"I was just wondering where you were, for Mama told me you weren't in the saloon yet, and I could see Belle didn't find you in your study."

"You have tracked me down now," he said with a wry smile at her artlessness. "I expect you wanted to give me an opportunity to admire your new gown. It is extravagantly beautiful. Worthy even of you."

"Oh, do you like it?" she beamed. "It has ten yards of material in it, and took *forever* to make. It was shockingly expensive, but it doesn't pay to stint on a ball gown." She whirled around in a circle to let him view her perfection from all angles.

"Lovely," he said. Already his senses were sated with her beauty, and he took a step towards the saloon.

"It has these spangles on the underskirt," she pointed out, causing him to turn back to render more admiration.

"Very nice."

"And I have had these paste buckles put on my slippers. Mama ordered them from London, and we were so afraid they wouldn't arrive in time, but they did." She stuck out a dainty slipper to be gazed at.

"Very fine indeed, Sherry. Your Mama has done you proud."

"Oh, and do you like my hair?" she pressed on. "You

will notice I am wearing it in the Méduse. Mama thought it best, since you liked it before."

"Now, I think we have seen you from head to toe, have we not? You will put them all to the blush. Shall we go and join the others?"

Sherry could think of no other novelties to show him, and as he had nothing to say to her, she took his arm, and smiled blightingly at Belle as she paraded in, hanging on his arm.

For a moment, Belle's heart panicked. That proprietary smile! She had got an offer! She could not remain in doubt and immediately arose from her seat, in the middle of a conversation with the Duchess, and hastened to Sherry and Clare.

"What has kept you so long? It's nearly time for dinner."

"Clare has been giving me so many compliments; we have been standing in the hall these ten minutes together."

Relief surged in Belle's bosom. Not an offer then. She relaxed visibly, taking a deep breath. "Have you been to the ballroom, Clare? Isn't it handsome? How busy we have been, fixing it up for you."

"Yes, I have been in. It has never looked finer. Pray accept my congratulations and gratitude."

"The roses are half-wilted," Sherry said. "I noticed just now as I came in."

"In?" Belle asked. "Were you two outside?" This opened up alarming possibilities.

"No, *I* was out for a breath of air," Sherry confessed, then got her own back by adding, "and the roses are all wilted. You must have forgotten to water them."

Clare became bored with their squabbling and sauntered off.

"Now see what you've done," Belle said angrily. "He will go straight to Miss Fairmont. I don't know what he sees in her."

"Whatever it is, Peters sees it, too. He is always at her side."

"Oh, Peters—who cares for him?"

While they spoke of other members of the party, their eyes never left Clare, following his elegant black back, to see in whose direction he would walk.

"There, Honor has nabbed him on his way past," Sherry said, rather unnecessarily, as Belle could see it for herself. "And her Papa is come, you know. Do you think he was summoned to receive an offer?"

"I don't doubt he came in expectation of it, but I'll warrant he wasn't summoned. Clare was as surprised as we were at luncheon, when it was said Strayward was coming."

"I cannot think he cares for her, even though her papa is a marquis. Her gowns are frightful."

"Oh, Clare is not impressed by fine feathers," Belle laughed, running her eye over Sherry's elaborate ensemble. "Or spangles either." She turned and headed in Lady Honor's direction, wearing a rather plain gown herself. Sherry was right behind her, but by the time they reached Lady Honor, Clare had detached himself from her and taken the seat vacated by Belle, next to his mother. It was now impossible to sit at his elbow without asking a footman to drag up a chair for them, so they had to find a seat elsewhere.

Lady Sara and Ella had been watching their performance with interest and exchanged a silent, knowing glance. Ella also cast a few covert looks at Clare, but other than bowing to her upon his entrance, he had not singled her out at all. She was still thinking of the strange remark he had made in the rose garden, but he appeared to have forgotten it. A moment later the Marquis and his wife entered the saloon. Though it was now time for dinner, everyone had to wait while Strayward had another glass of brandy, and he was in no hurry to knock it off, either.

Foreseeing there would be no opportunity to sound Clare out on his intentions over dinner, for of course they'd have a lady between them, Strayward determined to do it before. Less shy than the young ladies, he did pull a chair up to Clare's side, and said in a low voice, "Deuced hard to get a minute in private for our little chat." Clare gave him a look of unveiled hate. He should have told him directly the first time he had no notion of offering for Honor. This was what came of being polite. "About Honor you know," Strayward added, discomfited by that cold face opposite him. *Silly old woman, his wife. Dead wrong about the whole thing.*

"You'd better finish your drink. I believe dinner is waiting."

"Yes, by Jove. We'll discuss it later, heh?"

"I can think of nothing you and I have to discuss, sir," Clare said frigidly.

Strayward tossed off the rest of his brandy, and everyone went to dinner. The first course passed easily, but when it was removed and the game birds and mutton served, Strayward returned to the attack, in spite of Lady Sara's body, which was lodged between Clare and himself. He was well laced with liquor by now, his head foggy. From across the table his wife kept staring at him, tossing her head and darting her eyes towards Clare, in a meaningful and commanding fashion.

"Devilish fine place you have here, Clare," he began slyly.

"Thank you."

"Fine old family too, the Beresfords. An old and noble line, like the Sedgleys."

"Yes, our title dates from Norman times."

"The old and noble families should stick together."

"They usually do," Clare replied offhandedly.

"Never been any connection between our two houses," Strayward went on. "Deuced odd when you come to think of it. I'm connected one way or another with twenty of the noble families, my wife tells me, and I daresay you are too, yet there's no connection between our two houses."

"Our political leanings perhaps account for it," Clare

suggested, wishing to stress their differences, and even more to change the subject entirely. "I hear Bathurst has . . ."

"I never talk politics with Whigs," Strayward stated flatly.

"By all means let us discuss something else. Do you think Bonaparte . . ."

"What I was going to say," Strayward interrupted loudly, "about our two houses, no connection between them. An odd thing."

"Yes, it is strange."

"Ought to make a connection," Strayward said, skating precariously close to his object now.

Clare willed down his rage. It was not only the idea that repelled him, but the man's pushing it in public, in a loud carrying voice. And he was so foxed there was no hope of giving him a set-down. "Nowadays, of course, peoples' feelings come into it. It is not like the old days when marriages were arranged."

He was quite sure Sara was smiling into her serviette, while she pretended to wipe her mouth. Further down the table, he encountered a look from Ella. He raised his eyebrows and shrugged his shoulders in a helpless gesture, and she frowned heavily at him. Then Peters, on her left, addressed some remark to her, and she began talking to him. This too enraged Clare for some reason.

Strayward kept talking on in this vein, very loudly, throughout the remainder of the meal. Short of telling him to shut up, there seemed no way of silencing him. No topic introduced could seduce him from his aim. And to add to the general horror of the meal, every person at the table but the Straywards was ill at ease. He received consoling looks from Tredwell and his Mama, but through it all, Honor shoveled in food, without saying a word to her partner on either side. One had to admire her *sang-froid*. Say that at least for breeding. Those other two commoners, Belle and Sherry, were rolling their eyes and giggling, while their Mamas scarcely ate a bite, for fear of missing a word. One more scandal to rock London, if Prattle ever got hold of it. Prattle too had her ears stretched, but no thought of publicizing this interesting interlude entered her head. Clare was fading from her column. His name had not appeared since the day Ella went to his orphanage, but what would have appeared by now in London was the column about Prissie—and how Ella dreaded the day it reached Clare's eyes. It would be in Dorset by tomorrow, but she would be gone before its arrival, as they meant to take an early departure.

Strayward continued, pushing the idea of the two houses being joined, in a manner becoming more obvious by the minute. Dinner was nearly over—the sweet half-eaten, and Clare hoped to get the ladies off to the saloon before Strayward put it into so many words, as he quite clearly meant to do. Certain members of the party had a strong desire to hear Strayward go his length, and when the tray of pastries was passed for the second time, Mrs. Prentiss accepted a cream bun, and Mrs. Sheridan a *mille feuilles* so the whole party settled down for another ten minutes.

"Lean forward and protect me, Sara," Clare said to his dinner companion in a desperate voice.

"Hiding behind a woman's skirts?" she teased. She hadn't enjoyed herself so for years.

"It's that or a public announcement that I have no desire to marry his daughter."

"You're for it, my boy. He has no intention of letting you off the hook."

"And I no intention of being caught."

"I say, Clare," Strayward broke in on their chat, straining his neck forward to catch a glimpse of his quarry. "As I was saying, Clare, what do you think of it, you and Honor?"

The entire room fell silent. Not so much as a breath or a tinkle of silver on china was heard. Everyone was on tiptoe to hear Clare's reply. "A delightful idea," he said, in a voice as smooth as silk, "but I fear my fiancée might dislike it."

Into the quiet a babble of voices was unleashed—questions, exclamations, even a shriek or two from the vicinity of the Misses Sheridan and Prentiss. Honor looked up in surprise, though she didn't say anything or stop chewing. Clare glanced at Strayward, who said only, "Oh, I see," in pretty good spirits, then turned his attention to his wine glass.

"Well done!" Sara congratulated Clare. He exhaled and clenched his fist in his lap to stop its shaking.

His relief was short-lived. An announcement of this magnitude was not easily forgotten. The ladies, and even the gentlemen, pressed forward enquiries as to the identity of the fiancée.

"No, an announcement is premature," Clare parried. "The lady has not accepted yet."

"Doing it too brown," Harley jeered.

"Too thick and rare," Peters seconded.

"Come on, out with it, Pa'k," Bippy urged. "Fancy we have a pretty good idea."

Upon hearing that he had not yet been accepted, Belle realized at once it was not Sherry, as she had first feared. On second consideration, she reached the conclusion that the only reason he had not been accepted was that he had not asked anyone. "Is she at this table?" she asked mischievously. Ever alert and scheming, she knew he had not offered, but felt he might very well offer for *someone* after this night's debacle. She was still in the running.

"What is that old saw about curiosity killing the cat?" he asked evasively.

"The old saw is 'Curiosity killed the cat, and satisfaction brought it back,'" she quoted laughingly. "It can't be Sherry; *she* would have accepted."

Clare directed a malevolent stare down the table at her.

"So would *you*," Sherry shot back.

"Oh, you are funning us," Belle continued. "Anyone would have you."

"What do you say to that, Miss Fairmont?" Clare asked.

"I disagree," she said quietly.

"It's *you*," Belle shouted in an accusing tone to Ella, her eyes flashing.

"This is one of Clare's little jokes," Ella replied, ready to sink from humiliation.

"I made sure it couldn't be *her*," Sherry said disparagingly, just as though Ella were not there.

It was Ella's turn to be furious. Her anger was about evenly distributed between Sherry and Lord Clare, who had put her in this hateful position.

"You are mistaken," Clare said quietly to Sherry, in a very cold voice. Every eye at the table flew to his face to read whether he was serious. This verified, the eyes slewed to Miss Fairmont. She felt very like a wild animal at Exeter Exchange, with the crowds staring at it for amusement.

"Well, and what is your answer, Miss Fairmont?" Belle asked.

"What is the question?" she replied.

"Will you marry Clare, of course."

"He has not asked me, and this is all a very bad joke."

"I knew he hadn't asked *her*," Sherry told Belle, in no inaudible tone.

Clare felt a pronounced desire to walk down the table and box Sherry's beautiful ears. "No, it is no joke, Ella," Clare said, smiling in embarrassment at such an unlikely manner of proposing. "It was very remiss of me to be sure, to announce our engagement before making a proper offer. *Will* you do me the honor to be my wife?"

"No, Your Grace, I will not," she said firmly. The whole table, including Clare, sat in a state of shock. Miss Fairmont laid down her serviette, pushed back her chair, and marched from the room, before the tears spurted out of her eyes. She had never been so angry, so *ashamed* in her life.

"I'll go to her," Sara said to Clare.

"No, let me," Clare replied, and excusing himself, he hastened out the door after her. He caught her just at the foot of the great stairway, on her way to her room.

"Ella, I'm sorry," he said, with a half-laugh at the mess he had made of it.

She looked at him as though seeing some strange and unpleasant sight for the first time in her life.

"You will live to be a good deal sorrier, my lord," she replied, in a tight, angry voice.

"If you don't kill me first. Come into the study. We can't talk here."

"We have nothing to say to each other."

"Come," he urged, clamping a hand around her wrist, and drawing her to the nearest room, a little study frequented by his Mama on winter afternoons. "I am damnably sorry, Ella. I don't know what possessed me to do it. It was Strayward being so persistent, and Sherry . . ."

"You had no right to drag *my name* into it. To embarrass and humiliate me in front of all those people!" She let her anger surge forth, as it kept her tears in check.

He put his two hands on her arms, below the shoulders. "Are you really *so* humiliated, to receive an offer from me?" he asked, in a soft wheedling voice, full of confidence.

"Yes! Such an offer, made in jest, to save your own skin!"

"But I was in earnest, Ella. I said we should continue our discussion again."

"Oh!" she looked to see if he was, if he could possibly be serious.

He laughed—a mixture of triumph and amusement, *tolerant* amusement. It never entered his head she would refuse. He had not meant to be offensive at such a critical juncture, but for her to receive such an odd proposal, and to see no humility whatsoever in the eyes of the supposed lover, gave a great deal of offense. "Well, you warned me you would not have me," he laughed, sliding his hands down her arms till he held both her hands in his, "but I will not hold you to it."

"Don't cringe in your boots, Clare. It does not become one of your monstrous arrogance. I do not mean to accept you, so you needn't worry."

He could not believe her to be serious. "I know you are angry with me for announcing it before you accepted . . ."

"And before you *asked*!"

"Well, that's what I meant of course."

"*Of course!* It is all one and the same to you. That is perfectly clear. You have only to ask any girl in the whole world, and she will have you." She wrenched her hands from his grip.

"With the possible exception of yourself and Prattle," he added playfully. He was used to having Ella give him a hard time.

"Well, we refuse you," Ella said angrily.

Her voice was so fierce that he looked at her face closely, and began to realize for the first time that she meant it. It had the effect of a hard blow to the stomach. The shock of so unexpected a thing momentarily knocked the wind out of him. A rising anger quickly followed the initial shock. "Shall we let Prattle speak for itself?" he asked scathingly.

"Oh no, Your Grace. No one is better qualified to speak for Miss Prattle than I." The fateful words were out in a rush of spite before she well considered their consequence.

"Am I to understand you are an intimate acquaintance of this vulgar gossipmonger?"

"I have the pleasure to be an *intimate* acquaintance."

"Then you will kindly tell her for me she is a vicious, underbred . . ."

"That will not be necessary, Your Grace. You have just told her."

While he stood, dumbfounded, she turned on her heel and ran from the room. In seconds he was after her, but by the time he reached the hall she was halfway up the stairs. "Ella! Ella, come back here!" he shouted angrily after her rapidly retreating figure. She didn't even look around.

Two footmen and a maid, their ears flapping, stepped forth from the dim recesses of the hall that had been concealing them, tacitly offering their services to bring her back, though it must have been pretty obvious that force would be required to do it.

"What are you doing here?" Clare demanded sharply, then walked away without awaiting an answer.

Before he had decided what to do, Sara came into the hall. She knew by his face that no satisfactory conclusion had been reached to the episode at the dinner table.

"Clare, you greenhead," she said baldly. "What possessed you to do such a thing?"

"Desperation," he answered with an equal directness.

"Strayward is the outside of enough, certainly, but you should have stuck to your guns and left your imaginary fiancée anonymous."

"She refused me, Sara," he said, his voice puzzled.

"Yes, and wouldn't you be in a fine pickle if she'd accepted!"

"But I meant it. Why do you think I did not?"

Sara's heart skipped a beat. She had dared to hope he meant it but had not thus far revealed to a soul that she did. In fact, she had just inferred to the guests at the table that it was all a little private joke between the pair of them, and Ella was angry at Clare's making it public.

"I hope I am not so *monstrously arrogant* as to pull a stunt like that on an innocent female."

"No, Clare, not *monstrously* arrogant, just arrogant."

"It is what *she* said."

"Did she indeed? But then I gather she didn't believe you meant it either."

"Of course she knew I meant it," he said, still angry at the realization. "And she said something else that wants some explaining too. Is it *possible* she is Miss Prattle?"

"Good God, did she tell you *that*?" Sara shrieked. Oh,

the fool of a girl, she had clearly lost her reason. Bad enough to reject the top marital prize in England, without incurring his eternal wrath as well. *No* hope of a repeated offer now.

"That is what I understood her to say, and I take your exclamations of horror as a confirmation."

The fat was in the fire. To make little of it was the best, the only way now. "She does it for a lark, you know. She was always interested in writing."

"You call *that* writing? It is muckraking of the worst sort. I am shocked you would allow her to so degrade herself, Sara. You should have known better."

Sara's well-coiffed hackles rose dangerously at this slur on her taste and guardianship. "You make too much of it. A little playful criticism of the social scene—no one takes it amiss but yourself. Indeed Lord Byron told me the other day he finds it vastly amusing, and thought Sherry— Richard Sheridan, I mean—to be the author."

"Lord Byron has not been mocked and scorned as *I* have been."

"True, but then Byron is not *yet* so toplofty as yourself."

"It is *unpardonable*, Sara, and you would do better to call your niece to account than to make excuses for her."

"I make no excuses, in fact, I add several items to the column myself, and so does Mama," she added haughtily.

One could only marvel at such gross impertinence. "Upon my word, I don't know what to say."

"You might try saying you're sorry," she suggested, with an imperious toss of her head.

"More sorry than you can know to have unwittingly invited Prattle under my roof. And I collect even *you* will admit *that* was an underhanded thing for her to do."

"That was wrong, but it was *my* fault. It was I who wangled the invitation."

"No, it was Tredwell. Does *he* know?"

"Indeed he does not. He was an innocent pawn. I fabricated the romance between them out of whole cloth to get you to ask her, and for that I *do* apologize."

Clare's temper was quick to rouse, but like most hot-blooded people, he exploded, then soon settled down. He was not without a sense of humor, and the thing had its humorous side, even if he was the butt of the joke himself. He had always liked Sara, liked the very *dégagé* manner of her that would pull off such a stunt as this. To see her looking penitent softened him, and when he replied there was less rancor in his voice. "I am relieved to see some shred of respectability still clings to you, Sara."

"I *am* sorry, Clare. It was beastly of me, but really she has hardly written a word about the odd time we have had here, hunting frogs and holding a jousting tournament . . ."

"Well she might refrain, when it was all her own doing!"

As this was delivered with a rueful smile, she dared to return, "She only suggested—it is for the *host* to provide entertainment for his guests, and you were sadly lacking there."

"You know how hastily this party was thrown together, and *why*."

"The *why* of it has succeeded at any rate. I trust not even Strayward will push the match now, after that leveler you dealt him. Lord, I nearly *died* laughing when you said, cool as a cucumber, your fiancée might dislike it. You are a complete hand."

"Too complete a hand for your niece's taste, it seems."

"I imagine it was the *manner* of the proposal she resented, rather than the idea itself. If you were serious, why did you not ask her before dinner?" It seemed there might yet be a hope of pulling the thing off, if she trod softly.

"It occurred to me. In fact, I was looking for her when I came down, but she was in the saloon, and there was no privacy."

"You were certainly leaving it to the last minute. You have been alone with her a dozen times these last days."

"It takes a little time to fall in love, Sara. I was by no means positive till she told me in the garden she wouldn't have me. I decided on the spot she would. But then Strayward arrived . . ."

"He is an inopportune devil. Er . . . am I to understand you *did* ask her before dinner?"

"No, I've just told you there wasn't time."

"But how did she come to refuse you then?"

"It was not a refusal precisely. She only said she wouldn't have me if I did ask her, and neither would Prattle. I wonder if she was trying to tell me then she was Prattle."

"Very likely," Sara agreed, without believing a word of it. Her mind was fully occupied with figuring how Ella had come to say anything so forward as Clare had just told her. They were clearly on a much closer footing than she had guessed. "What shall we do now?" she asked. She wanted to hear whether he was still desirous of marrying Ella, after that strong tirade against Miss Prattle.

His reply told her nothing. "She won't come down to the ball. It will be a headache, I expect."

"It would be best if she would come down, and let everyone see it was all a little joke, as I have been busily convincing your guests it was."

"I hope you may not have entirely convinced Strayward."

"He won't insist after this, surely."

"I shan't give him a chance. He's three sheets to the wind already and will likely go to his room."

"I hear the others coming," Lady Sara said, as the voices of the ladies leaving the dining hall was heard through the corridor.

"Try to get her to come down," Clare urged. Then he added, hesitantly, "Of course, we must not insist."

"No."

"You may tell her I shan't inconvenience her by re-peating my unwelcome offer," he added a little stiffly.

Sara's spirits sank to hear this, but she had to nip off upstairs before she was discovered in conclave with Clare by the others.

Clare returned to the dining room to take port with the gentlemen and was happy to see Strayward's head on the table, with stertorous snorts issuing forth. He had him lifted bodily from his chair by four stout footmen and carted off to his room. He had never been so happy to see a guest dead drunk and only wished he had passed out half an hour ago.

Sara mounted the stairs to do battle with her niece. She did not find Ella sunk into vapors on the counterpane, as she rather feared she might, nor even indulging in a bout of tears. No, she was swiftly and silently snatching her clothes from their hangers and wadding them into balls before tossing them into her traveling trunk, which stood open on the floor before her. Her face was composed into rigid lines of unroutable anger. Sara quickly scanned her mind for the best way to handle such a touchy situation and in the squeezing of a lemon formed her plan.

"So, Clare was right," she said, laughing light. "He made sure you would be too hen-hearted to meet the company below."

Ella paused, her green sprigged muslin in her hands, ready to be mussed up like the others. "Did he say so?" she asked, her eyebrows lifting.

"Yes, I told him I would try to persuade you to come down to the ball. I had hoped to pass his awkward pro-posal off as a joke but, of course, if you fly into the boughs and flee his house in the dead of night, there will be no hope of that. Well, he told me exactly how it would be, and he was right. This means I must miss the ball, too, of course, and I have been rather looking forward to it."

"What did he say?" Ella asked, disregarding Sara's spurious complaint.

"How did he word it exactly?" she asked herself, while hastily composing a quotation. "He said, 'Don't think she will have the bottom to face the masses. That would take more countenance than Miss Fairmont possesses.' Something of that sort."

"I don't pretend to match *him* for gall," Ella said coolly. Sara stored it up for repetition to Clare. He'd enjoy it. "You think the others at the table know it was a joke?" Ella asked.

Know it was a joke. So that was to be the game played. Very well, then. "They will know it if you go downstairs as though nothing had happened and behave normally to Clare." Such a black glare greeted this suggestion that Sara back-tracked, lest she lose the advantage gained by asking too much. "Oh, you need do no more than exchange a few pleasantries with him. He charged me to tell you you need fear no repetition of his proposal, if you *do* decide to go."

"No, that is a joke best not repeated," Ella replied, not emphasizing the word 'joke,' but making sure to use it.

Ella didn't know why she hid the truth from Sara. In one sense she was proud of it. Maybe he had only asked her to escape Honor, but at that same table sat both Sherry and Belle, either of whom would have snatched eagerly at any offer from him, no matter what grotesque form it took. They were both pretty, popular ladies. To have been preferred to them was something. Sara would give her the very devil for refusing and pinch on about it forever. She wanted nothing so much as to get away from Clare Palace and try to forget the whole thing.

And now getting away was impossible. A challenge had been issued—a challenge for her to match his own nerve and brazen out the curiosity of the mob. Upon consideration, it seemed the best plan. If it could be passed off as a joke, it would cause only a ripple in London; if not, it could be a tidal wave. The Duke of Clare's finally making an offer after all these years was singular enough, but to have made it to a very plain girl in public, and to have been refused, was indeed an event. He would never live it down. And why should she care for his embarrassment? He had cared little enough for hers.

Well then, call it charity. It might mitigate the last blow Prattle would deal him, when he read the account of himself seducing a servant. This low blow still to come bothered her more than the rest. He *had* been sincere in his offer, but he did not know she was Prattle when he made it and still did not know what was in store for him. She really ought to do what she could to atone for that.

"I daresay I made too much of it," Ella said, when she realized Sara was looking at her, expectantly.

"A good deal too much," was the unhesitating answer. "Clare is a great one for jokes, you know. Well, love, I think your hair wants some fixing. It looks quite disordered from your packing. I'll have Stepson come in, but you better get Bickles to repack those clothes, too."

"Yes. They *will* think it was a joke, won't they, Sara?"

"I'm sure they've heard you two teasing each other times out of mind. *He* thought you had a sense of humor to match his own. How shocked he must have been to see you so irate. I can't think what came over you myself, Ella."

"The others didn't think it was a joke. And that Sherry . . ."

"Too *farouche*. I could have killed her, and so could Clare. But it will all pass over if you can but buck up and make an appearance downstairs for a while."

"Yes. We'll leave *early* tomorrow, Sara?"

"It was our original plan, so that is no problem. I am eager for my Herbert. He'll be home by now, and the children too."

This return to mundane topics relieved the tension, and in fifteen minutes Sara returned from her room, ready to take her niece to the ball. The company from the countryside had begun to arrive in the meanwhile, and the opening minuet was about to begin. Clare was standing up with the Marchioness. Sara wondered how he had exchanged Honor for her. It was a sort of symbol of his not being expected to offer for the daughter she supposed. Ella's hand was sought by Peters, and within minutes the dance begun. Heads turned in Ella's direction. It was clear the dinner party was being discussed, but the interest waned when she was seen to be in good spirits. It took all her self-control to maintain a semblance of the spirits she by no means possessed, but she did it.

After the minuet, Sherry approached Ella. "Oh, Miss Fairmont, you must tell me, for I am dying of curiosity. Did Clare really mean what he said to you?"

How strong the temptation was to tell this beautiful, hateful girl the truth. "At dinner you mean?" Ella asked, as though she could scarcely remember.

"Yes, when you dashed out of the dining hall."

"It was a joke, of course, but I lost my temper with him, odious man, for making it sound as though he meant it."

"I was sure it was a joke," Sherry replied, then went in search of Belle to confirm that she had been right all along.

Belle had long since put the same question to Clare, and when given Sherry's story, contradicted it. "*He* told me he was very fond of Miss Fairmont," she informed Sherry.

"Anyone may be fond of her, but did he say he wanted to *marry* her?"

"Not precisely, but when I said I knew he was only roasting the poor girl, and it was too bad of him, he got very angry and said he could think of no one he would rather marry."

"And only look at the plain old gown she is wearing. I have seen it on her times out of mind. I can't think what he sees in her."

"Not a clotheshorse in any case, dear," Belle said sweetly, then turned away to smile at a particularly handsome squire's son she had had a charming flirtation with at the ghost party.

Ella avoided the Duke as long as possible, and as he seemed content just to know she was there—he did know that, for their eyes met several times—it was not difficult. But the time came, at last, when she must face him. A waltz had just finished. Ella was with Bippy, and Clare was with Sara, and at the music's end Sara led Clare towards her niece. Ella longed to run for the door but knew perfectly well that several pairs of eyes were trained on them; she steeled herself for the meeting.

She curtsied and said in a calm voice, "A very pleasant ball, Your Grace."

"Very nice," Bippy mumbled, and Sara too threw in some platitudinous compliment.

"You young ladies deserve the credit," Clare replied. "Your flower arrangements are unexceptionable."

"It was Belle and Sara who did that," Ella returned.

"Do you find it too warm in here? I could have some windows opened if you wish," Clare suggested, apparently as determined as the young lady to say nothing of interest.

Sara decreed it was not at all warm, and the elderly ladies sitting along the wall would not like a blast of cold air on their backs.

"I am not too warm," Ella added.

"Well I am, by Jove," Bippy said. "Think I'll go and get a glass of punch. Will you come with me, Miss Fairmont?"

She snatched at the chance to get away. "Yes, I am thirsty."

"You, Sara?" Clare asked.

"Let's all go," Sara decided, hoping to prolong the meeting with Clare and Ella that all might be witness to their continued friendship. Since it was possible to walk only two abreast across the crowded floor, no conversation was necessary between the feuding couple. Wine was brought to the ladies, and Sara decided to make one last desperate throw to reconcile them, or at least give them privacy to do the job themselves.

"Bippy, will you come with me to the study for a moment? There are ten minutes before the next dance, and I should like a nice quiet sit-down to rest my head and feet."

He could hardly refuse and in fact had no desire to do so, as it was not every day a fashionable lady of the first stare like Lady Sara requested his escort. They sailed off together, while Ella's heart first sank, then rose unaccountably to her throat.

"We should have one dance together, for the looks of it," Clare said, when they had been deserted.

"Do you think it necessary?" Ella asked, in the tone of one long inured to self-sacrifice in the common good.

"Preferable, not necessary," he returned, with an air of the greatest indifference.

"Very well."

"I expect I ought to thank you for putting in an appearance," Clare continued. "Your aunt tells me it was done to save my face."

"To save unnecessary gossip."

"And my proposal—no, no, don't cringe, I am not about to repeat it—is to be explained as a joke in very poor taste?"

"I think it best, yes."

"As you wish, though I still fail to see why you consider the mere *offer* such an insult that it must be kept hidden at all costs." His voice, formerly indifferent, was gaining emotion as he spoke, and Ella had to make an effort to keep her own calm.

"I am only thinking of yourself."

"One rejection is not likely to sink me entirely. Or perhaps my *monstrous arrogance* leads me astray in the matter?"

"I prefer we do it in this way," Ella said and gave no further explanation.

"If you will pardon my making a suggestion, Miss Prattle, you would do yourself a greater service if you admitted I had asked you. Yes, don't goggle—I give you

197

carte blanche to print it up in your column. It will not detract from your consequence to have refused me."

"No, indeed," she replied, goaded by both his tone and words, "to have *refused* you must be a strong testament to my judgment."

"It would help to counteract the infamy of your position as Miss Prattle, in any case."

"You cannot mean to *tell* anyone!"

"How unhandsome that would be in me. But there is no matching me for *gall*, you know." Sara, of course, had relayed that phrase to him.

"I came to your ball to try to make up for any harm I have done you as Miss Prattle. If you tell a soul, I will never forgive you!"

"And take a lifelong vengeance by scribbling the lot up in your column to bore society."

"You are *hateful*!" she said.

"This bickering is pointless. Let us go on to the ballroom, if you're up to it."

"I'm up to anything you are, so you needn't think me lacking in nerve."

"*I* of all people ought not to accuse of *that*," he returned, and they walked off together to the ballroom, to show the world by their scowling faces and utter lack of conversation with each other, that they were on the best of terms. They confirmed the lie by taking a cold, formal leave the minute the music stopped, and by not so much as glancing at each other during the remainder of the evening.

Still, they had been seen together, and so the affair passed over as a nine-hour's wonder. Neither the Sheridans nor the Prentisses had the least desire to puff Miss Fairmont up by bruiting such a story about, and the gentlemen were none of them keen gossips. Naturally both Miss Fairmont and Miss Prattle were mute on the subject, and so the principals scraped through with only their feelings battered.

Fourteen

The guests, with the exception of the Straywards, were all preparing to leave first thing in the morning. By setting out early, only one night would have to be spent at an inn, and even getting little sleep after a ball was preferable to repeating this experience two nights in a row. The young gentlemen had some thoughts of making London that same night. No private farewells were taken by anyone. Clare and his mother went to the lawn to give and receive thanks and wave their handkerchiefs as the various vehicles bowled down the drive. Ella was not distinguished from the others by either more or less attention from the host. If his smile was a shade less warm for her than for some of the others, his Mama's was warmer, and Ella could not even have the satisfaction of feeling slighted. She leaned back against the squabs of the carriage, heaved a vast sigh of relief, then immediately bounced forward to have one last look at the grounds as the trip home was begun. Crazy Nellie's Tower, tilting a little, the Oriental Pavilion, the pond—each dredged up a memory, and brought a lump to her throat. She would see them no more. It was a sad end to the visit, but at least it was an end, and the process of forgetting could begin.

Sara, eager to discuss the visit, took one look at the Friday face on her niece and refrained from discussion. She closed her eyes and pretended to sleep, though her mind was busy with schemes to throw the pair together when they got back to London. Clare would not be far behind them, she surmised.

The Duchess was not so considerate of her son. He too looked to be in a bad skin, but she lit into him the minute they were reseated at the breakfast table, over a fresh cup of coffee.

"Now, Master Jackanapes, I would like you to tell me what you meant by last night's disgraceful performance."

"It's no point pretending you refer to anything but my proposal to Ella, I suppose?" he replied.

"No point in the least. What possessed you to do such a *ramshackle* thing to the poor girl?"

"Strangely enough, I did not consider an offer of marriage a ramshackle thing. I am at a loss to know why it has everyone in the boughs."

"It was the *way* of it, Patrick, so public and unseemly, to a shy girl like Ella. Belle Prentiss now, or Sherry, would have been in alt. Belle would have answered you in verse on the spot and painted up a picture of it afterwards to set on the wall. Sherry would have run to a mirror to admire the stars in her eyes, but *Ella* ... And besides, no one seems to think it was a *real* proposal, and to make fun of her with a *mock* proposal—but I know that's not what you meant, whatever the others think."

"I hope I am not such a loose screw as that."

"Well, of course you ain't, Pat. It's this Prattle creature who has given you such a black reputation."

"I hold Prattle largely responsible," he replied curtly.

"Still, that is in no way Ella's fault, and you have treated her shabbily. Now, I have been thinking what it is best to do," she continued contentedly, "and I think you must run up to London as soon as we get the Strayward ménage blasted off, and make it up with Ella. Lady Sara will stand your ally."

"No, that is quite impossible," he said firmly.

"Nonsense. Nothing is impossible if you set about it in the right way. You took her by surprise. You *must* have. She was not expecting an offer on such short acquaintance. No person of any sense or sensibility would credit you were serious anyway, just blurting it out like that, out of the blue. And speaking of sense and sensibility reminds me, don't forget to get Miss Austen's books for me. Oh, Pat, the very thing! I have Miss Fairmont's copy of *Pride and Prejudice*. What an excellent excuse to call on her!"

"Have you indeed?" he asked. From the interested tone, the "quite impossible" seemed to be now capable of consideration at least. "Certainly it must be returned," he allowed.

"Yes, there is nothing so annoying as losing a favorite book. And very likely *she* took your book on Kant with her and will have an excuse to see you too or, at least, write a note."

"No, she will most certainly have left it behind."

"I'll send a boy up to her room right now to see. Arking!" She executed the command, and in five minutes Kant's *Critique of Pure Reason* was being handed to her.

"Gudgeon," she grumbled.

"*She* is not looking for an excuse to be in touch with me," Clare pointed out.

"I wonder how soon we might expect the Straywards to leave," he said, looking at his watch. Leaving in his curricle, he might even overtake Sara's coach before they got to London.

"He got to bed early enough," the Dowager replied meaningfully. "Passed out at the table, I suppose?"

"Yes, he can't have kept his head up two minutes after the ladies left."

"Pity he didn't conk out before dinner, pest of a man. Really they are too pushing for anything. I wonder whom they'll sic Honor onto next."

There was no time for a reply. The entire Strayward family came into the room together at that moment. The answer was soon discovered, as soon as everyone had said good morning.

"We are dropping by Welmere on our way to London," Strayward told them. Welmere, the family seat of Lord Buchan, Earl of Buchan and Baron Rawdon, could by no manner of computation be considered as "on the way to London," being twenty-five miles due north. "Buchan ain't engaged or anything, is he?"

"Not to my knowledge, sir," Clare answered promptly, a vast weight slipping from his back. A great fear had seized him that Strayward would return to the attack on himself, once he saw he was not really engaged.

"How old a man would you say he is?" the Marchioness asked.

"Not a day over forty," Clare replied, skimming a mere ten years from the man's probable age.

"That's all right then," the Marchioness said. Honor was twenty, give or take a year.

"Are they Tories, Papa?" Honor asked, with the intention of insulting the Duke.

"Funny thing, that. Don't know what they are," the papa replied, frowning.

"Tories," the Dowager informed them, though she hadn't the least notion what they were.

"Good," Honor replied, feeling herself to be very witty and sarcastic. She then dug into a hearty breakfast to sustain her till they reached Welmere.

Clare entertained the hope that he would be able to get away within the hour, but the dilatory family sat discussing Buchan, his relations, Welmere, and relevant matters for an hour, and then startled the host and hostess by asking to be shown the library. Clare feared a long wait was in store, but it was only one book they wished to see. They asked Mr. Shane for *Debrett's Peerage*, and the three of them poured over it, quite shamelessly discussing the points of Welmere, and whether Buchan was up to Lady Honor's weight, genealogically speaking. He was inferior to Clare in all but politics and availability, but they settled on him nonetheless.

"We'll cut up to Welmere then," Strayward decided.

"Do you know him at all?" his wife asked.

Clare and his Mama exchanged a wild eye and were hard pressed to keep a straight face.

"If he's a Tory, I must have met him," the husband replied, and with this hypothetical acquaintance they finally went, to impose themselves on a stranger for an unspecified length of time.

"I don't believe what I have just seen and heard," the Dowager said, when they were alone.

"Old Buchan is fat and gouty, and might very well relish a young morsel like Honor," Clare returned, smiling.

"And will he be to her taste? The right flavor anyway—Tory."

Back at Grosvenor Square the next afternoon, Ella gave a deep thought to her position and came to a conclusion. The Season was nearing completion. She would continue being Miss Prattle till June 1, to complete her contract with Thorndyke. Information would be gathered from Sara and her grandmother, for she herself would go no more into society. Naturally, Clare's name would not appear in the column. She had already set on Lord Byron as his successor. On June 1 she would return to Fairmont, to return no more to London, but to occupy herself with the long-delayed start on her novel. This left two interminable weeks to be endured before her departure.

Clare got a late start from his palace, but arrived in London very shortly after Sara and Ella, with the help of his well-matched grays. He went home, changed, took up Ella's copy of *Pride and Prejudice* and decided to have lunch at a club before making his call. Lady Sara, eager to go out and make up for lost time by a few visits, had the carriage called and took her mother with her. Ella stayed home, giving instructions to the butler to say she was not at home. So when the Duke came with her book in his hands, it was taken by Greeves, who informed His Grace he would make sure Miss Fairmont received it. When pressed for information as to where Miss Fairmont might be found, Greeves prevaricated that "the ladies" were out visiting. Some considerable driving about town was required before Lady Sara's town chaise was spotted, but not much looking was necessary to see Ella was not in it.

Clare pulled up and exchanged polite inquiries as to the safe arrival back in town of his guests.

"We are fine," Sara told him happily. "Ella is at home. She decided not to come with us." She hoped he might take the hint to go and see her, if such was his intention, while she was alone.

"I see," he said and soon drove off. What he saw, of course, was that Miss Fairmont had left instructions she was not at home to him, and he took instant umbrage. A few acquaintances waved to him as he passed, and one friend hailed him up for a chat.

"Hear you've been having some gay old times at Clare," Mr. Best roasted, with a leer.

"Ah, you have been reading Prattle," Clare laughed, though any reminder of that character stung him. "Well, I fear it was only an indifferent visit," he admitted.

"For the *guests* maybe. We read *you* was pretty well entertained with your Hebe. Who is she, eh? And more importantly, old boy, did you bring her back with you?"

"I beg your pardon?" Clare asked, searching his mind for what this seeming *non sequitur* was all about.

"Oh, you're a sly one. You left her behind to polish the golden apple, eh? That was too bad of you, Clare. One of us would have been glad to take her off your hands. Any of *your* lightskirts would be worth a look. Well, toodle-oo. I'm off to Tatt's."

Clare drove home in a quandary, at a complete loss to understand the remark. Before he reached Belgrave Square, another friend made comments of a similar cast. Whatever Ella had written, it obviously had the town in an uproar.

He demanded the last week's copies of the *Morning Observer* the minute he was in the door, and went to his study to peruse them. The early copies he had already seen at Clare. The next couple seemed innocuous enough. He was not best pleased to read of himself as being slightly less than an indifferent jouster, but it could by no means account for what was being said around town. Then his hand fell on the fatal paper, and picking it up he read:

. . . We have good reason to believe that the three young ladies are no more than a smoke screen to cover his true reason for deserting us in mid-season. It is no goddess he is wooing, but a mere Hebe. We have it of a first-hand witness at C——e that the damsel is unlikely ever to wear a coronet, a mobcap being her present headgear. Are you all agog to see Hebe? You *may* have the opportunity, when the dreary party at C——e breaks up, if His Grace has not tired of his new protégée by then, and decided to leave her behind with her dustrag, to polish the golden apple for next year. Ho hum, now for some *interesting* news.

The paper fell from his hand, and he stood staring at it, as though it were a live, terrible thing. His lips were white with fury, yet he sat down calmly and sorted through the remaining papers. A few mild comments about his house party, but no further reference to Hebe. His anger was bad enough, but added to it was a sense of confusion. *What on earth was she talking about?* Miss Prattle's barbs always stung, but even if misdirected, there was some truth behind them. This, the worst she had ever written, was completely fictitious. His first impulse was to drive over to Grosvenor Square and demand an explanation. This was closely followed by the memory of his last visit. He would not be admitted peacefully and wouldn't give her the satisfaction of causing a brawl on her doorstep, to be duly recounted in tomorrow's column, no doubt. He grabbed up a pen and dashed off a note.

MISS FAIRMONT:

I would like an explanation of this impertinent piece of libel, or it will be necessary for me to take legal action.

Yours respectfully,
PATRICK BERESFORD
DUKE OF CLARE.

He tore the offending column from the paper, folded it into the envelope, and sent it off to Grosvenor Square.

The column was read in other quarters where it caused a great excitement and various plans. The Dowager had read it the day before, shortly after her son left, and wondered with a shrug what Miss Prattle had misunderstood this time. Less emotionally involved, her mind was more precise, and she soon hit upon Prissie Muckleton as the Hebe referred to. The story obviously had come from the palace, and she wondered which of her guests had stumbled on Prissie. She settled on Belle Prentiss as the likeliest perpetrator of the story. Sherry saw it, and wondered for ten minutes what a Hebe was, but she eventually reached the same conclusion as the Duchess. She would make it a point to tell Clare *she* was not the one who told on him, and it sounded very much like Belle Prentiss.

Belle, innocent for once, read it and was more amazed than any of them. She knew herself to be innocent, and knew as well that the only one she had told was Ella Fairmont. The gentlemen and Sherry were automatically cleared of suspicion. At first, she thought Ella had mentioned it to someone, which was bad enough, but a checking of the date on the paper, and a computation of the time required to write a letter to London, and the story to percolate to Miss Prattle and be reported soon satisfied her that the story had gone directly from Miss Fairmont to the paper. There was no other way to account for its being printed so soon. She smiled with an anticipatory satisfaction and began laying her plans.

It *must* be Ella, but she would verify her suspicion before presenting it to the Duke. *Then* they would see how he liked Miss Fairmont and her clever pen. Nothing would be more likely to give him an abhorrence of the girl. An unacknowledged admiration for Ella was there, too. Who would ever have thought her capable of such a splendid stunt? All these years she had been going about to parties without claiming the least interest, and here she was Miss Prattle.

It was read at Grosvenor Square, too, not very long after Lady Sara returned from her drive and visits. She went to her niece's room, her eyes flashing fire, and said, "What is the meaning of *this*, my young lady?"

Ella told the story of Prissie Muckleton and Belle Prentiss in a confused, distracted manner, with such abject self-accusations that it was pointless to chastise her further. She was clearly on the edge of nervous collapse.

"Oh, Ella, what a shame! And he this very day asked for you when I met him. He cannot have seen the column then. How came you to *do* it?"

"I didn't *know*! It was the very next day that the Duchess took us to the orphanage and explained everything, and it was too late then to stop Thorndyke from publishing it. Sara, what am I to do?"

"I think your best bet is to make immediate tracks to Fairmont, and I shall do my possible to conciliate him."

"Yes, yes! I can't *ever* face him again."

"My God, Ella, and you might have *married* him!" Ella did not bother to deny it.

"He hadn't read this when he asked me."

"Oh, it is out of the question *now*. This goes much beyond the bounds of what is forgivable. I only hope he will not blame *me* for it."

"Tell him it was all my doing. He will know it anyway."

"I wonder that Thorndyke printed such a thing."

"He would not doubt it when he knew we were *there*, at the palace."

"Well, I am surprised it did not occur to *you* to doubt it, but it is too late for that now."

While they were still discussing their dilemma, a maid came to the door with a note for Miss Fairmont. "It's from *him*," Ella said, looking at the crested envelope.

"For God's sake, open it. He has seen the column."

Ella's fingers were trembling so that she handed it to Sara. "You read it. I can't."

Sara tore it open and read the curt message. "He means to sue, and who shall blame him?" she said, handing it to Ella, who read, shook in her shoes, and handed it back.

"He wants an explanation. What shall I say?"

"You'd better tell the truth. I shouldn't think he even knows what you were talking about."

"Oh Sara, must I tell him I was gossiping with Belle? It is so vulgar . . ."

"Not so vulgar as repeating the gossip to the whole town! I wonder you should scruple at private scandalmongering."

"You wrote in the column, too," Ella reminded her.

"I know it. You needn't remind me. We are in this together—Mama, too, if it comes to that. Don't worry that *we* mean to desert you."

"Will you help me write him an explanation? Perhaps if I apologize . . ."

"Certainly you must apologize. I think it will be better if we go to see him."

Ella's eyes widened in horror. "No! I couldn't face him in person. It must be a letter."

"You may be right. We must take great pains with it—wheedle him into a good humor if we can."

"Yes, and tell him I mean to give up the column."

"My dear idiot! That goes without saying. What you must do is let him see you were jealous of what Belle told you. He would not be so inhuman as not to forgive jealousy. He told me once it was the easiest of all vices to pardon."

"No, I shan't tell him I was jealous!"

"This is no time for standing on your high ropes, my girl. Every wile must be used."

"I *refuse* to write that."

"Well, I think perhaps it will be best if *I* write the letter, dear. You are in no fit case to be composing. Leave it all to me."

"I wish you would do it. But don't tell him I was jealous."

"If you say so," Lady Sara said agreeably, but when she had written a reply, she did not trouble to show it to Ella for approval, but sent it to Belgrave Square with the greatest speed.

It was read with a similar speed, and sufficiently smoothed the ruffled noble feathers that no thoughts of suing were pursued. There was even a hint of satisfaction on Clare's brow as he read that Ella had been plunged into a positive *ague* of jealousy upon hearing Belle's story. He was not happy that the answer came from Lady Sara rather than Ella, but softened to read that the poor girl was prostrate on a bed of sorrow. He would let her stew a few days and then call on her. But upon consideration he thought he had still to repay her for not being home to him. He would ignore her for a week—resume with his other flirts, and give her jealousy time to ripen. Not cut her, of course, or pretend in the least that he was angry. He would be civil but distant, and enjoy himself hugely when they chanced to meet in public. He realized perfectly well that it was an odious trick, but Miss Prattle deserved it, whatever about Miss Fairmont.

He looked forward with pleasure to the Ottley's rout that night, and felt a sense of letdown when neither Lady Sara nor Ella appeared. He thought then that he ought to have acknowledged Sara's letter, and told them he meant to drop the matter. Very likely they had stayed away because he had not made known his intentions in that regard.

The next morning he wrote Sara a short note accepting

her story and apology, and casually slipped in that he would likely see her at the Opera. In fact, he did see Lady Sara, but not her niece. Ella, she said, was not feeling quite the thing. A bout of flu, she feared. He thought it more likely it was a bout of pique that he had not been to see her, and accepted the lie without a blink.

"There's a lot of it going around," he said, then excused himself to go and admire Sherry's latest gown. He stayed with her for five minutes, confirming out of the corner of his eye that Lady Sara was not oblivious to the fact.

He had to hear from several other members of society what a sly old dog he was, keeping his new flirt out of the city, but he assured them one and all he was not through with her yet.

Ella stuck by both of her intentions. It was not necessary to go to Fairmont since Clare had forgiven the column, but she stayed at home, and said not a word about him in the few remaining pieces she had to write. Lady Watley and Sara told her what was going on, and she faithfully reported what was told her, so long as it did not involve Clare.

Patrick was becoming impatient with her long absence, but had decided he would not go to call till he had the pleasure of paying her off in public first. He flipped through his invitations each day, deciding where she was most likely to be, and though he frequently encountered Lady Sara, he never inquired for her niece, nor did he see her.

Ella was despondent and bored. It proved impossible to write a novel when she was so completely wrapped up in her own predicament, but she sat with the blank pages before her, doodling and telling herself she was planning an outline. She was surprised one afternoon, a week after returning to town, to receive a call from Belle Prentiss. Next to Clare, she could not think of anyone she would less like to see, but curiosity and ennui conspired to have the visitor admitted to her presence.

Belle, like Clare, looked in vain at every social gathering for Ella and, unlike Clare, took the bull by the horns when a week passed and still she had not seen her. "I hear you have not been well, Ella, and decided to make a sick call. I am happy you are not in your bed."

"Oh, no, I am not that sick. That is—I am recuperating, you know."

"You look pulled. Well, I am come to cheer you up, and tell you all the latest *on dits*." She proceeded to do this, though there was little Ella had not already heard from her family sources. "Wasn't it a shocking thing that Miss Prattle got hold of that story I told you at Clare? I can't think *who* could have told her."

Belle looked closely to see how this comment was received, and was very well satisfied with the glint of malice it elicited from her listener. "I wish you never had told me," Ella was goaded into saying.

"Oh, Ella, it was *you* who leaked the story to Prattle, and everyone thinks it was I. Sherry accused me of it to my face."

"I am sorry you had to take the blame. It happens I did mention it, but I had no notion it would get talked around so."

"I see Prattle has quit writing about Clare. Byron is her latest target. I am surprised Prattle has not let the world know the baron's latest folly."

"What is that?" Ella asked, with a certain eagerness. Neither her grandmother nor her aunt provided her with the sort of *little* follies she delighted in writing up.

"Oh, haven't you heard? But you have been sick, of course. Everyone is saying he washes his hands and face in pure cream each morning and night, and that is what accounts for their beautiful color. He has such a romantic, pallid complexion, hasn't he?" This was pure fabrication, mentioned to not a soul but Ella, and its subsequent publication in 'Miss Prattle Says' would constitute Belle's proof of the author's identity.

"Does he indeed?" Ella asked, smiling. "How absurd."

"Yes, the very thing Prattle would revel in. I am surprised she hasn't taken him to task over it. But I daresay she will."

"Oh, yes, I shouldn't be surprised to read it any day now, since Prattle has taken up Byron."

Belle stayed half an hour in all. Before leaving she said, "Now that you are better, will you be going to some parties before the season is over?" She wished Miss Prattle's exposure to be as public and humiliating as possible.

"No. No, I still feel a little weak."

"What a pity! I had hoped we might see you at Almack's closing dance. But then, of course, Clare won't be there, and I bet *that* is why you aren't bothering to go to it." The Duke, she felt very sure, *would* be there, but she had a sharp idea it was a reluctance to meet him that kept Ella out of society. Really, she was a widgeon of a girl, to be so discomposed at that odd dinner party they had all attended the last night at Clare Palace.

"I believe the Duke is still in town," Ella said.

"Yes, but he was telling me he must go to Dorset the morning of Almack's last assembly, so he won't be at it."

"I see."

Belle took her leave, barely able to keep in her delight at having so successfully completed her mission, and Ella, lacking one item for that day's column, wrote up a bit on Byron's supposed use of cream in his toilette. She wrote:

> L—d B——n may be content to *eat* vinegar and potatoes to restrain his spreading girth, but on his beautiful exterior such stinting is not practiced. We have it that he uses pure cream instead of water to attain that maidenly complexion. He should try drinking it, to counteract the acidic quality of his conversation.

Without a backward thought, she sealed up the paper and sent it off to Thorndyke.

As the second week since the party in Dorset

progressed, and still Ella remained immured within the walls of her aunt's mansion, Clare became impatient. His anger with Miss Prattle had been overcome, and he even took to scanning her column every morning to see what she had to say. He thought she might resume a more restrained mention of his own activities, but it was all Lord Byron now. He laughed with the rest of London at her roasting of him, but some jealousy was beginning to blend with the laughter. She was paying entirely too much attention to this handsome poet. And where the deuce did she see him and discover what he said and did, for she went nowhere these days.

He chanced to encounter Byron once at Manton's Shooting Gallery, and teased him a little about Miss Prattle.

"No, I don't mind," the poet replied airily, looking dangerously handsome with his jacket tossed off, and his waistcoat hanging open. "It's *my* opinion, Clare, that she's actually in love with me. Such an excess of passion as she displays can't be all hate. There's bound to be some love mixed up in it. There's little difference between love and hate in any case. Two sides of the same coin. It's their indifference you have to look out for. Just stir a woman out of her indifference, and you can do anything with her."

"You take an optimistic outlook. I was not so flattered when she pilloried me."

"You should have been. Why, you have only to look at whom she chooses for her targets. You, me, Hartington—dashing beaux, all of us. She don't bother sticking her knife into any but handsome, young bachelors. I think you're jealous I've cut you out."

It was so near the truth that Clare naturally contradicted it violently.

"You've a right to your opinion," Byron continued, "but if the truth of the matter ever comes to light, we'll see it's some romantic young chit that's doing the scribbling. And pretty fine scribbling it is, too."

"You don't subscribe to the theory I've heard mentioned that it's Lady Caroline then?"

"Lord, no, it's ten leagues above her style. Madame de Stael is more like it—but I still think it's some *young* chit."

This conversation gave rise to some unpleasant reflections on the part of Clare after he had left the Shooting Gallery. There was some truth in it, and the part most likely to be true was that Ella had diverted her attention to Lord Byron and had become indifferent to himself. Not once had his name appeared since his return to town.

He purposely performed a few rash and foolish acts to try to prod her into resuming her guardianship of him. He set up a race to Brighton with Alvanley, with a prize of one thousand pounds. This would have been worth two paragraphs at least when he was in favor with Miss Prattle, but she ignored it entirely and did a column on the indecency of the current vogue among ladies of damping their gowns. He won the bet with Alvanley and started a story, untrue but widely circulated as fact, that he meant to institute an annual pig race on Hampstead Heath with the proceeds. Harley dashed out to his country seat and put all his swine through their paces, to select the likeliest one to garner him the first prize. But Miss Prattle feigned ignorance of the whole affair and took on the debutantes that day, to warn them of the dangers of trotting too hard during the Season. Not more than three outings a day should be undertaken, she advised.

Back at Clare Palace, the Dowager Duchess of Clare waited on tenterhooks for word from her son. She received none, nor did she get her books by Jane Austen, for that matter had completely slipped Clare's mind. She did hear, however, that Clare was making an ass of himself in London, and in an excess of impatience she had her traveling coach hitched up and put to for the wearisome journey to London. *I'll pretend I came for the King's birthday party on the fourth of June,* she thought to herself. *It will please old Charlotte.* She arrived in

Belgrave Square in the late afternoon of the day of the closing assembly at Almack's. Though it was nearing dinnertime when she arrived, she found Clare at home, making no preparations to go out, nor to receive guests.

"What, moping around the house?" she asked.

"I've been out every night since I got here and decided to stay home and rest. Everyone will be at Almack's tonight, and I'm not in the mood for it."

"I have been hearing very strange stories about you, Patrick. I didn't mind the race to Brighton. Congratulations, by the by. You must have flown to have beaten those famous grays of Alvanley's."

"Sixteen miles an hour."

"But to be setting up a *pig* race, love. So vulgar. Couldn't you have made it a horse race at least?"

"That was a faradiddle, Mama. Of course I am not setting up a pig race."

"Well, it is what everyone is saying, for I had letters from Aunt Sophronia and also your cousin Henry Wyatt, and they wrote of it as quite a settled thing. In fact, poor old Muggins is running the porkers at home till they'll be as tough as white leather when it is time to slaughter them." Clare smiled, but the effort only emphasized the haggard lines, the weariness in his face.

"Do you know what surprises me," she continued innocently, "is that Prattle has stopped taking you to task. She is becoming quite derelict in her looking after you. It is all Lord Byron now. Is it true that the silly young fellow eats nothing but potatoes and turpentine?"

"Vinegar, Mama. Turpentine would kill him."

She shuddered. "I can't think what the world is coming to. But the real reason I am here, of course, is to discover what progress you are making with Miss Fairmont and also to see why I have not received my books."

"I *am* sorry, Mama. It completely slipped my mind."

"Slipped your mind? But my dear, did you not dash off here for the specific purpose of making it up with her?"

"About the books, I mean," he explained. "We'll go

down to Bond Street tomorrow and see if we can't find them."

"Ella will tell me where to go," she said, to get the conversation back on its proper track.

"It won't be necessary to bother Miss Fairmont," he replied.

She directed a look of disgust at him, and said "Cloth head," in a derogatory manner.

"Actually, she has not been well," he said, feeling some excuse necessary for his inaction.

"And you have never heard of a pen and a piece of paper, I suppose? Certainly one would think them strangers to you for all the letters you ever write *me*."

"These things are best done in person," he said.

"Yes, and they are best done *now*, before she goes home, for the Season is all but over, and you may be sure she will be bolting right home to Fairmont if she is in queer stirrups."

"Yes, well, I had pretty well decided to call on her tomorrow."

"What's wrong with tonight?"

"I won't want to leave you alone your first night in town."

"That is about the most hen-witted thing you've said yet. I had no idea I would find you home and had planned to go early to bed, after two days' jostling along the potted roads, and spending a night at a very noisy inn which prevented me from closing an eye. In fact, I mean to retire the minute I've had a bit to eat, so I'm not to be your excuse."

"Very well, shrew. I'll go over to Grosvenor Square after dinner. Lady Sara and Lady Watley will be at Almack's, I fancy. The closing assembly. They won't miss that."

"And remember to ask her where I am to get my books, too."

"I mean to make an invitation from you to call on her tomorrow my excuse. You can ask her then."

"Lord, what a muddle you're making of it, Patrick. You don't need an excuse to call when you're offering for a girl, and certainly not such a lame-brained excuse as that. It doesn't make a bit of sense."

"You're a lot alike, you and Ella. Always right there with the moral support and ego builders when a fellow most needs them."

She laughed merrily. "We shall all deal famously. You won't need Prattle with me and Ella to keep you in line."

He opened his mouth to tell her he would have Prattle too, but she spoke before he could do it. "And by the way, I have something to tell you, or ask you. It was Belle Prentiss, I imagine, who gave Prattle that jumbled version of your Hebe. The butler told me Prissie was talking to her the night she landed in from the village. I'd give that one a sharp set-down if I were you."

He was in some doubt as to whether his mother would like Ella so well once she knew the truth. In fact, he was not quite positive he would tell her. "Tell me, Mama, what exactly is your opinion of Miss Prattle?"

"Oh, an upstart and trouble-maker. Some vulgar person, I have no doubt. Why, do you know who she is?"

"The rumor is that she is a young lady. Pretty well thought of, in fact, socially speaking."

"Then she's a fool, to be risking her reputation by carrying on the way she does."

"But if she could pull it off . . ."

"Then I should love to meet her!" she said.

Patrick smiled but saved his surprise. If Ella refused him, he would keep her secret. There was no hoping his Mama would do it.

Fifteen

The last two weeks since returning from Dorset had dragged by very slowly for Ella. When Sara asked her, merely as a matter of form, if she planned to attend the closing party at Almack's that evening, Ella surprised both herself and her aunt by saying she would go. "Clare will not be there, you know," Ella said. "Belle told me he left for Dorset this morning."

It would be in the nature of a farewell to fashionable London for her. Her last look at all the people she had been writing about over the years. She dressed with care, borrowing Stepson for the arranging of the hair, and putting on a new gown not quite finished in time to take to Dorset for the visit—a pale green with dark green ribbons pencilled in a double line round the hem. She had new gloves with no fingers out too, from the shopping spree occasioned by the visit to the Palace, and felt a pang that Clare would not see her in her new gown, for she looked rather better than usual. They set out, the younger lady with no very high hopes for the evening, since the only person whose presence could please her was guaranteed to be absent.

Clare had some hazy notion of asking Ella to accompany him to Almack's if she accepted his offer of marriage, and with this in mind attired himself in the formal satin breeches and black coat required by the place. He learned, of course, at Grosvenor Square that the ladies had already gone to Almack's.

"Miss Fairmont also?" Clare asked.

"Yes, Your Grace."

Remembering that the butler had tinkered a little with the truth on a former occasion, Clare asked if he would mind just to make *sure* Miss Fairmont was not at home.

"No, she's *really* not here this time," the butler said, with a knowing wink, and no shame whatsoever. So Clare proceeded to Almack's, looking forward to his evening with a deal more pleasure than Miss Fairmont was doing.

The evening began much as usual. Ella and Lady Sara arrived early, but the rooms were already three-quarters full. Ella glimpsed all around, taking her last look at all her old characters. There was Lord Petersham, forced to wear something other than brown for once; Prince Esterhazy who might even possibly have shared a carriage with his wife, though it was unlikely; the whole ménage from Melbourne House; a generous sprinkling of young hopeful maidens, eying the bachelors, who were eying them. The whole column tomorrow would be devoted to this party. Really everyone was here, for no one would be so *farouche* as to give a ball on the night of Almack's closing party. Yes, everyone was here, and why did the place seem so empty and uninteresting?

There was a noticeable shifting of eyes to the entrance door, and Ella too looked, thinking to herself, it must be Lord Byron. She had not spotted him in the throng. But the gentleman who had stepped in and turned so many heads was not Lord Byron, but the Duke of Clare, with Bippy Tredwell in tow. Ella felt weak. "Sara, it's *him*! We must leave!"

"Don't be such a ninnyhammer. Do you think he is going to stand up and announce to the room that you are Miss Prattle? If he comes this way, smile and say 'good evening,' and you may be sure he will not give you the cut direct. He always says a few words to me."

"I can't face him. I'm going."

"And how do you plan to get past the door without pushing him aside?" Sara asked. She had a good point, for Clare had not moved from the door, but stood with his quizzing glass raised, scanning the room, obviously looking for someone. Ella was positive of two conflicting facts: he was most certainly looking for her, and he was most certainly *not* looking for her. In either case, he would have difficulty to find her, for she had got behind her aunt, and buckled her knees so that no portion of her body was visible to him.

"Ella, for God's sake, stop acting like a confirmed lunatic," her aunt said sharply. Ella straightened her knees and turned her back to the door. "He's not coming this way," Sara assured her, and she risked looking towards him.

True, he was not coming towards them, but Bippy Tredwell at that point spotted Ella and raised a hand in salute. She smiled and nodded and watched, mesmerized, as he began tugging at Clare's sleeve and saying something to him. As he kept looking at them from time to time during this interval, it was but logical to assume he was informing Clare of their whereabouts. But Clare refused to hear him. He looked everywhere in the room but at them. Ella hardly knew what to think. She had feared Clare would come to her, feared he would not, feared he would stare her down, or past her, or through her, but it had never occurred to her he would find her invisible. She was deflated and pretty soon angry as well. But Clare was in high spirits, smiling and talking to everyone with a greater degree of amiability than was common to him. When the minuet was begun, he asked Sherry to stand up with him, and Ella's hand was solicited by an elderly gentleman who was a friend of Sir Herbert's.

At the dance's finish, Ella went again to Sara, who said to her, "You see there is nothing to fear. He doesn't mean to behave in any way differently from before."

"He never acted like this before!" Ella objected.

"I mean before we went to Dorset. He had a few words with me, just before the dance began."

"Did he say anything about me?"

"No, I mentioned you were here, and he just nodded. He did not appear in the least angry."

So far from being angry, Clare was enjoying his game of cat-and-mouse very much. He had decided on the third dance as the one for which he would seek Ella's hand.

For one hour he would let her fume, and wonder what he was up to. He was sorely tempted to go to her after the minuet, but Emily Cowper accosted him, and getting away proved impossible. At the end of the second dance, Belle Prentiss, who had arrived late, came up to him, her eyes sparkling. Ella observed this, as she observed every move Clare made, by a judicious and very brief toss of her head in his direction, rather as though she were lifting a curl from her forehead.

"I was wondering if you would be here," Belle said to Clare.

"As you see, I *am* here," he replied, fearing that Belle would entrap him for the next dance. His impatience to go to Ella was becoming acute.

"Everyone is here tonight. It hasn't been such a squeeze since the first assembly. There is Sherry, looking fine as a star in yet another white spangled gown. Harley and Peters are on their way in; I passed them just now. Oh, and there is Lady Sara and Miss Fairmont. Quite a re-gathering of your house party."

"Yes."

"Which reminds me, Clare, of the most *amazing* thing I have discovered," she ran on, slipping in as if incidental the main reason for having sought him out.

He looked up with a minimum of interest, expecting to hear some dull bit of gossip and wondering how soon he might excuse himself.

"I have uncovered Prattle, and what do you think? It is Miss Fairmont."

She had his full interest now, but was hard put to account for the violent expression he wore. "Nonsense!" he said.

"No, it is true, I swear. But I must tell you how I tricked her. I was very cunning and devious. I *suspected* her when I read that odious piece in the *Observer* about your having a lightskirt at Clare. I bet you thought *I* was responsible for leaking that out, but the only one I told

221

was Miss Fairmont, and *that* is what first made me suspicious."

"Why did you tell her?"

"Because I—oh I don't know. We got to talking one day as girls will do, and I told her. I didn't think it would do any harm, for I thought she could be trusted. And then when I figured out she must have sent the story direct to the paper, for there wasn't time for it to get around in the normal way because it appeared so soon, I set about confirming my suspicion. I told her a whisker, just a silly little thing about Lord Byron, to see if it would show up in Prattle. I said he bathed his face and hands in cream, and that is what makes them so white. When I read it in Prattle the *very next day* I *knew* it must be she."

"It doesn't necessarily follow. She may have told someone."

"No, she was pretending sick, and not going out at all, and it was in the *very next day*. I believe she must have jotted it down the minute I left. It was the last item in her column."

"Whom else have you told?" Clare asked.

"Only a few. I just got here. I mentioned it to Sally Jersey *en passant*, and Byron was with her. He dashed off to tell Lady Melbourne . . ."

"I take it you are awaiting my praise for this piece of meddling?" he asked, in the angriest voice she had ever heard.

"You should be thankful, after the things she has written about *you*."

"The *worst* she ever wrote about me was a lie promulgated by yourself. Clever, as usual, Miss Prentiss, but not so clever as my Miss Prattle. *She*, I think, has you beat on all suits."

"Well, she is not half so clever as you seem to think, for only look how I have caught her. And you needn't think you can hush this business up, for the room is buzzing with it already."

The merest glance around them confirmed this boast. Clare heard it with an impassive face, only the pinching of his nostrils giving any indication of his fury. His mind rapidly raced ahead to what must be done now. Within ten minutes Ella would be in a state of siege. Old Drummond-Burrell, for instance, wouldn't hesitate a moment to ask her to leave, or *tell* her. Already heads were together in groups, fans raised, and eyes staring towards Ella. He knew at exactly what moment she became aware of it herself. Saw her face take on that frightened look, trapped. She's going to panic, he thought. He turned to Belle—he had forgotten she was there in that instant of planning, yet the delay between their two speeches was hardly noticeable.

"Oh, no, I have no thought of hushing it up. I must go and congratulate her." On the words, he stepped forth, and Belle was left, stunned. She knew for sure now what she had suspected all along. Clare *loved* Miss Fairmont. She herself had wasted the better part of two seasons chasing him as hard as she could and refused a flattering offer from Sir Geoffrey Cunningham not three weeks ago. Well, she would never get Clare now, but she doubted Miss Fairmont would get him either after tonight. She smiled ironically and followed Clare across the room with her eyes, to judge by their expressions what transpired between them.

Ella was on the far side of the room, and already one of the patronesses was making a hurried path towards her—Mrs. Drummond-Burrell, the most intractable of the lot. She reached Ella before Clare, and was just saying as he approached, "Lady Sara, the most bizarre rumor is running around the hall—nonsense, of course, but I *must* ask you . . ."

Clare barged in, heedless of his manners. "Good evening, ma'am," to Mrs. Burrell, and again to Sara, "and a very good evening to *you*, Miss Prattle," to Ella.

It would be difficult to decide which of the ladies was

the most shocked. All three wore dazed, stupefied looks and were beyond making an answer.

"My dance, Miss Prattle, I think?" he said, again repeating that awful name.

Ella looked at him, her brown eyes accusing, hurt, and questioning. "I don't . . ."

"But Miss Prattle, you *did* promise me first waltz, when you were so kind as to visit me at Clare. How can you have forgotten?" He turned to the patroness. "Now tell her, ma'am, the *least* she can do to repay me for all those dreadful things she keeps writing about me, is to keep her promise to waltz with me?"

Drummond-Burrell finally spoke, but it was not to do as Clare bid her. "Are you Miss Prattle?" she asked Ella directly in a firm voice.

Ella opened her mouth, but no sounds came out, and Lady Sara too was struck dumb by the enormity of the situation. "But, of course, she is," Clare smiled brightly at the old tartar, as he folded Ella's arm into the crook of his own and patted her confined hand with his own free one. "Making a May game of us all, the naughty girl. She wants a good scolding, don't you think, ma'am?"

Mrs. Drummond-Burrell thought she wanted a deal more than that, but her mind was so disordered at this show Clare was acting that she hardly knew what she thought. The outrage Miss Prattle had been perpetrating for the last three years demanded the highest degree of contumely and censure, the latter to be administered by a public expulsion from the hallowed halls of Almack's. Yet the main butt of Miss Prattle's odium had been the Duke, and here was *he*, positively drooling over the sassy chit. If *he* meant to stand behind her, it would be difficult for the rest of society to ostracize her.

"But, of course," Clare rattled on, seeing the indecision on the patroness's dour face, "I collect *you* cannot quite disapprove of my Miss Prattle, when she has called those co-patronesses of yours to account, as I have often heard you do so yourself, ma'am."

This was one column of Miss Prattle's of which the strict patroness had approved, especially as it had been mentioned that the other patronesses ought to look to herself as a model of propriety. "I could not like to see it done in such a public way," she advised Clare, with an indecisive look at Ella.

"I am sorry, ma'am," Ella said weakly. Lady Sara just stood, wordless, and let Clare handle the matter.

Mrs. Drummond-Burrell hesitated. There were two points in Miss Fairmont's favor. The general tone of her column was highly moral—she reported on wrongdoings only to rail against them. And of much greater importance, there was the Duke, smiling at her in a besotted manner, fondling her hand, and calling her *my* Miss Prattle. Her decision—and Ella's fate—hovered on the razor's edge, till Clare stepped in and gave it a push.

"Shall we forgive her this once, ma'am?" he asked playfully, his whole demeanor indicating that he had forgiven her long ago—and took the patroness's forgiveness as a matter of course.

Politics at Almack's as elsewhere was the art of the possible, and old Mrs. Drummond-Burrell was too astute a politician to put herself in check. Where Clare led, society followed, and if he led away from Almack's, the place would lose much of its *ton*. "Well—if you say so, Clare. You're the one she has most often written about." She gave an uncharacteristic bark of laughter, the first and only ever heard to escape her lips in all her long years at Almack's. "But mind you mend your ways, Missie," she warned, then sailed off to be the first to announce she had taken Miss Prattle to task and that she and Clare had decided to give her one more chance.

"Well!" Lady Sara said when she had gone. "If I don't suffer nightmares from this, it will be a wonder."

"I remarked it all left you quite speechless," Clare replied. "Miss Prattle, they are beginning our waltz." He already had her arm in his and pulled her to the dance floor. She had hardly the strength to stand up, let alone waltz.

Immediately they were alone, his mood of reckless cheer left him, and in fact he found nothing to say.

"Why did you do it?" Ella asked in a shaken voice.

"I should have thought you'd be too thankful to look a gift horse in the mouth."

"You must have told. It *had* to be you. No one else knew."

To ears awaiting soft words of gratitude, this accusation of such a base nature was a jolt. His nerves, though he didn't show it, had suffered from the pass with Drummond-Burrell, and it didn't take much to nudge him into anger. His arm fell from her waist, and he was about to turn and walk away when a startled glance from the Countess de Lieven brought him to reason. He put his arm back around her waist, stiffly. "You have the temerity to say that to me, after that last column you sent in from Dorset!"

This outrage had momentarily slipped Ella's mind. Reminded of it now, she turned crimson. "I am sorry about that. It was very bad of me."

"Kind of you to say so."

"It was a horrid thing to do."

The simple word "horrid" had nostalgic memories for Clare. It seemed somehow an integral part of Ella Fairmont. Glancing at her in a mood mollified a little by memories and her timid voice, he softened even further to see how stricken she looked. Ready to fold up and die away. "Buck up. It will soon be over," he said gruffly.

It was not a phrase to give reassurance to one already convinced life was over for her. "I have been wanting to apologize for that," she added, so weakly that he had to strain his ears to hear her.

"Apologize for *thinking* it, not writing it. How *could* you, Ella? But it was that damned Belle Prentiss who set you on to that track."

"I cannot blame anyone but myself, but if *you* didn't tell about my being Prattle, who did?"

"I most assuredly did not tell, and in future I should be careful of printing any items given me by Miss Prentiss, if I were you."

Ella saw no way in which Belle could have known, yet she would not believe it was Clare when he had explicitly denied it. It *had* to be Belle. She had unearthed the truth somehow. "Does everyone know?" she asked.

"I doubt there's a person in the room who doesn't know by now."

"I am ruined! Please, I must go home."

"What—all your gall deserted you? If you care tuppence what people may think of you, you'll stay." All this altercation went forward while they danced, and Clare even smiled occasionally at others on the floor.

"I *don't* care. Please, let me go."

"And what about Sara? A fine thank-you to her for carting you around town these four years! And to myself, for trying if I can to save your reputation. Think of someone other than yourself for a change, Miss Fairmont."

These harsh words and the even harsher tone in which they were delivered shook her out of her fit of despair. Clare *hated* her—that much was indisputable—but if he thought her a despicable, underhanded conniver, he might at least be shown she was not craven. She repressed the urge to flee and said in a stronger tone, "Yes, I must stay, for Sara's sake."

"Try if you can to manage a smile while you're about it. Everyone is looking at you."

To smile under such circumstances was too tall an order, but she tried manfully. It only emphasized her misery. Clare felt a strong inclination to waltz her out the door and take her home, as she wanted. To get her away from the prying eyes. But they had to go on living in this world, with these same people, and if they were put to rout now, the future would be infinitely worse than it could be.

"We'll have this one dance—talk to a few people who matter, then I'll take you home," he decided. She was clearly not up to facing the whole night.

"Thank you," she said. He feared she was on the verge of tears. That last "thank-you" had been uncharacteristically meek. Sympathy at this point would send her over the edge.

He said brusquely, "For God's sake, don't turn into a watering pot on me."

"No, I won't," she said, still too meek to please him, and her eyes were flooding up.

"Come now, I expect better than this from Miss Fairmont."

She blinked back the tears and made answers, largely irrelevant, to what remarks he could think of to say to her till the dance was over. Ella looked about for Sara when the music stopped, but Clare, discerning her intention of getting away, held her arm.

"Shall we tackle your new love first?" he asked.

"What do you mean?"

"Byron. Might as well get it over with, don't you think?"

"I *couldn't*!"

But Byron, like everyone else at Almack's, was eager to meet Miss Prattle, and upon intercepting a smile from Clare, came hurrying over.

"Now tell me, Clare, was I correct or not in my surmise regarding Miss Prattle?" he said, looking at Ella in a teasing manner out of eyes which had been described by another poet as something like the windows of heaven. Even with the troubles besetting her, Ella took a moment to admire them.

"Are you ever wrong, George?"

"Not in my judgment of literature—and women. I take those two areas as my own special province."

"With such a bare-faced assertion as that, I quite tremble to make you known to my special friend, Miss Fairmont."

"Alias Miss Prattle," Byron took her hand and raised it to his lips. Ella's heart fluttered, and Clare bristled to see her falling under the poet's spell. "I have been longing to make your acquaintance, ma'am," he replied, looking deeply into her eyes.

Some jumbled phrases were made by Ella. "Never have I regretted my inability to dance so much as tonight," Byron continued, glancing at his club foot, while the others politely looked elsewhere and pretended not to know what he was talking about.

"Well, I have decided to forgive Miss Prattle," Clare said after a moment's uncomfortable pause, "and if she asks you very nicely, George, may I count on you to do the same?"

"Oh, I forgive her anything, so long as she doesn't take to printing the truth about me."

"I am sorry," Ella said.

"But I find it less easy to forgive *you*, Clare. I made sure Miss Prattle was in love with *me*. I am much more interesting, you know," he turned to Ella, with a bantering and dangerous smile. "We literati ought to stick together, don't you think? These dull clods of Corinthians have no appreciation of the finer things in life. May I call on you tomorrow, and ask your opinion on some verses I am presently composing?"

Ella smiled in delight, and Clare replied, "Unfortunately, old man, Miss Fairmont is already engaged to ride out with me. And now I shall forcibly drag her away, before you make some other rendezvous."

"Ah, but we writers can arrange things by letter, eh, Miss Fairmont?"

Clare did drag her away then, in a state of alarm.

"Oh, he is *charming*," Ella enthused. "I never saw such eyes, with lashes a yard long."

"There are Harley and Peters," Clare pointed out, welcoming any distraction.

"By Jove, I always knew you was up to anything, Miss Fairmont," Peters began. "Is it true you're Miss Prattle?"

"It is all too true," Clare said, happy with the way in which the revelation was being taken. "Pulled the wool over all our eyes."

Harley had other fish to fry. "Been wanting to ask you about this pig race," he said to Clare. "I've got myself a porker—a young sow, clocked her at eight miles an hour—over a short run of course. Whom do we see about entering?"

"Don't believe everything you read," Clare told him.

"Read? I don't read anything. Wideman told me about it. He says it's to take place in a month's time, and I think you ought to advance the date, for July is getting pretty hot to be running a pig."

Into this discussion Miss Sheridan appeared, so lovely that all talk was suspended. "Everyone is saying you are Miss Prattle, Ella. Can it possibly be true?"

"I'm afraid it is," Ella confessed.

Sherry smiled at her. "You will want to mention *I* was the first one Clare stood up with tonight. If you are wondering what this new hairstyle I am wearing is called, it is the Victime. Quite an old do, but I have decided to bring it back into fashion. Isn't it lovely? Do you like it as well as the Méduse, Clare?"

"Did I fail to compliment you on it when I stood up with you for the first dance? How very remiss of me. It is charming."

"It is, isn't it? But very few could wear it. Mama said in the olden days ladies used to wear a little red ribbon round their throats, to remind people of the guillotine, but I think that is *horrid* and wore this blue one instead."

Clare dragged Ella away as soon as possible and engaged various groups in conversation. Not everyone was so well pleased with Miss Prattle as Lord Byron and the crew from the house party, but there were no direct cuts, and with the Season about over, he thought talk would have time to die down over the summer.

"Can I go now?" Ella asked.

"Yes, I shall take you home. We'll say you have the

headache—or perhaps it will be better if Sara has a headache, and you take her home. We have scraped through pretty well, I think, and shan't give anyone the satisfaction of saying you have a headache."

Sara accepted without a blink that she had a headache. She had placed their fates in Clare's hands and was well pleased with his handling of the mess. "It's no more than the truth, for I think this knife jab in my temple is the onset of migraine."

"I'll call your carriage," Clare said. He took them to it as well, then returned to continue his charade for another hour, before going to Belgrave Square with a splitting headache himself.

Sara, despite her migraine, gave Ella to understand that she had been treated much better than she had any right to expect by Clare, and she hoped she was grateful to him.

Sixteen

A night's indifferent sleep proved efficacious in curing all the headaches involved except Belle's. Hers would linger for a few days, till she formed the excellent notion of trapping Lord Harley, now that she knew from experience at the Palace what sort of girl he liked. That she was not that sort of a girl mattered not in the least. She was nothing if not versatile, and very capable of entering into the interests of a Corinthian.

At Grosvenor Square, Lady Watley was treated to a recounting of the night's events and entered, with Sara, into hopes that Clare might yet come up to scratch, if only Ella would not do something foolish.

"Well, she won't do it with the column," Sara affirmed, "for I mean to write it myself. This is the end of the contract, thank God! I wouldn't renew it for all the tea in China."

"We'll both stay home today," Mrs. Watley said. "We'd be asked a million questions if we showed our noses out the door, and we can keep an eye on you-know-who, too, to see she don't decide to slip away to Fairmont, or something equally foolish. Just like her to vanish when things are going so well."

"I don't mean to budge an inch from the house, and if he comes to call, I shall make sure she has her hair combed and something decent on."

"Where is she anyway? She's usually down before this."

"She's up and dressed. Writing on the magnum opus, I expect."

"I don't dare ask what it's all about."

"It's about twenty pages of doodling right now, for she hasn't put a word on paper since we came back from Dorset, in spite of the hours she's spent pouring over it."

In her room, Ella was not even pretending to write this morning, but pacing back and forth, wondering if Clare really meant to drive out with her today, as he had indicated to Lord Byron. Surely he would not just leave things like this. She had subjected the preceding night's events to exhaustive scrutiny and realized at length what Clare must have grasped in a moment. Once the secret was out that she was Prattle, he had acted in the only possible manner that might have saved her skin. That he had pulled it off at all was a feat of no mean proportions and that he had done it for her, after her abuse of him, could indicate nothing but continued regard. It was incredible, but no other possibility could account for it. His ploy might very well have failed, and if it had, he would have looked the greatest fool in the kingdom, to have gone on befriending her when everyone else cut her out. In short, he had staked his reputation to save hers, and while she did not place so high a value on her reputation as he seemed to, it was the act of a generous man.

Sara would have been relieved to know what care was spent on her niece's toilette that morning and that Stepson had been asked to do the recalcitrant hair. When all was arranged, there was nothing to do but wait, in an agony of suspense, for Clare to come.

Before he could come, Clare had to wait and explain to his Mama why he had not better news to report than he had.

"Well, am I looking at an engaged man?" the Duchess asked her son, before she even took her place at the table.

"I'm afraid not, Mama, but you're looking at one about to pop the question."

"Four hours wasn't enough time for you to screw yourself up to the sticking point?" she asked. "I couldn't get to sleep. Heard you come in after twelve. I was going to ask you then, but I knew I wouldn't get any sleep if you had failed."

"Things fell out somewhat differently than I expected. She was at Almack's, you see, and there was no privacy there to ask her."

"No, well, it ain't the best place, I'll grant you. How was the assembly?"

"More exciting than I expected. I was wishing you were there; I could have used you."

"You've developed a charming way of expressing yourself. I don't advise you to use that particular phrase when you're making your offer to Ella."

"No, Mama."

"What do you mean anyway, you could have *used* me? I don't trip the light fantastic so well as I used to, and I can't think you were lacking for partners."

"No, but when it was revealed that Ella is Miss Prattle, I would have been thankful for your power with a setdown," he smiled agreeably.

"What! Patrick, quit bamming me. You cannot mean . . ."

"Oh, yes, I have known it for some time now."

233

"And her so sweet butter wouldn't melt in her mouth. Oh, the minx! Just wait till I get my hands on her."

"Take care, Mama. You are speaking of your future daughter."

A loud laugh escaped his mother's mouth. "Am I indeed? Well in that case, I shall limit myself to one hand. And you still mean to have her?"

"Certainly. She can make good use of *me* now. You see I am willing to be put to use myself, with no objection whatsoever."

"And do you mean to sit there and tell me you managed somehow to get the patronesses to *accept* her? Walking on water is nothing to this. I begin to think I've sired a magician. Tell me the whole, at once."

He did so, and they both enjoyed a triumphant laugh at his brass. "Well, it seems to me the poor girl has suffered enough for her little prank, and I shan't add to her discomfort by saying another word. Get on over there now and ask her to marry you. She can hardly refuse after what you've done."

"No—I feel she is *beholden* to me, after that."

"And bring her back here after. I have a hundred questions to ask her."

"And I have one to ask you. Will you go and lure Sara and her mama from the house for me? Sara is a darling, but I fear she will be hanging around to crow over last night, and I am just a little impatient after waiting so long . . ."

"You took on the assembled patronesses of Almack's and the whole of London society, and yet you are afraid of Lady Sara Mantel. There is no understanding you, Patrick. I'll go, though. I want someone to talk to about it."

Before too many moments, the Dowager was deposited on the doorstep at Grosvenor Square, and though the two other ladies were surprised to be urged so strenuously to go for a drive on a day that was really not at all pleasant, for the sky was overcast, they agreed. Sara went up and told Ella where they were going.

"Did she invite *me* to go?" Ella asked.

"Well no, but you were not there. Why don't you come down and say 'good morning' to her? It would do you a world of good to be seen in her carriage."

Ella agreed, in some little trepidation. "Ah, Miss Prattle!" the Dowager said, laughing merrily. "Busy writing up your column, are you?"

"No. No indeed, I am not doing anything."

"Well, I am glad to see you, for I want to inquire of you where to get those books by Miss Austen. Hatchards, is it?"

"Yes."

"Well, shall we be off, ladies?" the Duchess said to the others, quite markedly omitting Ella from the invitation.

"Perhaps Ella . . ." Lady Sara said.

"No, she will not want to come. She is much better off where she is. Nosey Parkers will be saying things to her, you know."

There was nothing for it but to go, and Ella sat alone, worrying that her column had given the Duchess a disgust of her. She was about to return to her room, when the butler came to the door, after first telling Clare with a twinkle that she was here this time, right enough.

He stepped in, nervous and unsmiling at the ordeal before him, for making an offer of marriage is no easy thing for anyone.

"Good morning," Ella said, quite giddy with nerves herself.

"Good morning," he replied.

"I have been wanting a chance to thank you for last night. It was so very kind of you."

"Mama tells me it was the height of impudence, and it would have served me well if we'd both been shown the door."

"She—she was here a short while ago. I'm afraid she is not very well pleased with me."

"She'll come around. *I* am pleased. You carried it off

very well. I was afraid there at one point you were about to knuckle under."

"And so I should have if *you* hadn't ... It was very kind of you, and I want to thank you."

"You already have. But that is not why I am come."

She stared, flushed, sat down, then arose again immediately. "No," she said, at length. "You mentioned to Lord Byron that we were to go out—or something of the sort."

"Byron! You were quite taken with him, I think."

"Oh, yes. So very . . ."

"Charming?" he supplied.

"Handsome, I was going to say. But charming, too."

"He is become quite a favorite with Prattle, I have observed."

"But I could not go on writing about *you*! You know I could not."

"Not even when I bet Alvanley a thousand pounds and won. Nor when it was said I was to set up a pig race?"

"You had much better use the money for your orphans!"

"Mama spilled the soup, did she? And here I was counting on the surprise of that unknown benevolence on my part to—"

"What?" she asked, breathing a little faster.

"Why, to win favor in Miss Prattle's eyes," he replied, coming a step closer."

"I cannot think why you should care what *she* thinks! She is horrid."

"Do you know, I am beginning to like her excessively. I was quite cut up when she abandoned me for Byron."

"Oh, you are fooling! You know she is *horrid*!"

"Ella!" he laughed shakily and reached out his arms for her. She ran a step forward and went into them.

"Oh, Patrick, I never meant to make such mischief," she said, in a strangled voice, her head against his shoulder.

"Now, now. There is no harm done. With our combined gall, we will stare them all out of countenance."

This arrogant phrase was delivered in a caressing tone, while his hand stroked her hair.

"We?" she asked, lifting up her head to look at him.

"We. You and I, the Duke and Duchess of Clare," he said firmly.

"Patrick, you have not even asked me this time!"

"Yes, this time I am taking the question as well as the answer for granted—it is this *monstrous arrogance* of mine that gets a little out of hand at times."

"Have I not taught you *anything*?" she asked, laughing.

"A great deal, you *horrid* girl, and now I will teach *you* to play fast and loose with my affections. Byron indeed!" he said, just before he bent his head and kissed her quite ruthlessly.

"Say you'll have me, Ella," he urged in a coaxing tone. "Now that you've given up tongue-lashing and deriding me in public, you must become my own private Miss Prattle, to keep me in line."

"I should begin your reformation by insisting on a proper offer, Your Grace," she warned teasingly.

"Oh, damn!"

This harsh interjection quite naturally surprised Miss Fairmont, till she too heard the sound of wheels in the street and followed Clare's gaze out the window, to see his Mama's carriage pulling up outside the door.

"They're back already," he continued. "She must think me a speed demon to have had time to be accepted—make an offer already."

"Patrick! Is *that* why she came, to get rid of Sara and grandmama?"

"Yes, much good it did me." Already the three women were alighting and looking towards the house. Then, very quickly, Clare said, "Miss Fairmont, Ella—darling, will you do me the honor to be my wife?"

"I must consider the matter," she replied with an outward calmness she was far from feeling.

Glancing to the window, he reminded her urgently, "You have about two seconds in which to consider it."

"That will be enough. I suppose I must accept."

He flashed one very brief, happy, and triumphant look at her before going to the saloon door and turning the lock on it. Ella looked on at this irregular behavior with interest.

"Do you mean to barricade the windows, too?" she asked. "Must they come down the chimney like Père Noël?"

"No, shrew, they will come in by the door as soon as I am through with you." Already the sounds of the outer door opening and female voices raised in discussion were heard. With no further waste of time, Clare strode to Ella and pulled her brusquely into his arms. He kissed her with passion and, she feared, considerable expertise, for he seemed to do it very well. Their thoughts were overridden by feelings for some seconds, and when he released her a disquieting silence reigned in the hall beyond. Observing this, they looked a question at each other, but soon decided to put the interval to good use, and resumed their embrace with no demur whatsoever on the part of Miss Prattle, who obdurately derided fast conduct in young ladies.

With a breathless "Oh," she pulled back at last and looked to the door. Silence still prevailed in that direction. He reached for her again, but she pulled back. "I cannot imagine what they will think," she whispered.

"Unless I am mistaken, they will have a pretty good idea what to think," he replied, putting an arm about her waist and pulling her towards him.

"Patrick—stop it at once! We must unlock the door." She tried to pry his arm loose but found it to be unmovable.

There was a rattle at the door at this point. He kissed her ear briefly, and removed his arm but held to one hand as he went to the door and unclasped it.

"Were you locked out?" Ella asked, pink with shame. "I cannot think how the door came to be locked."

"It happens all the time when it is slammed shut," Sara lied glibly, with a knowing look at her niece.

"Well, slowpoke, did you get it done this time?" the Dowager demanded of her son.

"Slowpoke? I cannot think you have even been around the block," he countered.

"Patrick, you cloth head, you cannot mean you have *still* not asked her? Must I do it for you?"

Clare glanced at Ella. "You will observe this assumption of a positive answer is a family failing. I have not only *asked*, Mama, but been accepted. Two quite different matters, you know."

"I detect the firm hand of Miss Prattle in that answer," the Dowager said approvingly. Her words were overborne by the delighted exclamations of Lady Sara and Lady Watley, and a general volley of congratulations and kisses exchanged.

"Well, I think this occasion calls for a glass of champagne or something," Sara decided. Then she laughed gaily. "I little thought when I wangled us that invitation to Dorset, Ella, that I should find you a husband." The wine was delivered to the saloon, and the Dowager called for a toast.

"It's the man who gets stuck with the job of coming up with some suitable words, I believe," she said to her son.

Clare lifted his glass. "It's the height of bad taste to drink to oneself, I suppose, but for this one occasion I mean to take the rules and bend them a little . . ."

"That's nothing new," the Dowager said aside.

"Thank you, Mama. May I continue now, or must I box your ears first?"

"You have your work cut out for you, Ella," she warned, with a pleased grin. "I doubt if even *you* can make a silk purse of this sow's ear."

"The heel of your own foot, Mama. As I keep *trying* to say, I would like to propose a toast—to the Duke and Miss Prattle."

BESTSELLERS